RETURN TO THE MADNESS

Book Two of the Promises Series

A Vietnam War Novel

Glyn Haynie

For information about this title or to order other books and/or electronic media, contact the publisher:

Glyn Haynie
www.glynhaynie.net
glyn@glynhaynie.com

ISBNs:
Hardback: 978-1-7340260-2-3
Paperback: 978-1-7340260-3-0
eBook: 978-1-7340260-4-7

Printed in the United States of America.

Typesetting: ebooklaunch.com

Final Proof Editor: Dr. C. K. Phillips

Cover Designer: Suzette Vaughn

Cover Photograph: Don Ayres

Author Photograph: Shannon Prothro Photography

BOOKS BY GLYN HAYNIE

RETURN TO THE MADNESS,
A Vietnam War Novel (Book 2)

PROMISES TO THE FALLEN,
A Vietnam War Novel (Book 1)

WHEN I TURNED NINETEEN,
A Vietnam War Memoir

SOLDIERING AFTER THE VIETNAM WAR,
Changed Soldiers in a Changed Country

FINDING MY PLATOON BROTHERS,
Vietnam Then and Now

CONTENTS

RETURN
TO THE
MADNESS

PREFACE

I found writing *Promises to the Fallen* fulfilling and rewarding. It gave me the means to tell about an infantry platoon's day-to-day struggle with survival, conflict, and death in Vietnam. In the year 1969, fascinating characters that I became fond of and that I related to developed. I believed I accomplished what I set out to write about the Vietnam War.

I left the keyboard to gather dust, with the computer screen blank. I thought I had finished writing. It had never been my intention to write a series to *Promises to the Fallen*, but the question "What happened to Eddie Henderson?" was asked many times.

After several months of sitting around the house, I, too, started to wonder what happened to Sergeant Eddie Henderson. In the Epilogue of *Promises to the Fallen*, I wrote about him and his family thirty-five years later—believing this stated his fate after Vietnam. However, the urge to tell about his marriage, along with his second tour in Vietnam, seemed to take hold.

No longer could I let Eddie Henderson fade into the darkness. I sat at the desk with the keyboard at my fingertips. The computer screen began to fill with words.

Sergeant Eddie Henderson's story is not over . . .

CHAPTER 1

BACK FROM INDIANAPOLIS

The darkness reminded Eddie Henderson of the night that his best friend, Mitch Drexler, died in his arms.

Through the haze of his memory, he saw the enemy rushing their bunker firing AK-47s, throwing grenades—then the satchel charge that exploded, killing Mitch. He remembered the smell of blood, the cries for help while he held Mitch as the life drained from his body. Eddie recalled the promise made to Mitch before he died—the promise he didn't keep.

He and Mitch had gone through training together, and Eddie stayed with his parents while they were on leave before reporting to Vietnam. He wouldn't have made it this far if it wasn't for Mitch. The two friends watched out for each other and protected one another from the Viet Cong—until that fateful night that the enemy killed Mitch. Not only did Mitch die during the attack on Hill 100, but the enemy killed his squad leader, Sergeant Stahl, and the platoon medic, Doc Wheeler.

Eddie's life was forever changed.

While the Mustang sped along the highway, tears rolled down his cheeks. He wiped them away. Eddie hoped his girlfriend, Cheryl, didn't notice the sob that escaped from his throat.

He glanced at Cheryl, taking in her features—round, emerald-green eyes, perfectly spaced, with a small, upturned nose and full lips. When she smiled, dimples appeared. Eddie reached across the seat and stroked her long red hair.

The drive from the Oakland International Airport had taken thirty minutes. Finally, she steered the car into a parking spot in front of the red brick, four-story apartment building close to the Berkeley campus. Cars drove by as Cheryl opened the driver's door and then quickly stepped to the ground in one motion. Her only focus was to get to Eddie. She stood on the curb before he eased out of the car.

Cheryl looked into Eddie's eyes. "Are you okay?" She grabbed his hand. "You've been quiet . . . You've seemed distant since you returned from Indianapolis."

Eddie squeezed Cheryl's hand and then pulled her into his arms. "I'm sorry, I don't mean to be." He held her tighter. "I've been thinking about Mitch, that's all." His eyes flashed as he diverted his gaze from hers.

"I know those memories won't go away, but you have to remember that it wasn't your fault he died. You know that, don't you?" Cheryl brushed a strand of hair from her eyes. "The enemy—not you—killed him."

He pursed his lips and momentarily held his breath. "Yeah, you're right." However, he knew he could've done more to save Mitch. *I should've blown the claymores. If I had, the outcome might've been different*, he thought.

He turned while reaching into the back seat to grab his piece of luggage. The weight of the bag reminded him of the disassembled rifle it contained along with the reason he carried it. The memory of Mitch's wife, Sandra, and Billy Matheson, embracing and kissing danced before him—he had failed Mitch.

After he shut the car door, Eddie put his arm around Cheryl's shoulder while guiding her toward the entrance of the apartment building. When they walked through the building doorway toward the apartment, Eddie pulled her in closer. Her smell, along with the warmth of her body, calmed him.

Once inside the apartment, Cheryl locked the door. "You want anything to eat or drink?" She threw her jacket across the chair.

"No, thanks. I'm not feeling well." Eddie wiped the sweat from his face. "I hope it's not the Hong Kong flu."

"How long have you been sick?" Cheryl put the back of her hand on his forehead. "You're hot and your skin feels clammy."

"I've been feeling bad the last couple of days. But it really hit on the flight back home." Eddie kissed her on the cheek. "I'm going to bed."

"Go ahead." Cheryl stood at the open doorway with a concerned look. "I'll join you in a couple of minutes."

•

Cheryl picked up items scattered around the apartment. Her head jerked toward the bedroom, acknowledging Eddie's moan. "Having another nightmare? I'm coming."

Eddie's moan was slightly muffled.

Cheryl ran to comfort him but tripped and caught herself by grabbing the sofa and then bolted into the bedroom. "Eddie, I'm here." She put her arms around him. He jerked away from her. "My God, you're soaking wet. You're hot with a fever."

Eddie opened his eyes. "I'm . . . I'm sick." He wiped at the sweat pouring down his face.

"We need to get you to a doctor." Cheryl struggled to get him out of bed.

With trembling hands, Eddie buttoned his shirt. He leaned against the edge of the bed to put on his pants. Cheryl held him while he stepped into his penny loafers. She led him down the apartment steps to the car.

While he rested against the rear fender, she opened the door. Eddie then collapsed on the seat. "Move your leg. I need to close the door." Cheryl lifted his right leg. After positioning him into the car, she slammed the door and dashed to the driver's side.

Cheryl stumbled getting into the car and quickly started the engine before slamming the door. "You don't look so good." She pulled into the traffic and then headed west.

Eddie moaned, wiping at the sweat that covered him. He felt his body shaking uncontrollably. "I'm going to puke." He rolled down the window and heaved onto the pavement. Cheryl maneuvered through the traffic, heading toward the hospital. "I'm sorry," he whimpered.

She concentrated on her driving. "It's okay. We'll be at the hospital in a couple of minutes."

Within ten minutes, she pulled into the emergency room entrance. Cheryl slammed the gear shift into park, and was at the passenger door in seconds. "Lean on me. I'll help get you inside."

"I can walk." Eddie stumbled out of the car. "Shit, I don't know if I can." His knees weakened beneath him.

Cheryl wrapped her arms around Eddie to support him. "I got you. Walk with me."

While she struggled to get Eddie inside the emergency room, an orderly ran out to help. "He's really sick." There was panic in her voice. "Thank you. Please hurry."

The orderly grabbed his arm. "What's his name?"

Cheryl ducked under Eddie's right arm to help support him. "Eddie . . . Sergeant Eddie Henderson."

HE WAS RIGHT

It had been five days since Eddie's entrance into the hospital. His room was well illuminated and had a polished, white tile floor that reflected the sunlight streaming through the large window.

Eddie rubbed the crust from his eyes and then stared through a feverish fog at his surroundings. "Where am I?" His voice quivered as he spoke. "Cheryl?"

Cheryl peered into his eyes. "You're at the hospital." She took his hand, pressing it against her face. "You're sick."

"The hospital?" Eddie muttered. "What happened?" He licked his dry, cracked lips.

"The doctor says you have malaria." She kissed the back of his hand.

While he looked around the room, Eddie wiped at the sweat. "Malaria!" With a small grin spreading across his face, he said, "Damn, I should've listened to my squad leader, Sergeant Stahl, and taken the orange pill." They laughed at his attempt at a joke.

Cheryl grinned. "Well, maybe you should've."

She placed the straw between Eddie's lips so he could drink from the large cup. Water dripped down his chin. "I needed that."

After Cheryl wiped his chin, she climbed onto the bed. She slid next to him, with their bodies touching. "You've been here for five days."

Eddie's eyes went wide. "Five days!"

"Yes. I've been worried." Cheryl snuggled in closer.

"I'm sorry." Eddie squeezed her.

"Good morning," a voice at the doorway announced.

Cheryl stood with blood rushing to her face. "Good morning, Doctor."

The doctor walked to the foot of Eddie's bed. He picked up the medical chart and reviewed it. After several minutes, he placed it back on the bed rail. In silence, he leaned over Eddie while placing a stethoscope to his chest, and then he listened. Next, he took Eddie's wrist while he timed his pulse. "It appears the medication is working. I'll discharge you in a day or two."

"Great, Doc. You saying I'll be fit in a couple of days?" A smile tugged at Eddie's lips.

The doctor released Eddie's wrist and then placed the stethoscope around his neck. "You won't be a hundred percent for a couple of weeks." He stepped back. "I'll notify your commander."

He stared at the doctor. "My commander?"

"Yes, your fiancée told me you're in the Army." The doctor glanced at Cheryl. She blushed until her freckles were no longer visible, diverting her eyes to avoid looking at Eddie.

"Yes, she's my fiancée." Eddie beamed when he looked at Cheryl.

She shot a glance at Eddie, pleased with his response. "Was that a proposal?"

"I believe it was." Eddie's grin spread ear to ear.

"Yes! I'll marry you." Cheryl leaned over the bed, kissing Eddie on the cheek.

The doctor laughed. "I'll leave you two alone." He turned and eased out of the room, closing the door behind him.

After the doctor left the room, Cheryl said, "I told him you were my fiancé. That way, I could stay with you." She bent down to kiss him. "Are you mad?"

There was a tingling sensation that traveled the length of his body, the right kind. Although he hadn't thought of it, Eddie realized that he wanted to marry Cheryl. Whatever lay ahead for both of them may be a challenge, but the love he felt for her was worth any risk. His smile grew as he stared into Cheryl's eyes.

"No, of course not." He grabbed her hand. "How can I be mad at the woman I'm going to marry?"

Within seconds, guilt coursed through his body. He couldn't undo his decision to re-enlist and return to Vietnam. But to tell her now was the wrong time.

Cheryl giggled after she kissed him again. "I almost forgot." She walked to the television. "You need to watch this." She reached up, pushing the power button. Next, she rotated the channel selector to the NBC channel. "This has been playing all morning."

Eddie sat up in bed. "What is it?"

"You'll see." She walked back to his bed.

The static on the television cleared. Eddie saw a crowd of thousands on the UC Berkeley campus. "No, not another war protest."

Cheryl remained quiet, intently watching the television screen.

Then Eddie recognized the student talking while holding a microphone. "It can't be." He wore an army fatigue shirt over a black T-shirt with blue jeans and sported a full beard. "I'll be damn. It's Professor."

"Yes, it is." Cheryl held Eddie's hand. "The commentator said Professor is protesting the war but wants everyone to treat the returning soldiers better."

"Good for him. I remember when we came back from 'Nam, he said he would." Eddie tightened his grip on Cheryl's hand.

He recalled that the platoon nicknamed Calvin Cox Professor because he was the only college-educated man in the unit. Deep down, Henderson thought he liked the name. Even with their age difference, they became close friends.

Memories of Professor searching for the enemy soldier that killed his brother, Bobby, surfaced. Eddie recalled how Professor checked each body of a dead VC or NVA soldier to see if he was the one. He felt sad for Professor because he never did find him.

•

The next morning a soldier from the Presidio of San Francisco, an army post, knocked on Eddie's hospital door. "Sergeant Eddie Henderson?"

Eddie sat up to prop the pillow behind his back. "Yes." He studied the soldier, wondering why he would come to his room. "Hope I'm not in trouble." He smiled.

The soldier grinned and entered the room. "No, you're not in trouble, Sergeant." He stopped at the foot of the bed. "I brought your paperwork to sign you in from ordinary leave until you've recovered from your illness."

"You mean recovered from malaria." Eddie lifted his left brow.

"Correct." He handed Eddie a multipart form and a pen. "Sign this form to start your medical leave. Now, your sick time won't count against your ordinary leave time."

"What's today's date?" Eddie took the form.

The clerk glanced at his watch. "It's March sixth."

Eddie signed in the signature block. Next, he entered the date. "Is that it?"

"No." The clerk handed him another form. "Now sign this form to sign in from medical leave. Doing this puts you back on ordinary leave two weeks from now."

Eddie signed the second form. "Any other papers to sign?" He handed the paperwork back to the soldier.

"No, Sergeant. You report to Fort Lewis April fifteenth to depart for Vietnam." He tore off a page from each form. "Here are your copies." He handed the pages to Eddie.

"Thanks." Eddie took his copies.

The clerk held out additional paperwork. "These are your amended orders for Vietnam." Once Eddie took the orders, the soldier asked, "Any questions?"

"I guess you covered it all." He handed the clerk the pen. "Thanks for coming out here to help me."

"Sergeant, my honor." The soldier almost stood at attention. "Welcome home." He did an about-face, passing Cheryl as he left the room. "Good morning, ma'am."

Cheryl showed her beautiful smile. "Good morning."

She gave Eddie a quizzical glance while she fluffed his pillow. "What was that about?"

Eddie looked out the window. "The Army needed me to sign some paperwork. That's all."

"Oh, that was nice of them to come to the hospital." She smoothed his hair. "You can go home tomorrow." Then she pulled the cotton blanket up to his chin. "Comfortable?"

Eddie lay in bed, staring into Cheryl's green eyes while enjoying the attention he received from her. A wave of guilt washed over him. *I'll tell her when we get home.*

TIME TO CONFESS

Once home, the guilt ate away at Eddie. The remorse he felt washed over him like ocean waves hitting him hard, knocking him backward. He hoped it wasn't too late to be honest, to tell her about his return to Vietnam.

Cheryl kissed Eddie on the cheek. "I bet you're happy to be home."

Eddie flopped into the overstuffed chair. "Yes, and I'm glad to be out of the hospital."

"Do you want anything?" Cheryl walked toward the kitchen.

"No, thanks. I'm good."

While he sat in the chair, his foot began tapping faster and faster. Eddie held his breath, waiting for her to return. Each second seemed to last an eternity as he listened for her footsteps returning to the living room—the shame he carried for not telling Cheryl earlier loomed over him.

He ran his fingers through his thick hair. "We need to talk."

Cheryl stood in the kitchen doorway, opening a beer. "What's wrong?" She tilted the bottle allowing the beer to flow down her throat. After she lowered the bottle, she wiped her mouth with the back of her hand. "You don't want to marry me, do you."

He stood and walked toward her. "I love you. I want to marry you." His arms circled her small waist. "But you may not want to marry me."

"Why do you say that?" She brushed his hands away, escaping from his grasp.

"I'm going back to Vietnam." Finally, he said it. "I've wanted to tell you but haven't found the right time."

Cheryl stepped back. They stood facing each other. He sensed the silent panic take hold of her body and thought he could hear her heart racing. Eddie wondered if she would scream, hit him, or run for the door. He didn't want to lose her.

She crossed her arms while stomping her foot. "That can't be true. You've only been back a short time." Anger smoldered in her eyes.

"I re-enlisted. I'm going back next month." Eddie reached for her.

Cheryl stumbled backward, pushing his arms away. "Oh, Eddie, why didn't you ask me first?"

Eddie took a step forward. "I don't know. I have to go back. I need to go back." He pulled her close to him. "Will you wait for me?"

She stared out the window with tears streaming down her face. The silence made Eddie's legs go weak while his stomach turned over. He waited.

She rested her head on his shoulder. "I want to marry you." She held on tighter. "Why do you feel the need to return to Vietnam?"

While Eddie thought of his time with the First Platoon, regret crept through every nerve in his body. He longed to be with his brothers and, in some way, to stop the bloodshed, save them from death. The remorse he felt ate at him each day.

Eddie stared at the floor. "I need to return to my platoon brothers. Maybe I can help them survive. I shouldn't have left them."

Cheryl stepped back. "If you let guilt consume you, you'll never have peace. What's done is done. Returning to Vietnam will not undo Mitch's death. That will be with you forever, no matter what you decide."

"I know it will. But I still need to go back." He looked into her eyes, searching for her understanding and acceptance. "Shit, Cheryl, I no longer have a choice. I re-enlisted, end of story."

Eddie thought he saw steam coming from her red, freckled cheeks every time he opened his mouth. He knew Cheryl struggled to contain her anger. She picked up the framed photograph of Eddie and her taken when they first met in Hawaii. She stared at it for a moment and then hurled it against the wall. Eddie ducked, watching the frame and glass explode when it hit.

"Come on, Cheryl, calm down; you don't need to get this upset. Just calm down."

She mentally snapped and grabbed his arm. "Calm down! Don't you dare tell me to calm down." Cheryl took a deep breath and then released her grip, staring at him. "Arguing with you is pointless because you're determined to return to the war."

Eddie watched her face change from rage to hurt. "Damn, Cheryl, you can argue with me all night, but I still have to go." Eddie reached for her hand. "I'm not saying that I'm born for this, but I wish you would be proud that I dare to do what I think is right."

"I am proud of you." Cheryl took his hand into hers, pulling him close. "I don't want you to die." She clung to him to keep him from leaving. "I'm not happy that you're going back, or even re-enlisting, but I'll wait for you." Cheryl whispered in his ear, "You better come back."

A DAY TO REMEMBER

Cheryl, with her mother, made all the arrangements for the wedding. She decided on an intimate wedding in a small ballroom at a local hotel. Eddie was agreeable. He wanted to invite the Drexlers. Professor agreed to be the best man.

The day before the wedding, Eddie drove to the airport to pick up Mitch's parents, John and Martha Drexler. Since his own parents died over a year ago, they'd become his adopted parents.

He knew how much they missed Mitch and was surprised in the way they welcomed him into their family. Even during his visit, after he returned from Vietnam, Mr. Drexler became angry, as a father would, when he told him that he was returning to the war.

When he drove into the arrival area, Eddie spotted the couple standing next to their luggage. The car rolled to a stop in front of them. In one motion, Eddie opened the door, jumping from the vehicle. In a long stride, he headed toward the Drexlers.

Mrs. Drexler held her arms out, and Eddie walked into her embrace. "Oh, Eddie, you look good." She pushed him back to get a better look at him. "I bet you put on some weight."

He stood tall with his shoulders back. "Yes, ma'am, I have, about twenty pounds."

Mr. Drexler stepped in front of his wife. He took Eddie's hand in a firm grasp. "You do look good, Eddie." He shook it vigorously. "You even look like you're taller."

"Thank you, sir." Eddie pulled his hand away, rubbing it. "It's great seeing you again. Thanks for coming."

Mrs. Drexler beamed as she placed her hand on Eddie's shoulder. "We wouldn't miss your wedding." She stepped closer. "We want grandchildren."

Eddie felt his blood race to his face, but he managed a grin.

Mr. Drexler put his arm around his wife. "Now, Martha, I told you not to talk about grandchildren." He looked at Eddie with a mischievous grin. "But grandchildren would be great."

Eddie averted his eyes to the ground. "Let me load your bags. Then we'll head for the hotel." He picked up the two oversized matching suitcases. "Wow, you sure packed a lot."

"You never know how the weather will be in California." Mrs. Drexler crossed her arms in front of her chest and gave Mr. Drexler a stern glance.

Mr. Drexler avoided her look. "I told her not to pack that much for a two-day visit."

"She's probably right," Eddie said over his shoulder while he struggled to the car. "The weather is always changing."

Eddie placed the luggage into the trunk. "Mr. Drexler, you can sit in the front seat. Hopefully, you'll have enough legroom," he said. After he opened the passenger door, Eddie helped Mrs. Drexler into the back seat. "I hope it's comfortable enough for you. It's a short ride."

With her hand, she brushed her gray hair back. "It will be fine. I haven't ridden in a Mustang before."

When Eddie settled into the driver's seat, Mr. Drexler placed his hand on Eddie's arm. "Son, from now on, please call us John and Martha. Forget all that mister or missus crap."

Eddie laughed. "Yes, sir." Then he wheeled the car into the traffic, heading toward the interstate.

While looking in the rearview mirror, Eddie said, "We're going to meet this evening at seven in the hotel restaurant for dinner."

He looked at the road and then back into the mirror. "Cheryl will be there. I can't wait for you to meet her." He grinned. "Oh, her parents too."

Martha raised her voice over the roar of the road. "We're excited to meet her too."

"Guess who else is coming?" Eddie glanced at John.

John shook his head. "Who is it?"

"Professor will be there. He's looking forward to meeting you." Eddie looked at the road then back at John.

John's eyes went wide. "I can't wait to talk to him."

Eddie shot another look in the rearview mirror. "I invited Rocky, too, but he can't make it."

Martha leaned forward with her hand on Eddie's shoulder. "That's a shame."

The car fell silent for the rest of the trip.

•

"We're here." Eddie coasted the car to a stop at the hotel entrance. He jumped from the car and bolted to the passenger door. He held it open for them.

After John rolled out of the car, Martha made several attempts to get her body to move forward but failed each time. "This is harder than I thought it would be." She giggled while holding her arm out for help.

Eddie grasped her arm. "Come on, I'll give you a hand." With a slight tug, she popped onto the entranceway.

While they waited, Eddie retrieved the bags. "You go get checked in. We'll meet you at the bar at six." He handed the two suitcases to the porter and then slipped him a tip. "We can spend some time together before everyone gets here for dinner at seven."

Martha placed her hand on Eddie's arm. "Who's all coming for dinner?"

"Me, Cheryl, her best friend, and her parents. Oh, Professor too." Eddie put his arm around her shoulder, giving her a gentle squeeze. "That's who will be at the wedding too."

He watched John and Martha follow the porter into the hotel.

•

The Mustang swung into a parking spot not far from the front door of the hotel. Eddie ran around to the passenger door, opening it for Cheryl. When she stepped onto the cobblestone drive, Eddie noticed her long slender legs supported by heels that matched a short, dark-green skirt that contrasted perfectly to her light-green blouse. Her soft, shiny red hair hung below her shoulders, and her green eyes twinkled as if she was flirting with him.

Eddie stood transfixed while staring into her eyes. "Damn, you're beautiful!"

Cheryl's cheeks suddenly turned red, the color nearly matching her freckled skin. "You're such a gentleman." She looked away to find a distraction.

The doorman held the door open for the couple to enter the hotel. They walked directly to the bar. When they arrived, Eddie heard a voice calling, "Over here, over here."

A smile crept across his face. "Cheryl, there they are." He waved back to acknowledge he saw them. "That's Mitch's parents, John and Martha Drexler."

They maneuvered through the tables, with Cheryl in the lead. She reached the older couple first and walked into the arms of Martha, giving her a loving hug. "It's nice to meet you. I've heard so much about you two." Next, she turned to hug John.

Eddie reached across, giving both a brief hug. Then, he pulled a chair out for Cheryl.

Martha sat staring at the young woman in front of her. "Oh my, Eddie, she is beautiful."

Cheryl smiled with her even, white teeth showing while her green eyes sparkled.

Eddie beamed. "She's not only beautiful but intelligent too." His chest stuck out as he gazed at Cheryl. "She graduates from the University of California this summer."

Martha took a sip of her drink, looking over the rim of the glass at Cheryl. "What will you do when you graduate?"

"I'm going to teach high school math." Cheryl beamed with excitement apparent on her face.

"Oh my goodness." Martha set her glass down. "I hope you'll still be able to have children while working."

Loud laughter from their table resonated throughout the restaurant.

The four talked while having cocktails. The conversation was mainly about Eddie and Cheryl's future. On her second drink, Martha grasped Cheryl's hand. "Cheryl, we want grandchildren."

John almost choked on his drink. "Martha, I told you."

"Oh, John, you do too." Martha glanced at her husband with a mischievous grin. "You told me."

John picked at some lint on his jacket. "Let's give the kids a break, okay?"

After the laughter subsided, Cheryl squeezed Martha's hand. "I don't know when, but I'm sure you'll have grandchildren."

Martha finished her drink. "What will you do while Eddie is in Vietnam?"

The conversation at the table became quiet.

Cheryl picked up her glass, twirling the ice. She took a long drink. "I'll wait." The twinkle in her eyes disappeared. She listened to the chatter along with the laughter around the bar area, but her disappointment was firmly etched on her face.

Eddie immediately put his arm around her sagging shoulders to comfort her, but the guilt of returning to Vietnam weighed heavily on his mind. Even if he wanted to, he couldn't undo his decision.

"It's time to eat." He stood to change the subject.

The two couples walked the short distance to the restaurant.

While standing at the entrance, Eddie felt a hand on his shoulder. Then he heard a whisper in his ear. "Hello, Sergeant Little Fella."

Eddie recognized the voice. He spun around to face Professor. "Man, it's been too long."

The two embraced like two brothers seeing each other after a long absence.

"Thanks for coming." Eddie stepped back. "Look at you, hair getting long. Damn, a full beard already."

Out of the corner of his eye, Eddie caught John staring. "John, this is Professor."

John reached to shake hands.

Eddie continued, “Professor, this is Mitch’s dad, John.”

Professor stepped toward John. “Mitch was a hell of a man. A good friend.” He ignored John’s extended hand and embraced him.

Martha heard the conversation and pulled Professor into her arms without saying a word.

Eddie waited. “Okay, Martha, you can let go now.”

“Oh my, it’s so good to meet you at last,” she cried.

Cheryl latched on to Professor’s arm. “It’s great to see you again. Thank you for coming.”

After a brief hug, Professor said, “I wouldn’t miss it.”

She squeezed his arm tight. “Why didn’t you tell me Eddie re-enlisted? Hell, he’s even going back to Vietnam!”

“Ouch!” Professor flinched from her fingernails digging into his skin. “That wasn’t my place to tell you. It’s Eddie’s responsibility.”

Cheryl released her firm grip on Professor’s arm. “Fair enough.” She grinned at him.

An attractive redhead sitting at a table in the far corner waved. “Cheryl, over here.”

With pride, Cheryl said, “That’s my mom.”

Everyone took a seat at the large round table. After Eddie made the introductions, the festivities began to celebrate the marriage of the young couple.

•

During the party, Eddie cornered Professor. “I need to ask a favor.”

“Sure, anything.” Professor placed an arm around Eddie’s shoulder.

Eddie turned to face Professor. “I want to make you my emergency contact.”

“I have no problem with that.” He had a quizzical look on his face. “Why not Cheryl?”

After lighting a cigarette, Eddie offered one to Professor. “If I get killed or wounded, I want you to tell Cheryl. I don’t want a stranger knocking on the door, handing her a telegram.”

“Hell, nothing’s going to happen to you.” He allowed a nervous laugh to escape from his lips. “You live a charmed life.”

"I'm serious." Eddie took a long drag from his cigarette, blowing the smoke skyward.

Professor's mouth pointed into a frown as sadness reflected from his eyes. "Okay, I'll do it."

"Thanks. It means a lot." Eddie stepped forward, giving him a brief hug.

"I have a question for you." Professor inhaled deeply from his cigarette. He released a cloud of smoke. "What happened in Indianapolis?"

Eddie seemed surprised by the question. "I had dinner with the Drexlers. They asked about Mitch." He glanced toward the doorway. "We got along well. John did get mad when I told him I was going back to Vietnam."

Professor put the cigarette out. "Come on, what about Billy Matheson?"

While Eddie thought about what to say, his eyes went dull. His mind wandered back to that cold February night and the promise he didn't keep. It was still fresh in his memory how he looked through the scope with the crosshairs centered on Billy's forehead.

"Well?" Professor furrowed his brow.

Eddie eyeballed Professor. "I did see them. Sandra is pregnant." He looked at the floor. "I didn't do it. I couldn't keep my promise to Mitch."

Professor watched the twinkle in Eddie's eyes grow fainter with disappointment.

"Eddie, that's a good thing. You're not a killer." Professor hugged his friend. "Let's get back to the party."

The two platoon brothers joined the group seated at the table, celebrating the upcoming wedding.

•

The next afternoon, the groom and best man stood in front of the preacher. Eddie nervously waited for Cheryl to enter the room. He wore his dress Army uniform with his awards and decorations displayed, and Professor wore a dark-blue suit.

Eddie patted Professor on the shoulder. "You look uncomfortable wearing a suit."

"I am. I prefer jeans and a T-shirt."

Eddie smiled at the maid of honor, Pam, as she stood across from him, appearing calm. Then he glanced at John and Martha, sitting on the left side of the room about twenty feet behind him. Martha smiled and waved at Eddie. Cheryl's mom sat next to them with an empty chair next to her for Cheryl's dad.

"Here Comes the Bride" began to play. Eddie straightened, looking to the rear of the room.

"Are you ready?" Professor whispered.

Eddie watched the side entrance as Cheryl and her dad walked arm in arm into the room toward the front. She wore a white, full-length gown that revealed her soft, fair shoulders. Cheryl had her long red hair pulled into a French-braided bun, but he saw only her smile and gleaming green eyes. He knew she was having her fairy-tale moment.

"I am," Eddie stammered. "She's beautiful."

•

Cheryl rolled onto her back, staring at the diamond ring on her left hand. "Can you believe we got married yesterday?" She nudged Eddie.

"It seems like a lifetime to me." Eddie rolled over to face her.

Cheryl giggled, punching his arm playfully. He laughed and then pulled her in for a hug. Her laughter gave way to a sob.

"I was only kidding." Eddie flashed a comforting grin

Cheryl's sobs became louder as she rolled onto her side. "I know." With her back to Eddie, she stared out the window, watching the sunlight filter into the room. "I don't want you to go back to Vietnam."

"I'll be home before you know it. Hell, we can meet in Hawaii for R and R." Eddie tickled her side. "Won't that be fun?"

She didn't respond, remaining still. Eddie sensed the sadness run through her, traveling through every inch of her body. He understood that she might feel helpless about him returning to Vietnam, but what could he do?

"I don't want you to leave." Cheryl rolled into his arms, crying. "We only have a week left together." She held him tighter. "What if you don't come home?"

He knew there was nothing he could say to quiet her fears. He remained silent.

Each morning as the sunlight slipped through the bedroom window, Eddie lay on the bed with his eyes open, using the stillness to get ready for the trip back to Vietnam. Of course, he knew it was a useless exercise. How can anyone prepare to return to the madness of war?

CROSSING THE POND

From a deep sleep, Eddie bolted upright in bed. "Mitch, I'm coming; hold on!" He flipped to his side, falling to the floor. "Where's my rifle? I can't find my rifle!"

Cheryl slid out of bed. She sat on the floor in front of him, as she had done many times over the weeks. "Eddie, it's okay. You'll be okay."

He jerked away. "Help Mitch!"

She took his hands into hers. "Eddie, you're home. You're safe. It's me, Cheryl."

He sat upright, looking around the room, sweat dripping down his face. His pounding heart pushed blood through his veins until he thought it would explode.

She cradled him in her arms. "It's okay. It's okay." She rocked him softly.

He gasped. "Shit. I'm sorry, Cheryl."

"It's okay. We might as well get up. We have four hours before your flight leaves." Tears trickled down Cheryl's cheeks as she turned to head to the kitchen.

After a leisurely breakfast, Cheryl walked around the apartment, picking up, dusting, and organizing. Eddie sat on the sofa, drinking coffee while watching her.

"Come sit with me." Eddie put his cup down. "Take a break."

Cheryl opened the closet door to hang a sweater. "If I stop moving, I'll only think of you in Vietnam." She shut the door. "Why did you volunteer to go back?"

He felt trapped between two conflicting needs—his need to stay with Cheryl and the need to return to the men that he wanted to help. His confliction tore at his heart; he didn't want to be disloyal to Cheryl or his platoon brothers. The choice he made was before his marriage. He had to return.

Eddie walked toward her. "I've told you. I need to." He didn't understand, either. It was a feeling deep in his gut that drove him to return. "Please wait for me." He reached out to her.

She walked into his arms. "Of course, I will." She cried harder.

After they embraced in silence for several minutes, Eddie said, "I need to finish packing. We need to leave in thirty minutes."

"That soon!" Cheryl buried her face into her hands, sobbing louder as he walked into the bedroom. She managed to stumble toward the sofa, falling in a heap onto the soft cushion. Cheryl stared at the bedroom entrance while tears trickled down her cheeks. In a short time, she heard the lock snapping on the duffel bag.

A shadow came through the doorway, followed by Eddie. "I'm packed. All ready to go."

"You look handsome in your uniform." Cheryl managed a smile. "Let me wash these tears away. I'll put some makeup on. Then we can leave." She kissed him on the cheek as she passed him. After five minutes, Cheryl strolled from the bedroom without any evidence of her crying—except for her puffy eyes. "Let's go." She passed Eddie, heading for the apartment door.

They sat in silence during the drive to the airport. Feeling uncomfortable with the quietness, Eddie turned the radio on and a song blared: "*Where have all the flowers gone . . .*"

Cheryl started crying again. "Oh, not that song."

"Yeah, I guess not a good song to play." He turned the radio off.

In what seemed like seconds, Cheryl turned onto the airport road. After five minutes, she parked the car. Eddie eased out to the pavement and slung the duffel bag over his shoulder. With a quick pace, Cheryl walked around the Mustang.

"Let's go." She reached to touch his hand.

With a loving grin, Eddie wrapped his arm around her. "You're beautiful."

She remained silent as he guided her toward the airline's check-in counter.

Once Eddie checked in, he left his bag with the ticket agent. They strolled along the long corridor to the gate. "We still have an hour." He surveyed the walkway for a restaurant. "You want to eat?"

Cheryl shook her head no. She latched on to his arm with both hands, and they continued to the departure gate. It seemed like they sat for a short period when Eddie heard the announcement to board the flight to Seattle. He looked at Cheryl as tears streamed down her cheeks.

She wiped at the tears. "Wait a minute—I have a gift for you." Cheryl reached into her purse and pulled out a photograph. "This is the wedding picture of me that you loved." She handed him the picture.

"I do love that picture. I'll always carry it." As he looked at the photograph, he detected her scent. "It smells like you." He smiled.

"I put a drop of my perfume on the back." Cheryl's eyes twinkled as if flirting with him.

Eddie chuckled. "Now I can look at you and have your fragrance while I'm gone." He put the photograph into his pocket and then held out his hand. "Come on, hug me." He flashed his boyish grin.

"Who can resist that face?" She took his hand, allowing him to pull her from the seat.

Eddie wrapped his arms around her. He smothered his face into her neck. "I love you." He lingered, wanting to capture her aroma to take with him.

"Please be careful; I love you too." She squeezed his body into hers. "I'll write every day."

Eddie kissed Cheryl for a long time. He stepped back, looking into her eyes while flashing his boyish grin again. "I'll see you soon in Hawaii." Eddie turned to board the airplane.

•

The flight to Seattle was uneventful. Once he arrived, Eddie went to the USO. A young female worker greeted him, "Good afternoon, Sergeant. Are you going to Fort Lewis?"

"Yes." Eddie fidgeted with his garrison hat. "Where's the bus?"

"It's waiting outside. Go through the exit on the right." She pointed in the direction. "The driver will leave in five minutes."

"Thank you." He followed her instructions, going through the doors. Within minutes, he boarded the bus. It all seemed familiar to him.

As he walked along the aisle, he noticed the young faces of the soldiers he passed. Most didn't have campaign ribbons or a Combat Infantry Badge. They held the rank of Private First Class. It was a sure indicator that they were FNGs, heading to war for the first time. *Poor fucking new guys!*

Within four hours of arriving at Fort Lewis, Eddie stepped onto another bus for the airport. A soldier looked up from his seat. "Hello, Sergeant."

When Eddie sat down, he noticed that the soldier glanced at his jungle fatigues, eyeing the Combat Infantry Badge sewn above the US Army tag, and his Americal Division patch on the right shoulder of the shirt. "You going back?"

"Yeah." Eddie closed his eyes to get some sleep during the ride to the airport.

Once the bus stopped in front of the airliner, Eddie knew he would board the waiting Pan Am Airways aircraft to fly to Cam Ranh Bay, Vietnam. He stood with the other soldiers. Eddie walked to the bus exit door and then stepped down to the pavement. He strolled toward the stairs to board the plane. While he walked past the occupied seats, Eddie noted more fresh young faces. He felt a tinge of excitement as he remembered when Mitch and he flew to Vietnam a year earlier.

After he passed fifteen rows, Eddie found a vacant seat next to a sergeant. He wore an Americal patch on his right shoulder. "This seat taken?"

A combat brother, he thought.

"No, have a seat." The soldier shifted to his left.

"Thanks." Eddie stowed his bag and then flopped into the seat. "You ready for the long flight?"

The sergeant glanced up with a smile. "Yep, no other choice, is there?"

While waiting to take off, Eddie sized up the black sergeant sitting next to him. He knew his last name was Johnston because of his name tag. With his dark hair cut short, square jaw, and clean-shaven face, he didn't appear any older than Eddie. Johnston was a big man with broad shoulders and muscular arms, which gave the impression that Eddie was much smaller. He appeared aloof. Eddie assumed he didn't want conversation.

Eddie decided to leave him alone in his thoughts. That's what he wanted too. He fell asleep, staring at the photograph of Cheryl.

•

As the aircraft slowed, the pilot announced, "Buckle up, we are landing in ten minutes."

Eddie snapped on his seat belt as he looked past the soldier sitting next to him to see out the window. The sunlight was bright. He could see lush, green mountains and then the blue-green water of the South China Sea appeared as the plane turned.

Johnston shifted in his seat while looking out the window. "It looks the same."

"I wonder if the smell has changed," Eddie muttered.

With a big belly laugh, Johnston said, "I doubt it." He turned, smiling at Eddie. "That smell will never go away."

A light flickered, and a bell sounded. "Hang on. We're going in fast," the pilot announced.

The nose of the airliner dipped sharply as the plane dropped like a rock.

Eddie held on to the armrest. "This seems familiar."

"It does." Johnston grabbed the seat in front of him.

After the wheels thudded against the airstrip, the plane coasted along the runway. The pilot braked hard, throwing the passengers forward as the aircraft stopped. A loud gasp escaped from the soldiers. For most, this was their first experience landing at an airfield in a combat zone. Eddie peered out the window. He saw three green buses stop near the plane.

When the aircraft doors opened, an Army sergeant ran up the stairs. He picked up the airplane's handset. "You will board the buses waiting outside the plane. Officers on the first bus. Enlisted on the second and third buses." He released the button, taking a breath. "Okay, let's move."

The servicemen stood, talking, the volume of their voices getting louder by the second. They shuffled along the aisle toward the door. Once Eddie reached the doorway, he walked down the stairs. He boarded the second bus. Johnston followed him, flopping onto the seat next to Eddie.

Eddie stared out the window at the view. "The smell is the same."

"It is." Johnston wiped at the sweat running down his face. "The heat feels the same too."

"Some things never change." Eddie shifted his weight in the seat. "Hell, we've sat next to each other for a full day. I only know your last name, Johnston."

Johnston leaned forward while stretching his hand out. "Carl Johnston, from Detroit."

"Hello, Carl Johnston from Detroit." He shook his hand. "I'm Eddie Henderson from Ashville."

Once loaded, the buses drove to the in-processing area for replacements. Eddie didn't wait long to board another airplane; along with Johnston, there were twenty-five more soldiers going to Chu Lai. He knew he was going back to the Americal Division.

•

After four hours, the C-130 airplane made a steep dive. Within minutes, the wheels hit hard. The plane rolled along the Chu Lai runway. The pilot halted not far from a large hangar. Once the aircraft came to a standstill, the rear ramp lowered.

A bus stopped near the C-130 as the soldiers disembarked. Eddie was the first out. He stood on the runway, taking in the heat along with the smells of Vietnam. To him, it felt like he was in an oven. The smell was hard to identify, maybe rotting vegetables, mold, exotic food, and animals all rolled into one odor. The hair on the back of his neck stood on end. Fear gripped him. *What in the hell did I do?*

He had a change of heart. The old fears he believed that he left behind began to remind him of war and death. Soldiers walked off the airplane past Eddie as he stood on the runway, absorbing all that was Vietnam.

Johnston turned to face Eddie. "You coming, Sergeant?"

"Yeah." Eddie looked dazed. "Yeah, I'm coming."

Once the bus was loaded, the driver closed the doors. He drove to the Combat Center. It was at this location that the replacements received in-country training before reporting to their unit. Eddie observed the white beach with the blue-green water of the South China Sea on one side, while the other held rows of identical one-story buildings. They were built with plywood, painted green, running four feet high on all sides. Screen covered the next four feet up to the slanted tin roof. Sandbags were stacked against the plywood up to the screen for protection.

As the bus entered the compound, the driver drove under a sign that read, "Welcome to the Americal Division – Combat Center."

The bus stopped next to a large one-story building, referred to as the Replacement Depot. It had the same design as all the other buildings, Eddie saw while on the bus. Across the road was the South China Sea, with the small waves lapping at the white sand of the coastline.

Eddie, with the rest of the soldiers, strolled through the open doorway of the large building. He walked across the sand floor. After passing many of the benches that filled the building, Eddie chose one farthest from the door. Now, he waited for his assignment.

A NEW ASSIGNMENT

A short, slender corporal entered the building. "Listen up!" With long strides, he walked to the center of the room. "Quiet."

Eddie noticed right away that the corporal wore a Combat Infantry Badge. He had the look of a seasoned grunt. The soldier's eyes got his attention—it was his faraway stare that Eddie recognized. The corporal had witnessed the horrors of war. A position at the Combat Center was his reward for his time served in the jungle, a *rear job*, where it was safer.

"When I call your name, come up here." The corporal lifted his clipboard to read from the roster of names. "Sergeant Henderson, Sergeant Johnston."

The two sergeants looked at each other, nodded, and then they approached the corporal. He reminded himself that he would no longer be called Eddie. He was Henderson again, the Army way, with last names.

"What's up, Corporal?" Henderson asked.

"You two are going to Bravo Company, Aero Scout Detachment, of the One Hundred and Twenty-Third Aviation Battalion." The corporal used the clipboard to point toward the front of the building. "There's a jeep waiting for you out front." He looked at them to make sure they understood. "Any questions?"

"Aviation Battalion?" Henderson wiped the sweat from his face. "You sure?"

With a chuckle, the corporal lowered the clipboard. "Yep, good luck."

Johnston rubbed his chin. "That's weird for two infantry guys to go to an aviation battalion." He turned for the open doorway.

The two sergeants walked out of the building.

"You guys the replacements for Bravo Company?" The jeep driver peered over the steering wheel.

"Yep, we are," Henderson replied.

"Throw your bags in the rear and hop in." The driver put the jeep into gear.

After he threw his bag into the jeep, Henderson heard a familiar sound. *Whop! Whop! Whop!* A Huey helicopter with a large red cross painted on a white background located on the nose flew low over the Combat Center, heading to the division hospital.

Henderson eyed the chopper. "I'll never forget that sound. Now I know I'm in 'Nam."

Johnston glanced upward. "Brother, I'm with you. It's a dustoff. Hope they get the wounded to the hospital in time."

Without another word, they climbed in the jeep. The driver mashed the gas pedal while shifting gears. He drove north to the Detachment Headquarters, at the far end of the firebase to Ky Ha Heliport. After a short ride, he pulled in front of a building that appeared like all the other structures they had seen. One-story, painted green, with screening halfway to the tin roof. Soldiers before him had stacked sandbags at the bottom half. The sign in front of the building read Company B, 123rd Aviation Battalion. They jumped to the ground and grabbed their bags.

Henderson opened the screen door. "After you, Johnston."

A tall, lanky man stood behind a desk. The desk appeared to sit too low for the soldier. "Can I help you?"

"We're reporting to the unit." Henderson stepped forward. "Sergeants Henderson and Johnston."

The clerk picked up a sheet of paper. "Got your names here." He walked around the desk. "Wait here. I'll tell the lieutenant you're here." Before he turned away, he gave Henderson a smile that went from ear to ear.

Johnston glanced at Henderson with a raised eyebrow. "What's that about? You know the guy?"

"No, I've never met him." Henderson rubbed his jaw while watching the soldier walk into the office.

The clerk stepped out of the doorway. "You can go in now." Again, he smiled at Henderson.

Outwardly, Henderson appeared calm; however, the clerk's antics began to irritate him, like a wool blanket covering his body. "Is there a problem, Private?" Henderson demanded.

"Sergeant Henderson!"

The voice coming from the office sounded familiar, but he couldn't place it. He shrugged as he walked through the doorway with Johnston following. Henderson stopped fast, causing Johnston to walk into him.

"What the hell?" Johnston blurted.

"Hello, Sergeant Henderson." The lieutenant stood, extending his large black hand.

Henderson ignored the hand. He stepped forward, embracing the lieutenant. "Damn, I never thought I would see you again." Within a second or two, he let go, stepping back. "Sorry, sir."

He noticed that Lieutenant Brighton appeared older, with deep wrinkles in his forehead. Although his eyes seemed sharp, he had that faraway look to him. His left hand looked as if it had a small tremor. Henderson imagined the war was getting to him.

While his cheeks flushed red, Henderson thought he should make the introduction. "Sergeant Johnston, this is Lieutenant Brighton." They shook hands. "He's the best damn officer in the Army." Henderson took a deep breath. "He was my platoon leader during my first tour."

Brighton chuckled. "Take a seat." He gestured for the two sergeants to sit in the wooden chairs that faced his desk.

Henderson sat in the chair. "I'll be damn."

Brighton moved his muscular six-foot frame with ease to the chair behind his desk. He slid it out, sitting with his elbows on the desktop.

"Sergeant Henderson, I noticed you're wearing a wedding ring. Did you marry that girl you met on R and R?" Brighton rotated his band of gold around his left ring finger.

With a smile spreading across his face, Henderson said, "Yes, sir. She's the one. Her name is Cheryl." He removed a photograph from his breast pocket. "Professor was the best man." He slid it across the desk.

"No shit. How's he doing?" Brighton appeared surprised.

"Doing good. He's back at Berkeley, protesting the war."

"No shock there." Brighton handed the picture back to Henderson. "Cheryl is a beautiful woman. You're a lucky man."

"Thanks." Henderson's chest puffed a little bigger. "She is." He took a quick look at his favorite picture before putting it away, but not before he caught a whiff of her perfume.

"Let's get down to business." Brighton stacked some papers on his desk. Then he stared out the window as he took a drink of coffee. "Our platoon performs reconnaissance, rescue, and grab-and-snatch missions. It's pretty new to the division." He looked over the rim of his cup with a sober stare. "The unit is responsible for securing downed helicopters, rescuing the crew, along with any passengers." There was a hesitation as if he remembered a terrible event. "Sometimes it's a recovery mission."

Henderson leaned forward in his chair. "It sounds interesting." He mopped his face with a handkerchief. "How did we get selected?"

When Brighton leaned back in his chair, he held up two sheets of paper. "I saw your orders. Johnston's too. I'm always on the lookout for experienced people." He lowered the chair back on all four legs as he placed the orders on a stack of papers. He took another drink of coffee. "I knew you would be a good fit.

"There's one caveat; you will need to go through a training course." Brighton stared at both men. "It's nothing you can't handle. In a nutshell, you'll learn advanced first aid, rappelling, evacuating wounded or dead crew members, along with the task of rigging downed birds for retrieval, plus training in small-unit tactics."

Brighton rose from his chair, placing his hands on the desk. "The platoon's primary mission is grab-and-snatch missions. That's where a squad lands, taking a Viet Cong or North Vietnamese Army soldier captive. Sometimes, it's the equipment or weapons we want." Brighton sat back down. "Your squad will do rescue missions. The other three squads will go on the snatch missions."

Brighton leaned back in his chair, lighting a cigarette. "Go ahead, light up if you want." He took in a deep drag, releasing the smoke into a dense cloud.

"Damn, LT, I didn't think you would ever let us smoke." Henderson removed a cigarette from the Marlboro pack.

"Thanks, sir." Johnston took a cigarette from his pack of Kools.

After he inhaled another drag, Brighton continued, "Bravo Company has one platoon of infantry. I'm the platoon leader." He chuckled. "The men are known as Animals."

"Now that's interesting." Henderson sat up in his chair. "How many soldiers in each squad?"

"A squad leader with five soldiers. We're a little short of personnel. Henderson, you'll take the First Squad. Johnston, you'll be in the First Squad until another squad leader position comes open."

Henderson leaned forward as he wiped the sweat from his forehead. "No problem, LT."

As if he was sizing him up, Johnston rubbed his chin while he stared at Brighton. "I'm in, sir."

"Great." Brighton leaned back in his chair as he called to the clerk, "Lewis, get Laurel in here."

Henderson heard a faint response. "Yes, sir."

Within a couple of minutes, a soldier came busting through the door. "What you need, LT?"

Laurel turned to look at the two guests sitting in front of the lieutenant. "Gawddamn it. Sergeant Henderson?"

Henderson jumped to his feet, grabbing Laurel in a bear hug. "How in the hell are you? How did you get with this unit?"

At first glance, Henderson thought Ray Laurel hadn't changed a bit from the day the eighteen-year-old reported to First Platoon during his first tour. With a small build, he still appeared younger than his years. His Southern accent stayed with him. However, he noticed the sadness in his eyes and the nervous twitch on the left side of his mouth. His innocence was gone.

Laurel strove to break the hold Henderson had on him. "LT took me with him when he left the field for this assignment." He struggled harder to break the hold. "Now you can let go of me."

With a loud laugh, Henderson pushed him back, letting Laurel fall free from the hug.

Laurel stepped forward to admire his old squad leader. "Sarge, you've grown an inch or two. I bet you put on thirty pounds. You're looking fit." Laurel stood smiling at Henderson like he found his long-lost friend.

It took a couple of seconds, then Henderson noticed Laurel's tooth. "Hey, man, you got a new tooth. Looks good."

"Yeah, I do. It took a while." Laurel slapped Henderson on the back. "Now I'm pretty."

"Okay, the reunion is over." Brighton laughed. "Laurel, get them squared away." He stood and walked toward the door. "Training will start tomorrow." He knew he was getting two excellent soldiers.

They left the office, heading toward the squad hooch. When they walked through the doorway, Laurel yelled, "FNGs coming in."

"Yeah, right." Henderson saw three soldiers lying on their bunks. "How's it going?" They didn't move or look up at the new arrivals.

Henderson surveyed his new quarters. There were six areas arranged with a small wooden writing table and chair, a steel bunk with a mattress, and a metal wall locker. Each sleeping space had a four-foot wall separating it from the next. In the center of the room was a table with five metal folding chairs. Four light bulbs hung from the ceiling, shining light throughout the large building. *This is better than the jungle.*

"Hey, guys, this is Sergeant Henderson." The three soldiers shot Henderson an indifferent glance. Laurel's eyes narrowed as his lips compressed. "Gawddamn it, he was my squad leader, mentor, and friend during his first tour. Hell, he taught me how to walk point too."

With that information, they stood to show respect for their new squad leader. "Welcome, Sergeant Henderson," they said in unison.

"This is Sergeant Johnston." Laurel pointed at him. "He's on his second tour. He'll be with us until a squad leader position opens."

The three soldiers nodded.

Laurel waved his hand at the three soldiers. "The big hairy guy is Bear. The small Hispanic guy is Little JJ. That leaves the man from California, Brian Cain."

The men met in the center of the large room and shook hands.

With quick strides, Henderson moved to an empty bunk. A pillow, two sheets, and a folded green wool blanket at the end of the bed. He began to stow his gear in the six-by-two wall locker. Johnston did the same.

After he put his gear away, Henderson faced his squad members. "Tomorrow, we begin training. Meet out front at zero six thirty. We'll go to the mess hall."

TIME TO SHARE

After the first training day, the squad strolled toward the hooch. They were hot, tired, and hungry. Henderson craved a cold Coke to wet his dry throat and quench his thirst. He laughed out loud as he remembered that Kool-Aid was his go-to drink when he was with the First Platoon.

For a brief moment, Henderson acknowledged how thankful he was to have this new job with Lieutenant Brighton. Hell, he had a roof over his head with a bunk to sleep in and a mess hall to eat his meals. They even had a fan in the room. Don't forget the cold Cokes and Jim Beam. He never imagined living like this in Vietnam.

Henderson wondered why Brighton extended his tour and took this position. Surely, he missed his wife and being in the world. Henderson smiled at himself. *Shit, what am I doing back here?* He realized that Brighton wanted to be with his men and make a difference. The same reason that he came back to 'Nam. He thought Brighton had aged considerably since he first met him over a year ago.

Once the six soldiers entered the room, Henderson reached into the ice chest and then tossed a Coke to each squad member. They took turns passing the opener to punch holes into the top of the can.

"Take a load off, guys. We'll go get chow shortly." Henderson opened his Coke.

Laurel sat at the table. "That was a hard first day of training."

Henderson glanced at Laurel and thought he looked older than his eighteen years. His time in Vietnam had affected him too. War weathered the softness he once had. He appeared the same young man he mentored, but his eyes told a different story.

"Hey, the training will be over before you know it." Henderson smiled and placed his hand on Laurel's shoulder. "This is better than being in the bush."

"You got that, Sarge. Not complaining." Laurel glanced up at Henderson with a wide smile.

"Damn, how many times did they have us rappel off that tower?" Cain scanned his friends. "I bet we did it twenty times."

"I guess we can do it in our sleep now." Little JJ laughed.

Bear put his muscular arm around Little JJ's shoulder. "It had to be easier for you because of your small size. Hell, I have a lot more weight to lower to the ground while hanging on to a rope."

"Size has nothing to do with it." Little JJ playfully pushed Bear back.

"Didn't you learn to rappel during your paramedic training?" Johnston eyeballed Cain.

"Yeah, Sarge, I did." Cain smiled.

Johnston laughed. "So that's how you made it look so easy."

"You got me there." Cain threw a pillow at Johnston.

Johnston caught the pillow before it hit him. "You gotta do better than that."

Henderson remembered the bottle of Jim Beam he carried from the world. He smiled when he thought of how he wrapped the bottle in two towels and stuffed it into the middle of the duffel bag. When he went through customs, the MP saw it but said nothing. He reached into his wall locker and pulled down the bottle of bourbon. "Hey, guys, gather around the table. Let's have a drink."

The men scrambled to the chairs. Bear slid the ice chest closer, while Little JJ placed six glasses on the table. Cain scooped ice into each glass.

"Those glasses look like they came from the mess hall." Henderson poured a healthy shot of bourbon into each glass.

Little JJ laughed. "They sorta let me have them."

"I bet they did." Johnston poured Coke over the Jim Beam in each glass.

Henderson held his glass up for a toast. "To the fallen."

The squad raised their glasses and said in unison, "To the fallen."

They took a sip of the mixed drink. Each man stared to nowhere in particular as if they remembered a brother that the Viet Cong had killed in battle.

"Hey, Laurel. We're all new to the unit. What happened to the original First Squad?" Henderson's eyes widened as if this was the first time he had that thought.

"Sarge, they all got killed. The squad was on a rescue mission. And the VC shot down their Huey when they were coming in for a landing." Laurel downed his drink in one gulp. "It was the first time an entire squad got killed."

Henderson sighed as the sadness crept across his face. "Man, that's hard to take."

The men sat around the table in silence.

Henderson stood. "We're going to be together for a year." He glanced at the group. "I would like for each person to share one thing that no one else knows about them."

"What for, Sarge? That's private." Bear looked down at the table.

"That's why. I'll be first." Henderson put his hand on Bear's shoulder. "During my first tour, my best friend, my brother, was killed on Hill One Hundred." He glanced at Laurel. "His name was Mitch Drexler, and he died in my arms with a hole in his gut. He may have survived if I'd blown the claymores." Tears formed in his eyes. "I miss him and think of him every day." Henderson stopped and surveyed the men of First Squad.

"During my last tour, I was a platoon sergeant." Johnston stood and winked at Henderson. "It was my responsibility to keep everyone safe." His gaze fell to the floor. "I directed the platoon into an ambush one day, and three men got killed. It was my fault." He flopped into the chair.

Cain placed a hand on Johnston's arm. "When I was a paramedic, we responded to a three-car accident. I ran to the first car that happened to be upside down." He rubbed his chin, and his eyes went dull. "I found a mother and daughter that were critically injured. I could only treat one of them." Cain leaned back in his chair and looked up. "I let the mother die."

"Damn, Cain, there was nothing you could do. I think you made the right decision." Johnston slugged his drink down.

"Well, mine isn't a combat story like you guys." Bear crossed his arms across his chest. "Now, you can't tell anyone." He scanned the faces of each squad member. "I killed a man in a bar fight. I didn't mean too. He pissed me off because he was fucking with my woman. And he pulled a knife on me." He smiled. "The judge told me to join the Army or go to jail. It was an easy choice."

"Holy shit!" Little JJ turned in his chair to face Bear. "I didn't know that about you. I think you're doing better keeping your temper in check."

"I guess it's my turn." Laurel stared past the men at the table. "It was the monsoon season, and I just started walking point. It was one of my first days on point." He made eye contact with Henderson. "I heard a scream and found that Sergeant Nash had fallen into a punji pit. It killed him." Tears clouded his eyes. "I should've guided the platoon better."

Eddie grimaced when he recalled in horror the day that Nash died. "It wasn't your fault, Laurel."

The men of the First Squad shifted their gaze toward Little JJ.

"I figure the littlest guy goes last." Little JJ smiled. "Hell, I thought I had it hard. I was adopted. That's why I have a white man's last name, Jackson, and the first name Juan." He took a long drink from his glass and then wiped the Coke away with the back of his hand. "Which I'm proud of, by the way. Shit, I've never been in trouble, either."

"Well, you got a bigger family now." Bear laughed and grabbed Little JJ around the neck.

The room went silent while the men were deep in thought.

"I know it was hard to share with everyone." Henderson looked at each man in the eye. "But you did it without hesitation because you trust every man in this room with your life." He downed his drink. "We're brothers and will die for each other. That's what makes us special."

He placed the Jim Beam back in the wall locker. "Let's go eat."

"Only nine more training days!" Johnston yelled.

•

The training period zoomed by for the First Squad. It was during the last training day, small unit tactics, that Henderson learned that Brighton had heard of Little JJ's marksmanship with the M-60. He sought him out to join the squad. At first, Henderson thought he couldn't handle the twenty-three-pound M-60 machine gun. Little JJ stood at five-feet, weighing one hundred twenty pounds with a solid, muscular build.

Henderson pointed at a berm to his front. "Little JJ, I want you to move forward twenty-five meters to that berm and then give covering fire for Bear as he moves to your position."

"Got it, Sarge." Little JJ took up a prone firing position.

When Bear hit the ground, Little JJ opened fire, hitting the targets to his front. After he jumped to his feet, he ran toward the berm, holding his M-60 in the underarm position like it weighed nothing, destroying every target to the front. Once at the berm, Bear ran forward while Little JJ continued to give covering fire, leaving no target unharmed.

Henderson's brows cocked upward. "Okay, stop firing. Damn, you're good!" Little JJ lived up to his reputation.

"Hey, Bear, you got some speed for a big guy." Henderson slapped him on the shoulder.

David Russel was a huge man with broad shoulders, held up by thick legs. The squad nicknamed him Bear because of his size and the hair that covered every inch of skin. Bear had a temper. He was known to lose it at the wrong time, but he could pick up an injured man with ease.

"Okay, let's call it a day." Henderson mopped his face with a handkerchief. "Training is over."

"Now, let's get real!" Johnston yelled.

THE FIRST MISSION

Henderson looked at the five soldiers sitting on the deck of the chopper. He signaled it was time. "Get ready," he yelled over the sound of the turbine engine.

Henderson felt apprehensive, being the first mission, yet unafraid. It was the jolt he needed to give him the courage to go back into battle if needed. The training was better than expected, and the squad appeared to mold together without any difficulty.

The six-man squad was ready to rescue the pilot.

A pilot without a crew flew the downed chopper, flying a test run after maintenance. Not long after the Huey flew outside the division firebase perimeter, it went down from a mechanical failure. Brighton sent the First Squad for the rescue mission.

The squad's modified UH-1D Huey hovered over the crash site, while four men, two on each side, dropped the ropes. Henderson had told the squad members earlier that they would rappel for practice. They rappelled to the ground.

Once Henderson's feet hit the ground, he unhooked from the rope and then looked in all directions, assessing the terrain. While he surveyed the area, the jungle closed in on him. Henderson knew he was back in Vietnam. It was all too familiar to him—the wilderness of the jungle, the smell of rotting vegetation—that caused his senses to go into overload. With the sun beating down on him and the humidity sucking the air from his lungs, he moved toward the downed helicopter.

While standing near the chopper, Henderson observed that the terrain reminded him of his time with the First Platoon. The jungle, bamboo thickets, and dense stands of trees that surrounded him could easily hide the enemy. His sense of spotting danger came to him as naturally as lighting a cigarette. As he scanned the area around the helicopter, Henderson thought of the many battles he had fought during his first tour and the brothers he had lost. He hoped that he wouldn't lose any friends this time.

From the rescue Huey, Johnston monitored the operation on the ground. Henderson kept Johnston on the helicopter because of his analytical skills and leadership. He could guide the action from the air or take over, no matter what happened to him. Mounted on the right side of the helicopter was an M-60 machine gun operated by Little JJ.

While watching the action, Johnston received the signal to lower the basket. "Little JJ, give me a hand." Johnston reached for the basket. Little JJ pushed the front of the basket into the rotor wash. He guided it while Johnston lowered it.

"It's going down smoothly," Little JJ said.

On the ground, Henderson scanned the area as his eyes darted. "Laurel, Bear, guard the trail that leads to the helicopter."

When Laurel reacted to the order, Henderson recalled during their first tour how well he performed as the point man for the platoon. He trusted his abilities. However, he was still unsure of Bear because of his temper, but Henderson heard he was fierce in battle.

Tense, Henderson surveyed the site again. "Let's move. Cain, with me."

"Moving, Sarge." Cain jumped to his feet, stretching his six-foot frame while following Henderson. The fifteen-pound aid bag bounced against his side, not bothering him in the least.

After Cain reached the pilot, he checked every inch of his body. "It looks like he dragged himself away from the chopper before he passed out." He opened his first aid bag and started to treat him. "Besides the head injury, he has some cuts and bruises." He looked up at Henderson. "This is one lucky pilot."

Henderson surveyed the damage and assessed the helicopter was totaled. After checking for any signs of fire, he turned his attention back to his medic and the pilot.

When Cain removed his bush hat, his short, wet blond hair fell free. He wiped at the sweat beading on his face and dabbed around his narrow blue eyes. Next, he rolled his sleeves higher, exposing muscular biceps and forearms, and then resumed giving aid to the pilot.

While watching Cain work, Henderson asked, "How did you get your medical skills?"

Cain didn't look up while he continued to work on the pilot. "I was a paramedic for the city of Los Angeles before being drafted. The Army trained me as a medic."

As the basket lowered, Henderson grabbed hold before it settled on the ground. "Your skills are impressive."

Henderson turned his attention back to the mission.

"Bear, over here, now." Henderson held the basket stable, allowing it to hit the ground.

He lifted his six-foot-three, two-hundred-and-thirty-pound frame with ease. Bear ran to Henderson with incredible speed. His M-16 appeared a toy in his large hands.

In seconds, Bear stood over the pilot, scooping him up with his powerful arms. "I got him." He gently placed the aviator into the basket.

Henderson looked skyward. He signaled Johnston to hoist it up to the hovering chopper.

"Laurel, fall back on us," Henderson commanded.

Once the basket was secure, Johnston transmitted over the radio, "Animal One, this is Animal One-two. Over."

"Go ahead, this is Animal One. Over." Henderson held the handset of the PRC-25 radio that Laurel carried.

"Animal One, heading to the base—will return. Over." Johnston waved down at the squad.

"Roger that, Animal One-two. Out." Henderson handed the handset back to Laurel.

While he surveyed the helicopter, he gave the squad members instructions to prepare a sling for the damaged Huey. The training paid off. They had the sling ready in a short period. After Henderson studied the terrain, he assigned the squad to their positions to guard the downed Huey until the CH-54A Skycrane arrived.

From his position, Henderson stared at the dense jungle. It appeared a forbidden green wall circled the clearing. The thick vegetation, smells, and the silence reminded him of the danger that he might face. The heat was suffocating.

Although he hadn't been to this area before, it brought back memories of his first tour, living in the jungle with Mitch and Professor. He recalled the many nights setting out claymores and flares, eating the evening meal of C-rations while bullshitting and enjoying the brotherhood they formed during that year.

It was at this moment that he allowed his mind to think of home. He removed the picture that he carried. A grin creased his cracked lips. After a minute or two, he slid the photograph back into his breast pocket. Memories of Cheryl flashed through his mind as his grin turned into a wide smile.

•

No more than ten minutes later, Laurel walked over to where Henderson was sitting. "Chopper coming to pick up the Huey."

Henderson scratched his head. "How long?"

Whop! Whop! Whop! The blades of the Skycrane slapped at the air.

"Now." Laurel pointed as he laughed.

Henderson gazed skyward. "Okay, guide him in, Laurel."

While Laurel talked with the helicopter crew, the squad attached the sling load to the thick cable. When they finished, Henderson signaled Laurel.

Henderson yelled, "Move from the Huey!" The squad scrambled away from the crash site. Laurel gave them the go-ahead to hoist the damaged ship.

Minutes after the Skycrane flew off with the Huey swaying under its belly, their chopper returned to pick up the squad. The pilot slowly lowered the helicopter. He hovered roughly one foot off the ground. Within seconds, the four squad members scampered aboard to sit on the metal deck. They sat with the muzzle of their M-16s pointing at the floor. Little JJ swiveled the M-60 looking for the enemy. After the helicopter lifted fifty feet, the pilot rotated the chopper one hundred eighty degrees. He flew toward Chu Lai.

•

The noise in the mess hall was deafening. Soldiers talked over the sounds of others amid the banging of trays. The First Squad sat at the same table in silence, attempting to enjoy the evening meal of roast beef with mashed potatoes. To Henderson, the mess hall meal didn't compare to his mother's or Martha's home-cooked roast beef with the trimmings.

The thought of the roast beef meal he shared with Martha and John Drexler made him think of his trip to Indianapolis several months past. The sigh that escaped from his cracked lips signaled the disappointment that he didn't fulfill his promise to Mitch. With another sigh, his shoulders relaxed; he knew his decision was the right choice.

Henderson glanced around the table at his men. He knew that there are soldiers who talk the talk, but after a short training period, he learned that the men of the First Squad walked the talk; his pride of the men washed over him. He beamed. Henderson thought the mission went well and the men came together as a unit.

Laurel glanced around the table. "Hey, guys, did you see all the signage for the division changed from the Americal Infantry Division to the Twenty-third Infantry Division?"

"It's because of Lieutenant Calley." Cain took a large forkful of mashed potatoes.

"Who's that? What did he do?" Bear asked.

"You don't know?" Johnston's mouth was frozen open in an expression of stunned surprise that he didn't know.

Bear slammed his hand on the table, making the trays rattle. "Hell, I wouldn't have asked if I knew."

"He's going to trial for murdering over a hundred villagers, mostly old men, women, and children." Cain shifted his gaze around the room. "His unit killed over five hundred people over two years ago, March sixteenth, nineteen sixty-eight at a hamlet called My Lai."

Little JJ brows creased. "Shit. Why did it take two years to take him to trial?"

No one answered the question. There wasn't a right answer.

The men at the table, all assigned to the Americal Infantry Division, looked down at their trays in silence. Laurel reached across his chest with his right hand. With a slight pause, he touched the Americal patch he wore on his left shoulder. Henderson could see the discomfort in his face with cheeks that flushed pink.

After five minutes of silence, Henderson lowered his fork. "Hey, guys, you done good today."

Everyone looked at Henderson without saying a word. Their beaming faces spoke for them.

Brighton stopped at the table where the First Squad ate their meal. "Tomorrow morning, clean weapons and get your gear squared away." He rubbed the sweat from his head. "Then, take the afternoon off. Maybe relax a little, but stay around the hooch in case we get a mission."

The men acknowledged that they understood.

Once Henderson swallowed the last of his meal, he stood. "Tomorrow is an easy day. Get some rest." He turned to walk away, hesitated, and turned back. "Don't relax too much; we could still get called out tomorrow."

HUEY NEEDS A MECHANIC

The men woke early, even though they didn't have training or a mission. Their inner clock told them it was time. Once they returned to the hooch from a leisurely breakfast at the mess hall, they began weapons maintenance. Although they had cleaned their M-16s after the last mission, the men went through the motion as if their rifles were dirty. Each squad member disappeared into his private thoughts; the room was quiet.

After Cain packed his cleaning equipment, he stood, stretching. "Let's play some poker." He strolled to his bunk, laying his M-16 on the wool blanket that covered the mattress. Without a word, the men quickly stowed away their cleaning equipment along with their weapons.

"Bear, clean the table off. I'll get us the drinks." Henderson headed for where he kept the Jim Beam. "Little JJ, get some glasses."

Johnston grabbed the ice chest. "I got the Coke."

"Five-card stud." Laurel dealt the first hand. "Ante up twenty-five cents."

After roughly forty hands, Bear threw his cards on the table. "I fold." For a moment, his eyes flashed with anger. "Damn, you're the luckiest guy I know."

"We Southerners were born with luck." Laurel laughed as he counted his winnings. "You're not out of money, are you, Bear?"

He stood over Laurel. "None that I'm going to give you."

"Oh, come on, now. Let me take some more of your money." Laurel slid his chair from the table.

Bear lifted Laurel out of the chair, holding him in the air, squeezing him hard. "You're not a cheater, are you?"

Laurel kicked his feet, gasping for air. "Gawddamn it, let me go."

"Okay, you little shit." He released his hold, letting Laurel fall to the floor in a heap.

The room burst into laughter.

"Well, I guess that's the end of the game." Cain picked up his money. "I need to write to my wife."

Henderson stood, wiping sweat from his face. "Good idea. I'm doing the same." He put the Jim Beam back into his wall locker.

Laurel and Bear joked with each other as they cleaned off the table.

•

An hour later, Little JJ woke from a nap. "I'm getting hungry."

"It's lunchtime." Johnston licked his lips. "I'm starving."

Without another word, the men of the First Squad strolled to the mess hall.

While Henderson ate, Brighton slipped into the chair next to him. "Got a mission."

"What is it, LT?" Henderson tilted back in his chair.

"There's a Huey down because of mechanical failure. The pilot managed to land, about three klicks outside the wire, without damaging the helicopter." Brighton looked around the table, making sure he had the squad's attention. "You'll be taking a mechanic with you. They believe they can repair the Huey in thirty minutes." Brighton rubbed his head. "You'll stay with him until he's finished."

Henderson slowly lowered his chair back until the four legs were on the floor. "How long before we go?"

"You need to get moving now." Brighton stood.

The men dashed out the door, leaving their trays on the table.

•

Within minutes, the squad was at the helipad, waiting to board the Huey.

Henderson greeted the mechanic with a wave. "I'm the squad leader. Climb aboard. Take a seat in the center of the deck."

The mechanic, a short chunky man, nodded that he understood. He grabbed his tools and scrambled across the metal floor to the location Henderson pointed to. While Henderson glanced around at the squad, he observed that they appeared anxious and on edge, but he knew they were ready for the enemy if they decided to attack.

After he adjusted his headset, Henderson said, "Ready to go."

"Taking off." The copilot turned in his seat to check his passengers. Henderson raised his hand with a circular motion, signaling they were ready to leave the helipad.

The helicopter lifted fifty feet off the pad. The pilot pushed the nose down heading toward the chopper in need of repair.

As they flew southward along the coastline, Henderson watched the waves roll toward the beach. It seemed peaceful. He made a mental note to go to the beach more often during his downtime.

When the Huey banked hard right toward the mountains, the squad took hold of whatever they could to keep from sliding. The ocean disappeared as the jungle-covered hills came into view threateningly over the horizon.

While Henderson took in the scenery below him, his breath got caught in his chest. He knew the fear was gaining on him as he breathed shallowly to release the tension. Henderson had almost forgotten what the jungles of Vietnam looked like, not to mention the enemy that hid in them. He curled his finger around the trigger of his M-16. Minutes later, the headset crackled, waking Henderson from his trance. "Going to land," the pilot said.

Henderson raised his hand palm down, motioning they were landing. The men stared down into the jungle as they approached the landing zone. There was tension in the air. No one spoke a word. Henderson looked at the faces, observing how the tightness of their jaws and shoulders reflected in one another. His belly had become tight.

Once the skids touched the ground, Henderson yelled, "Let's go."

Four of the men were on the ground within seconds. Bear turned, grabbing the mechanic's tool bag while he jumped to the jungle floor. The mechanic slid to the ground, falling face-first. Bear reached down, lifting him to his feet. Little JJ remained on board behind the M-60 to protect the crew. Johnston stayed aboard to guide the rescue from the air.

The downed Huey sat roughly twenty meters away. Henderson signaled the pilot that he was clear to take off. The aviator waved. As the helicopter rose skyward, the chopper rotated one hundred eighty degrees. He circled the area at a safe altitude while the squad worked.

Henderson scanned the crash site, deciding where the best locations to position the squad. "Laurel, stay near me. Bear, to the east, behind that berm." Henderson pointed toward the rise in the ground. Next, he directed Cain. "Move to the front of the Huey, about thirty meters."

"Roger, Sarge." Cain ran to where Henderson directed him.

"Hey, mechanic, with me." Henderson motioned for him to follow.

The mechanic ran toward Henderson, following him as he took long strides toward the chopper. About halfway, Henderson pointed at a small stand of trees. "Laurel, stay here and watch the rear."

When Henderson reached the pilot, he stopped. "How's it going? Here's your mechanic."

The pilot nodded at Henderson. "Watson, come here. Check this out," the pilot said to the mechanic.

"All business, I like that." Henderson wiped the sweat from his face.

While he scanned the jungle that surrounded the clearing, Henderson noticed the copilot and crew chief talking as if they didn't have a care in the world. "Hey, you guys think you should be watching for the VC instead of bullshitting?"

The two helicopter crewmen stopped talking. They looked at Henderson. After a second or two, they began talking again.

Again, Henderson turned his attention to survey the thick vegetation to his front. He thought that the mountains of North Carolina compared to the jungles in Vietnam were like a manicured lawn in an American subdivision. He recalled during his first tour how he had to hack his way through the vegetation with a machete, or crawl through on his hands and knees while the wait-a-minute vines grabbed him. Not to mention the giant mosquitos that attacked in hordes, wanting nothing more than to suck out all his blood.

Crack! AK-47 rounds ripped through the fuselage. The copilot and crew chief hit the ground, crawling under the helicopter; the First Squad opened fire in the direction of the suspected enemy position. Henderson rushed toward the Huey, taking cover by the cockpit. He squeezed the trigger of his M-16, sending round after round into the jungle.

From the concealment of the jungle, several more enemy rifles opened fire, rounds zinging overhead and thudding into the ground around the crew. Henderson flipped his selector switch to automatic, firing three-round bursts into the suspected area. Cain did the same. Within seconds, both men reloaded with a fresh magazine and continued to shoot at the invisible enemy.

After several minutes, Henderson stopped firing. He motioned for Laurel to come to his position. Laurel crawled the short distance with the radio on his back. He gave the handset to Henderson.

"Animal One-two, this is Animal One, come in lower, taking fire on the south side at the edge of the jungle. Need fire support. Over."

"You got it Animal One. Coming down now. Out," Johnston replied.

The helicopter descended, while Little JJ peppered the suspected area with 7.62 rounds from his M-60. The men on the ground saw the line of red tracer rounds as they streaked toward the ground. The rest of the men fired into the jungle too.

Henderson yelled, "Cease fire."

"Animal One-two, stop firing," Laurel transmitted.

"Roger that, Animal One." Johnston adjusted the headset.

All of a sudden, there was absolute stillness. The air didn't stir the grass or leaves. It was an unnerving tranquility. Henderson waited for what seemed an hour.

Laurel rolled on his side. "Sarge, it's been quiet for ten minutes."

Henderson glanced toward Laurel and smiled. "Okay, let's get finished. Then get the hell out of here." He rose to his feet.

Before he walked away from the chopper, Henderson looked underneath at the crew chief. "It would've been nice if you got behind that M-60 attached to your bird."

•

Within twenty minutes, the downed Huey blades began to turn slowly, then faster. The crew boarded the chopper. The mechanic scrambled onto the deck with his fellow soldiers. After a moment, the pilot signaled Henderson they were taking off. The helicopter lifted, flying for Chu Lai.

Laurel placed the handset to his ear. "Animal One-two, come on down. Take us home. Over."

"Roger that, Animal One. Over," Johnston transmitted.

The rescue pilot changed the pitch and reduced the throttle as the helicopter descended to the landing zone. While the chopper settled on the ground, the First Squad boarded, taking their assigned seats. The Huey lifted, flying the Animals home.

Once they were back at the hooch, the squad stowed their gear. Then the men cleaned weapons.

Henderson surveyed his squad. "I don't know about you guys, but I'm going to eat, then get some sleep." His lips tugged into a smile. "You guys did good today."

"Let's go." Bear grabbed for Little JJ. Little JJ was the first out the door, escaping the crushing hug from Bear. The squad followed behind at a leisure pace as Bear chased Little JJ to the mess hall.

CHAPTER 10

HUNTER-KILLER TEAM

On the Americal Division firebase, located outside the village of Chu Lai, the sun rose over the horizon, spilling sunlight on the division base camp. The pilot of the Loach, an OH-6 scout helicopter, started the engine. He shifted in his seat, looking at the hills behind the massive military installation. While the blades of the Loach began turning slowly, two soldiers climbed aboard. One was an observer, the other a gunner with an M-60; both put on their headsets.

The pilot turned in his seat. "The mission for today is to fly over the hills, not far from Firebase Debbie. We're looking for enemy forces moving supplies."

The two crew members acknowledged the mission with a simple response, "Got it."

Behind the Loach, two AH-1 Cobra gunships started their engines as the pilots checked their maps. The pilots, along with the copilots, were fondly called Warlords. The three helicopters would form a hunter-killer team where the Loach hunted . . . and the Cobra killed. The Loach flew low to the ground, hunting until the observer spotted the enemy, or it drew fire. Flying high overhead out of sight from the enemy, the Cobras would strike with their miniguns, 2.75 rockets, and 40-millimeter grenade launchers, destroying everything in their path.

When the blades of the three helicopters rotated faster, they lifted from the ground. The Loach shot off first, staying low to the ground. The two Cobra helicopters rose higher, climbing to 1,500 feet while following the Loach.

The hunter with the killers flew a predetermined pattern across the rugged terrain of hills, valleys, and thick jungle growth. It was another hot, humid day with the early morning temperature already at seventy-nine degrees and eighty percent humidity. The atmosphere aboard the Loach was relaxed, but the crew remained alert. The aviators relentlessly wiped at the sweat that dripped into their eyes.

Within twenty minutes, the observer spoke into his headset, "Spotted movement along the trail to your southeast."

"Gotcha. Going for a look." The pilot dropped altitude. Once he lost enough height, he banked left.

The observer peered intently out the canopy window where he saw movement. "I see ten enemy soldiers with packs on the trail moving south."

"I'm dropping red smoke on their position." The observer dropped a smoke grenade on the enemy position.

"Roger, I see the red smoke." The Cobra copilot peered toward the ground.

The copilot looked at the pilot as he adjusted his headset. "Firing on the red smoke."

Green tracer rounds pierced the sky, zipping all around the Loach. "Taking fire!" the pilot transmitted. The Loach pilot started evasive maneuvers to avoid the incoming rounds.

Within seconds, the two Cobras descended with their noses pointed toward the ground. Both pilots fired their miniguns and grenade launchers into the area covered in red smoke. The earth exploded at the suspected enemy location. Dirt, brush, and small trees flew through the air, blocking the pilot's view of the NVA for a short period. After several runs at the enemy, the Cobras sought a higher altitude.

The Loach pilot flew low at a reduced speed around the kill zone. "I see five dead. The rest must've skedaddled," the observer reported.

"That's a good day." The pilot shifted his weight to one side. He wiped at the sweat that dripped off his face. "Okay, let's move to the secondary search area."

The first Cobra pilot looked to the Loach. "We'll follow your lead, as always."

There was laughter bouncing through the headsets of the three helicopter crew members.

The pilot banked the Loach hard right, following a ridgeline toward the hilltop that must've been three hundred meters high. The sun was now over the horizon, its bright rays behind them. The observer and gunner were on full alert, looking for the enemy.

"Time check?" the observer asked.

The pilot looked at his wristwatch. "Little after zero six thirty." He veered to the east side of the ridge.

Pieces of fiberglass and metal of the Loach flew through the air. The helicopter started to buck. More incoming rounds punched holes into the small aircraft.

"What the hell! We're receiving heavy fire!" the pilot screamed.

The observer saw streams of green tracers flying toward the helicopter. "Bank left, bank left!" he shouted into the headset.

The pilot attempted to regain control of the Loach. "We're hit! We're hit!"

A rain of steel penetrated the jungle as the two Cobras fired their miniguns along with rockets at the suspected targets. "Get out of there." The lead Cobra pilot banked right.

"I've lost control. We're going in, hard." The Loach pilot fought the controls as the ground zoomed closer. "Mayday! Mayday!" The helicopter started to spin and thick smoke streamed from the engine. "Mayday! Mayday!"

The lead Cobra pilot watched in horror. "Pull up, Skeeter, pull up!"

While the pilot of the second Cobra watched the action, he banked hard left to follow the Loach as it headed to the ground.

THEY NEED HELP

The hooch door banged open, and then the overhead lights shone brightly. "On your feet, First Squad," Brighton ordered.

"What the hell." Bear rolled out of his bunk, hitting the floor hard.

"Chopper down. It's hot!" Brighton stood in the doorway with his feet spread apart. "VC are trying to get to them."

Henderson jumped to his feet, striving to clear his head. "You heard the lieutenant." He slipped into his uniform and grabbed his M-16. "Get moving."

A strange sense of self-doubt tugged at Henderson. There was a time he thought he knew how to survive the war that he didn't think twice before making a decision. But now, this seemed different.

It was his third operation since returning to Vietnam with a new unit. The two earlier missions were straightforward: a crashed chopper outside the perimeter; the other one was a Huey that landed because of mechanical problems. The squad had a brief enemy encounter at the second site.

While he looked around at his squad members, Henderson ran through all the procedures he had learned. This will be the first time the squad faced a large enemy force. When he turned to face Brighton, he shrugged off any uncertainty he had. He was confident he knew what to do as the leader. The squad was ready. *Hell, I walked point for a year. I can do this*, thought Henderson.

"Gather 'round." Brighton spread the map on the table.

He pointed at the area of the downed helicopter. "They're on this hilltop. It's a Loach with a crew of three." He stopped to survey the squad. "I don't know if anyone is injured or not. The Cobra's lost communication." He traced his finger along a ridgeline. "It was reported that a platoon of VC are moving on this ridge to get to the chopper."

After Henderson studied the map, he traced his finger to the hill. "The chopper can set down in this clearing. We can fan out to protect the crew from there." He adjusted his bush hat while looking at Little JJ. "You stay on the chopper with the M-sixty. Everyone else goes to the crash site."

"Got it, Sarge." Little JJ pursed his lips. "Wish I could go on the ground with you guys."

Henderson smiled at the machine gunner. "Maybe next time." He surveyed his squad. "Carry three LRP meals, twenty magazines, and two quarts of water." He hesitated. "Any questions?"

The soldiers stared at Henderson without responding.

He took that as they understood. "Okay, let's go." Henderson turned toward the lieutenant.

Brighton extended his hand to Henderson. "Good luck."

"Thanks, LT." Henderson reached out with his right hand to take Brighton's into his. Brighton shook Henderson's hand.

"You can handle anything that comes up. Don't worry."

Henderson nodded.

"Bear, make sure you have the C-4 and blasting caps." Henderson turned his attention back to the squad.

Bear shot Henderson an unsmiling look as if to say, *Why are you telling me that?* But instead of giving one of his usual smart-ass replies, Bear nodded. "Got it, Sarge."

The men quickly loaded their rucksacks with a poncho liner, rations, ammo, grenades, and water. Henderson was relieved that the weight of the ruck wasn't even close to what he humped during his first tour. Each soldier carried an M-16. No one wore a helmet—they wore an issued bush hat. Command determined that helmets were too heavy and too cumbersome. Laurel carried a radio on his back. The soldiers shouldered their rucksacks, waiting for the order to move out.

Without a word, Henderson walked out the door with the First Squad following him. While they jogged along the path that led to the helipad, each man was quiet, deep in thought. The modified Huey sat on the pad with its turbine engine roaring. In the cockpit, the copilot studied a map.

When Henderson glanced into the right window, he gave the pilot a wave. The First Squad usually had the same helicopter crew for their missions.

The men slid onto the deck of the Huey, each soldier finding their assigned position. Little JJ sat on the right side behind the M-60. Johnston tapped him on the shoulder as he sat next to him, facing the open doorway. Bear and Laurel scrambled to the left side, sitting on the deck with their feet dangling over the skid. Crunched together, Cain maneuvered in the middle next to Henderson. As he shifted to make room for Cain, Henderson thought him an excellent medic. A trustworthy soldier—he liked him.

Henderson slid on the headset. He spoke to the pilot through the microphone. "Lieutenant, we're all on the ship." The noise of the helicopter engine was deafening.

"Roger, Animal One. Ready to take off." The pilot turned in his seat to check his passengers.

Henderson looked at his men. He rotated his finger in a circle to indicate they were taking off. The helicopter shuddered and then lifted straight into the air, roughly one hundred feet. It banked right. The pilot flew south along the assigned flight path toward Duc Pho.

The copilot, a warrant officer, spoke into the headset. "Animal One, we'll be at the crash site in twenty minutes."

Henderson turned to look at the copilot. "Roger, sir." He then checked his watch to mark the arrival time.

•

While the chopper flew across the rice paddies, Henderson was deep in thought. He knew the Loach had a light aluminum skin that enemy rounds could easily penetrate, but he also learned that the helicopter had a robust structural truss that protected the people inside. The crew received training to remove or destroy the M-60 along with any electronics. It was usual for a Loach crew to walk away from a crash. Aviators often said, "If you're going to crash, crash in a Loach."

The radio crackled. "We're going in to drop you off," the pilot transmitted.

Enemy rounds zinged by the helicopter. One bullet tore through the cabin roof without causing damage. No one in the squad flinched. They knew there was nowhere to go. Henderson kneeled behind Laurel. While he studied the terrain, the downed helicopter, and the enemy positions, Henderson observed the three crewmen hidden by a small stand of trees firing at the enemy. The burning Loach appeared destroyed.

With sweat dripping down his face, Henderson transmitted, "Drop us behind the crew."

"Roger, heading down now." The pilot started a quick descent.

Little JJ opened fire with the M-60, sending a stream of 7.62 rounds into the jungle where the NVA hid.

"Stop about two feet off the ground. We'll jump from there," Henderson suggested to the pilot. Seconds after Henderson made his request, the Huey shuddered, sliding to a hover. "Now!" Henderson screamed.

Five of the squad members jumped to the ground as one.

The crew on the ground, along with Little JJ, provided covering fire for the squad.

The pilot flew the helicopter to a higher altitude while the two Cobra pilots unloaded their armament along the perimeter of the downed Loach.

Once on the ground, Henderson yelled to Johnston, "Stay here. Cover our rear!"

Johnston nodded. "Wilco." He ran, hitting the dirt in a prone position behind a berm for cover.

While they approached the helicopter, the remaining squad members put down suppressive fire. M-60, along with M-16 rounds, tore the jungle growth apart. The return fire from the enemy intensified. Henderson heard AK-47 bullets thudding into the earth in front of him. Some rounds zinged past, and explosions shook the ground.

Henderson fell to the ground, seeking cover. The jungle floor turned upside down around the clearing while the Cobras fired rockets. Three enemy soldiers ran from the protection of the jungle toward the helicopter crew.

"We're out of ammo," the downed pilot yelled at Henderson. The helicopter crew dug in deeper behind the trees.

Henderson fired three rounds, striking the NVA on the far left. The soldier stopped in midstride as a bullet ripped through his chest, and he fell in a heap to the ground. A burst of M-60 rounds flashed toward the earth, which took out the other two enemy soldiers. When Henderson looked skyward, he saw Little JJ give a wave. Henderson signaled a thank-you.

There was a burst of M-16 fire from his rear. "Laurel, go help Johnston," Henderson ordered.

With eyes darting around the perimeter, Laurel said, "Moving, Sarge." He jumped to his feet, keeping his body low to the ground, rushing to the rear of their position.

While he took in the situation, Henderson knew he had to get to the crew. "Cain, cover us. Bear, on me." Henderson felt a tinge of fear but shook it off. "If they need medical attention, I'll signal you."

"Go for it, Sarge. I got you covered!" Cain yelled.

Henderson jumped to his feet, taking off at a run toward the crew with Bear close behind him. Weapons discharged round after round from the jungle while they ran the last twenty-five meters zigzagging, striving to dodge the incoming bullets as they tore into the ground around them. The Cobras, Little JJ, along with Cain, emptied their weapons into the jungle.

After they fell to the ground next to the crew, Henderson and Bear panted like two dogs that had been playing fetch on a hot summer afternoon. Henderson removed his bush hat and wiped his wet hair back. Then he used a bandanna to mop his face.

For the first time, he noticed the amount of hair that covered Bear's arms, chest, and face. It appeared he needed to shake his body as an animal would after going into the water. That thought made him smile.

Within seconds, it became unnervingly quiet. Henderson hoped that the VC gave up and went home.

The pilot slid closer to Henderson. "What took you so long?" He chuckled while he used a dirty cloth to wipe at the blood that dripped from the cut above his right eye.

"You know us, sir. We like to take our time." Henderson used the Southern drawl he had lost several years ago. "Us being Southern boys and all."

The pilot laughed out loud. "You're on time."

"Anyone hurt?" Henderson looked at the other crew members.

"I have a broken arm." The gunner rested his back against a tree. Henderson noticed his right arm hung at what had to be an extreme angle.

The observer glanced toward Henderson. "I'm okay. Shook up, that's all." He wiped the sweat from the gunner's face and held a canteen to his lips.

Henderson turned to Cain. "Call for Laurel to take your position, then you come on over."

"Laurel, on me!" Cain yelled.

Within seconds, Laurel flopped next to Cain. "What's up?"

"Cover me. I'm moving to Sarge." Cain picked up his first aid bag and took a long, deep breath. "Now!" He darted toward Henderson's position without drawing enemy fire.

Cain slid to the ground next to Henderson. "Who's hurt, Sarge?"

"Check the gunner first. Think he has a broken arm. Then check the pilot. He has a cut over his eye."

"Roger." Cain crawled to the injured crewman. He opened his first aid bag, going to work on him.

Fifty meters from the group of soldiers was the Loach. Flames licked at the sky, and dark black smoke drifted to the clouds. Next, he surveyed the equipment scattered around the crew.

"Sir, did you get everything?" Henderson asked the pilot.

"Yep, we got it all."

Laurel listened intently with the handset against his ear. He rubbed his jaw. "Sarge, an infantry platoon is moving up the hill behind the enemy."

Henderson shot a look in the direction of the jungle. "How much time before they get here?"

Laurel picked up the handset. After a brief moment, he said, "About twenty minutes."

The silence exploded from the M-60 machine-gun firing. Without hesitating, Henderson hit the ground. He then peered through the trees but didn't see any movement.

Laurel had the handset against his ear. He grinned. "It was Little JJ. He got a gook trying to sneak up on us."

For the second time today, Henderson looked skyward. He gave Little JJ a wave.

"Okay, let's get the crew, weapons, and electronics ready to load." Henderson held a hand out to the pilot, pulling him to his feet. "Laurel, call our bird. Tell him to land in the field to our east." He looked around at the crew. "You ready?"

"Let's do it." The pilot glanced toward his men.

Henderson ran to the center of the field to guide the Huey to the ground.

Bear pulled the gunner into his arms and walked toward the chopper with the observer following. The pilot carried some electronics, trailing behind them. Laurel brought the Loach's M-60. The squad assisted the three crew members onto the waiting helicopter, and Little JJ kept a watchful eye on the jungle to his front. Henderson stepped back. He waved for the pilot to take off.

"Take cover behind the berm," Henderson instructed. "Johnston, join us."

They moved as instructed, taking up fighting positions with nothing to do but wait. The brush moved, twigs cracked, and a metal rattling sound echoed from the jungle.

"Movement on our right," Bear whispered.

Henderson turned to where the sounds were coming from for a better view of the area. "Get ready." All weapons pointed in the same direction.

The radio static crackled. Laurel listened over the handset. "Animal One, this is Charlie One-six. Friendly coming in. Over."

"Charlie One-six, roger. Come on in. Out," Laurel transmitted.

Henderson shot Laurel a questioning look.

"Friendlies coming in. It's the infantry platoon." Laurel put the handset away.

Several minutes after Laurel made the announcement, the platoon burst through the jungle into the clearing.

A sergeant stopped eyeing the Animals. "Heard you guys needed to be rescued."

"Hell no, we don't." Bear stood. "What gave you that idea?" He gave the sergeant an indignant stare.

The platoon of infantry, along with the rescue squad, burst into laughter.

After Henderson lit a cigarette, he inhaled deeply. "Everyone take a break, but stay alert."

Within minutes, the rescue helicopter landed. The infantry company kept the area secure, while Henderson's squad loaded onto the chopper for the ride back to Chu Lai.

•

With a slow, natural gait, the squad strode in silence from the helipad toward the hooch. Henderson turned to face his men while he walked backward. "Get cleaned up. Then get some chow."

Once at the mess hall, they sat at the table, forking in large amounts of food in an atmosphere that was somber—not because anything went wrong with the mission, or a squad member got hurt; sometimes quiet was a good thing. The quiet relaxed the mind. It allowed Henderson to think of Cheryl.

They finished eating at the same time. "Let's do some maintenance while we have the time." Henderson stood and headed for the door.

Once at the hooch, he glanced around the room at his squad members. "Okay, get your weapons cleaned. Don't forget your gear too." Henderson reached into his wall locker. He lifted a bottle. "I believe I have a bottle of Jim Beam to share."

"Gawddamn it, I'm ready to clean my weapon." Laurel grabbed his cleaning equipment.

The men laughed. They broke out their cleaning kits. The soldiers sat in a circle on the floor while disassembling their weapons. They neatly arranged each part on an individual towel to their front.

Henderson poured healthy shots of Jim Beam into the six glasses and topped them off with Coke. He handed each man a drink. "Great work today."

Bear tipped his glass back, taking a large gulp. He set his drink down. "Hey, Sergeant Johnston, why did you come back for a second tour?"

After Johnston took a slow sip of Jim Beam, he said. "Well, I'll tell you. I'm from Detroit. When I got back home, the manufacturer I worked for gave my job away." He took another sip. "I was pissed, but what could I do? Hell, I re-enlisted. I even volunteered to come back to 'Nam."

Cain threw his rifle down, knocking his drink over. "That sucks, man. They're supposed to hold the job for you."

"Not if you're a black man," Little JJ muttered.

Johnston shrugged, downing the rest of the drink. "Nothin' I could do." He frowned, letting the anger go. "I was going back to my old unit, kinda like Henderson, but Brighton offered me to join him. Here I am."

Henderson placed a hand on Johnston's shoulder. "I'm glad you stayed."

"How about another drink?" Johnston handed Henderson his glass.

"Anytime, my man, anytime," Henderson said.

Cain finished cleaning up the mess he made. "Hey, me too. Laurel spilled my drink."

"Bullshit, you did it." Laurel punched Cain in the arm.

When he finished pouring the drinks, Henderson said, "Let's get some rest. Tomorrow is another day." He handed a glass to Johnston and one to Cain.

After lighting a cigarette, Henderson walked outside to breathe the fresh ocean air. He stared at the million stars in the sky. His thoughts went immediately to Cheryl. "I need to write her a letter tonight."

A voice from behind him boomed, "Then you better get to it."

Henderson jumped from the steps landing in the sand. When he turned, he saw Cain standing on the porch. "Man, you scared the shit out of me."

After his laughter subsided, Cain walked down the steps. "I need to write my wife too."

"What's her name?" Henderson watched the water lapping at the beach in the moonlight.

Cain gazed in the direction that Henderson stared. "Dianna. She's terrific. She's the mother of my son, Ryan."

"Wow, you have a son. I didn't know." Henderson put his cigarette out. "Guess it's time for some shut-eye."

The two soldiers walked back into the hooch, where their friends laughed, talked shit, and were still drinking.

"Okay, listen up." Henderson raised a hand to get their attention. "We don't know what tomorrow will bring. Let's get some sleep." He picked up the bottle of Jim Beam and put it in his wall locker. "No more drinking tonight."

While Henderson lay on his bunk, staring at the ceiling, he strived to understand why he left Cheryl at home and returned to the madness of the war. When each day passed, it became evident that he wouldn't find forgiveness for Mitch's death in this godforsaken country. Henderson also realized that he didn't make a difference in the war, no matter how hard he wanted to. Even the men he served with would be okay without him. *Hell, First Platoon still humped the mountains around the firebase without him.*

A DIFFERENT KIND OF MISSION

At the Noncommissioned Officers Club, Henderson bellied up to the bar with Johnston. They ordered a Jim Beam and Coke as the song "Born to Be Wild" by Steppenwolf thumped in the background. Henderson could feel the beat vibrating against his body.

"Let's get a table," Henderson yelled.

Johnston grinned while nodding his head. He strolled over to a table in the far corner, away from the jukebox. The music stopped right at the moment Johnston yelled, "Let's sit here." His voice echoed around the room. The patrons of the club stopped what they were doing, gawking at the two soldiers. Johnston smirked while shooting the bird with both hands at the customers. No one challenged him.

"That was great timing." Henderson pulled out a chair.

"Wow, that does sound a lot better, doesn't it?" Johnston slid onto a chair.

A cute Vietnamese woman appeared at the table. "GI want to eat?"

"Sure." Henderson glanced at Johnston. "You want a steak?"

"Yeah, sounds good. I hope it's better than the mess hall steaks. They're tough as leather."

Henderson looked at the young woman. "We'll have two steaks, medium, with all the trimmings." She wrote the order down. He glanced into her eyes while sticking his lower lip out. "Can you turn the music down a little?"

"Yes." The woman disappeared into the kitchen.

"Carl, this is my treat." Henderson lit a cigarette.

The jukebox arm swung down, and a new record played "We've Gotta Get Out of This Place" by The Animals.

Henderson rolled his eyes. "I've gotten to where I hate this fucking song."

"At least she turned it down. I didn't think she would." Johnston stretched with his arms over his head. "Too bad the rest of the squad couldn't come with us."

Henderson reached across the table, thumping Johnston's stripes sewn on his shirt sleeve. "Hell, when they earn their sergeant stripes, they can."

"Yeah, you have a point. We need to get off by ourselves once in a while."

"We do." Henderson downed the rest of his bourbon. "You want another drink?"

"Now that's a dumb question." Johnston reached for his empty glass.

The Second Squad leader, Sergeant Hanson, wandered into the club. He stood at the doorway, scanning the room.

"Should we invite him to join us?" Johnston pointed at Hanson.

Henderson signaled Hanson to come to their table. "Sure, one more can't hurt." He waved back. Hanson, a six-foot, athletic soldier, approached the table as if he was marching.

"That guy is going to be a lifer," Johnston muttered.

Henderson smiled. "I'm sure you're right." He stood to greet him.

Hanson stopped at the table. "Can I join you?"

"Sure, pull up a chair. We ordered steaks. You want one?" Henderson sized Hanson up, attempting to figure out the soldier as he sat down.

"No, I already ate, but I'll have whatever you guys are drinking."

Johnston signaled the waitress that he wanted another round to include the third man.

Henderson made his assessment. "You didn't happen to stop at the club by chance, did you?"

Hanson looked down at the table. "No, I wanted to talk to you." He leaned back in his chair, staring Henderson in the eye. "There's a mission coming up that I can use your help with."

The waitress set a drink in front of each soldier.

"Well, I believe Lieutenant Brighton needs to make those decisions."

"He already did. It was his idea that I talk to you."

Henderson's eyebrows raised a notch. "Do tell."

"Well, do you want to know or not?" Hanson leaned forward, downing half his drink.

"I'm all ears, Hanson." Henderson picked up his drink.

"The Second Squad has a grab-and-snatch mission in two days. LT thought you would be a good fit because it's in your old area, the horseshoe."

"Why is the area called the horseshoe?" Johnston scratched his neck.

Henderson gazed out the window. "It's an area roughly one klick long and two klicks wide between the Song Tra Khuc River and the base of the Truong Son Mountains. The river curves around the mountains, creating a horseshoe shape, hence the name."

The memories of his time in the horseshoe flooded his thoughts. He recalled the day they rescued the American prisoner and the awful condition that they found him. It wasn't long after when the First Platoon bathed in the river and was attacked by the NVA, killing Flores. The fondest memory was boarding the helicopters heading to stand down in Chu Lai.

"Hold on for a minute." Johnston waved at the waitress. "Hey, miss, three more drinks over here, please." He surveyed the table. "Sorry, but this sounds like we may need another drink. Go ahead, Hanson."

He laughed. "You guys are a pair, aren't you?" Then he took a slow sip of his bourbon.

The waitress came back with the drinks. She smiled at the men as she set the glasses on the table.

Johnston grinned at Hanson. "Okay, we're ready."

"At last." He glanced at the two NCOs to make sure they were paying attention. "I was sayin' that we'll go to the horseshoe in two days. There's an NVA PSYOP's team that's transmitting propaganda along with music, disturbing the troops on Hill One Hundred. S-two confirmed that they would be near or in the horseshoe area the night after tomorrow, which is Thursday."

"Why don't we blow their ass away?" Johnston shifted in his chair.

Hanson's forehead wrinkled as his eyebrows came together. "Good question. Command wants the equipment. If possible, grab the NVA officer in charge of the team too." He set his gaze on both soldiers. "Therefore, a grab-and-snatch mission."

"I don't know. First Squad's training had been rescuing downed choppers. Not the type of missions you do most days." Henderson swallowed half his drink.

Hanson picked up his glass. "Look at this way—you'll get real training."

The three NCOs let go with a loud laugh.

"Damn it, let's do it." Henderson downed the rest of his drink. "What you think, Johnston?"

"I say go for it." Johnston touched Henderson's glass with his.

"Great. We'll meet at my hooch at sixteen hundred tomorrow for the briefing." Hanson tapped his glass to theirs. "Now, let's relax and have some drinks together."

They touched glasses again, but toasting the fallen this time.

•

After the briefing Wednesday afternoon, Henderson and Brighton walked outside together.

"You have any problems with Sergeant Hanson being in charge of the mission?" Brighton glanced at the First Squad leader.

Henderson slapped Brighton on the back. "Hell no, LT. He has a lot more experience with these missions than I have."

"Great. I believe you're ready for this mission." Brighton placed an arm around Henderson's shoulder. "Otherwise, I wouldn't let you go."

"Thanks, LT." Henderson turned, heading toward the squad hooch.

The rest of the squad had returned from the briefing. After Henderson entered the building, he heard laughter. He witnessed a lot of horseplay as the men prepared for the mission. Henderson scanned their faces, believing they looked excited to do a different task.

After the sun fell behind the mountains, Henderson fell onto his bunk. "Okay, no goofing off or staying up late. Hit the rack. Let's get some sleep. Tomorrow is a big day."

No one complained. Bear turned the lights off, and Johnston extinguished his cigarette.

•

When the sun rose over the South China Sea, Henderson opened his eyes. He pulled out the picture of Cheryl that was always with him. While staring at the photograph, he recalled her voice, her smile, her laugh, and her smell. "Good morning, babe." Henderson slid the picture into his shirt pocket.

He flipped out of bed, and his feet hit the floor. Henderson walked from bunk to bunk, shaking the First Squad members awake. "Let's go; time to get up."

One by one, the soldiers climbed out of their bunks, slowly getting ready for the day.

"Come on, guys. Need to move. We need to eat first. Then meet on the helipad at zero nine hundred." Henderson tied his boot laces.

Without conversation, the men dressed. When ready, they filed out the door, strolling to the mess hall. Breakfast was the usual meal of bacon, eggs, potatoes, toast, and coffee. On a good day, they had SOS, creamy beef gravy, on top of toast. The soldiers sat at the regular table, eating in silence. Each soldier was deep into his thoughts to mentally prepare for the mission. During this time, silence gave them strength. It was later that they would start talking shit.

Back at the hooch, the squad members gathered their gear. The two NCOs went around to the squad members, checking to make sure they had everything they needed for the mission. The essentials were ammunition, food, water, and first aid dressings. Each man would have a map of the area of operation with a compass.

"You guys look good." Henderson scanned his men. "Okay, let's head to the choppers."

Little JJ started playing grab-ass with Bear as they opened the screen door.

Laurel followed, saying, "Gawddamn it" multiple times.

Cain chuckled while walking in the steps of the three other soldiers.

"Let's go." Henderson tapped Johnston on the shoulder.

The two sergeants let the screen door slam as they stepped out the doorway, heading to the waiting chopper.

Once they arrived at the helipad, Henderson noted that there were two Cobras, a Loach, and two Hueys waiting for the two squads of grunts. The turbine engines of the helicopters whined as their blades rotated. The noise was deafening, and the fumes from the engines choked them.

"Let's go. Load up." Henderson pointed at the Rescue One chopper.

The squad boarded the chopper, scurrying to their assigned seating. Except this time, Little JJ would be going on the ground with them. Henderson noticed that Little JJ was excited more than any of the other squad members because he'd had to stay on the chopper for support on the other missions.

While Henderson adjusted his headset, he signaled the pilot he was ready. Out of the corner of his eye, he saw the Loach, and then Hanson's Huey, Rescue Two, rise into the air. Rescue One soon followed, and the two Cobras took off too.

When in the air, the Loach flew low to the ground, and the two Cobras flew roughly a thousand feet above him. The two Hueys flew several hundred feet above the Cobras. Henderson thought the four helicopters with the two squads of grunts were a formidable force.

After fifteen minutes in the air, the Loach flew low over the jungle canopy, searching the landing zone for enemy soldiers. The Cobras, along with the Hueys, waited until they received the all-clear. Even then, the Cobras would take up an attack position high over the landing zone, while the Hueys went in to drop off the two squads.

The landing zone was on a ridge with a small clearing, big enough for one Huey to land in the dense jungle. The pilots would drop the two squads roughly two klicks from the suspected enemy broadcast station. The plan was to stay hidden in the jungle until darkness came. While using the concealment of the night, the grunts would hump to the site of the broadcasting equipment.

"Rescue One, Rescue Two, this is Skeeter One. Landing zone all clear. Over," the pilot of the Loach transmitted.

"Roger, Skeeter One. Rescue Two descending to LZ. Over."

"Skeeter One, this is Rescue One. We're right behind Rescue Two. Over."

"This is Skeeter One; we have you covered. Good luck. We'll head back to the base once you're secure on the ground. Out."

Rescue Two came in first, with Second Squad jumping from the Huey before the skids touched the ground. Hanson moved his men into the jungle growth to protect the next chopper as it neared the LZ. Rescue One landed seconds after the first helicopter took flight.

"Let's go." Henderson signaled his squad to dismount. The six-man squad was on the ground, running toward the jungle, where Hanson waited.

"Everyone accounted for?" Hanson surveyed the squad.

Henderson stared at Hanson. "Yeah, they're all here."

"Okay, let's move single file down the ridge toward the valley." Hanson adjusted his rucksack.

"Get ready to move, First Squad." Henderson surveyed the area for the best route.

Hanson put his hand on Henderson's shoulder. "I heard you were a pretty good point man back in the day. Want to give it a try?"

"Yeah, sure, Hanson." Henderson's eyes darted toward his squad.

He didn't know if Hanson was challenging him or wanted him to walk point. But he wasn't about to say no to the offer.

"Laurel, stay behind me," Henderson said over his shoulder as he turned, facing the trail. Henderson wouldn't admit he was afraid, but he knew to be the point man was a job others couldn't or wouldn't do, not ever. The image of Cheryl flashed in front of him; this time, he had more to lose. He heard her voice, "You better come back."

He stepped forward along the narrow trail as if he had walked point every day since returning to Vietnam. Henderson felt the burden of responsibility weighing him down; his mouth was dry. A tremor in his hand shook while he grasped his rifle. His knuckles turned white.

The men fell in line, with First Squad following Henderson and then Second Squad following the First Squad. While they descended the hill, Henderson took slow, careful steps along the path. His eyes followed the trail and the surrounding growth, searching for any evidence of NVA or VC presence. The heat and humidity soaked his uniform and made breathing difficult.

After two hours, Henderson came upon a small clearing. He halted the patrol, kneeling while he scanned the jungle across the field.

Laurel came to his side and kneeled. "What's up, Sarge?"

Henderson looked around. "To be honest, I wanted to take a short break." He grinned. "There's a clearing to our front. Do you think we should go around or not?"

Laurel scanned to his left and then right. "Man, that jungle is too thick to walk through. Let's cross the clearing."

"My sentiments too. It'll save time."

Hanson approached the two soldiers. "What's going on?"

"Looks like we need to be in the open for a short period." Henderson directed his attention to the field.

The Second Squad leader surveyed the surrounding area. "Yep, I agree." Hanson pointed to a thicket of bamboo on the opposite side. "We'll move into the bamboo there. Let's move two at a time." He signaled for the squads to move forward.

Henderson stood. "Laurel and I will go first."

"Roger that. Move out." Hanson positioned himself to cover them.

The two squads ran across the clearing without an incident. They gathered on the other side of the field.

Henderson picked up the pace as he continued along the ridge toward the valley. Once he reached the preselected stopping point, he halted the patrol. They were roughly three hundred meters from their objective.

"Laurel, check it out." Henderson eyed the jungle growth.

"Roger, Sarge." Laurel quietly disappeared into the thicket of brush that was covered by low-hanging trees. The patrol waited. After a couple of minutes, he reappeared. "All clear, come on in."

Henderson signaled the patrol to move forward.

When the men filed into the concealed position, they dropped their rucksacks, ready for a break. The squads set out security without being told. Henderson removed his canteen, downing half the contents. With the trees blocking the direct sunlight, Henderson felt a sense of coolness floating across his body. He was amazed that sitting in the shade almost seemed like air conditioning in Vietnam.

Laurel plopped next to Henderson. "Sarge, you know we're near the hill when we were with First Platoon? It was when we found the Chinook helicopter crew chief."

"You're right, Ray. It's about three hundred meters west of here." Henderson slid his canteen back into the cover. "I often wonder how he's doing. Shit, being a POW had to be tough. I still remember when we found him; he was skin and bones, with sunken eyes, unshaven, dirty, and the uniform he wore was in rags. He looked like death warmed up."

The image of the broken soldier never went away.

Laurel clenched his fist. "I tell you what, Sarge; I ain't never going to get captured."

Henderson hoped his face didn't betray the fear he felt about being captured. That's why he was the leader—he could wear a mask of defiance and confidence. He knew there was a time to show his fear, his weaknesses, but this wasn't it.

"I'm with you on that. Let's make a pact to kill each other before we let that happen." Henderson eyeballed Laurel. "I'm serious."

"You got it, Sarge. We ain't letting them take us alive." Laurel stood, wiping sweat from his lip. "Let's eat; I'm hungry."

Within minutes, the men had C-4 burning to heat water for the dehydrated LRP meal. Once the water came to a boil, Henderson ripped open his spaghetti with meat sauce meal. He poured more than a pint of boiling water into the green bag that contained the spaghetti. After letting it sit for a couple of minutes, Henderson stirred the contents with his plastic spoon. He began shoveling in mouthfuls of the hot meal.

After Hanson lit a cigarette, he leaned against a tree next to Henderson. "Let's go over the details one more time." He took a long drag while he eyed Henderson.

"Sure, no problem." Henderson crushed his cigarette into the ground.

Hanson placed the map to their front. "At this clearing, we'll drop our gear. It's the pickup point. Leave one of your men to guard it." He traced along the crest of the hill. "Here is where your squad will set up. You guys will guard our backs."

Henderson's lips pressed together. "We can do that."

"I know you can. I want to make sure we are in sync with each other." Hanson took another drag and exhaled. "My squad will move in to capture the equipment and the PSYOPS officer. He starts his show at twenty-one hundred hours."

Henderson stood. "What do you know about the broadcast equipment?"

"All I know is that the system is big enough to transmit a klick to Hill One Hundred. S-two believes it's a portable system that the

NVA can move easily. Hell, Bear could probably lift it." Hanson laughed as he folded the map.

"I sure hope it's as simple as that." Henderson lit a smoke. "What if the mission goes sideways?"

"We'll call for air support. Then get the hell out of there." Hanson stood, wiping at the sweat running down his face. "I've been on harder missions than this. If you hear gunfire, send in one team only. Keep the other team for security. I prefer you to stay with the men on security in case I get hurt."

"Look, Hanson, you can count on me, along with the men in First Squad." Henderson flashed a grin for reassurance.

"I know that. Okay, let's get some rest until nightfall." Hanson placed the map into his pants pocket. "Oh, do you want to walk point to the objective?"

Henderson smiled. "Yeah, I can do that."

•

When the sun dropped behind the mountains, the patrol readied to move to the suspected NVA broadcast station. The plan was to move to the edge of the hill and wait for the first broadcast and then attack the guards. Once the area was secured, Laurel would call in the choppers to get the grunts. They were already on station, flying high above with the two Cobras. The Loach was with them too.

The men shouldered their rucksacks. Henderson walked silently along the trail toward their objective. The jungle growth and elephant grass were too thick to walk through. Henderson decided to throw caution to the wind and use the trail instead of risking making noise as they moved through the jungle. While the moonlight filtered through the trees, he took short hesitant steps along a well-worn path, leading the patrol toward the objective.

Once he was within one hundred meters, Henderson stopped, sliding his rucksack to the ground. The rest of the patrol did the same. They were a short distance from the pickup location. He observed the clearing to his west that was the designated landing zone. Small stands of trees and five-foot-high elephant grass covered the terrain toward the objective.

Henderson whispered to Little JJ, "Stay here for covering fire. Guard the gear."

Right at twenty-one hundred hours, the song "Where Have All the Flowers Gone" played, " . . . *soldiers gone? . . . to graveyards . . .*"

Henderson took notice. "I know that song. Can't believe they're playing it."

When the song ended, a voice in perfect English spoke. "American soldiers, you need to come over to our side. Help us get rid of the troublemakers that have invaded our land. If you don't, we will wipe you out, like we've done to all invaders before you." The speakers sent his voice over a great distance.

"Gawddamn it! That's some weird shit," Laurel whispered.

They played the same song again as the men crept toward the station.

"*. . . soldiers gone? . . . to graveyards . . .*"

The First Squad stopped to guard the front of the broadcast station. Henderson assigned their positions as Hanson with his men moved toward the enemy. Within a minute after Hanson left to capture the equipment, gunfire erupted. Henderson identified that it was M-16s firing. The shooting stopped as quickly as it started.

Henderson spotted three NVA running through the elephant grass toward his squad positions as they ran for the station.

"Hold your fire until they are closer," Henderson whispered.

As he shot a look at Cain, Henderson pointed to his right. Two more gooks were sneaking through a stand of thin trees toward the station. Cain nodded that he understood before he faced the direction of the approaching NVA. Now the enemy was coming from two directions.

Henderson heard a noise to his rear. When he turned, he observed Hanson pushing a prisoner out of the thick overgrowth, with Hanson's men carrying equipment behind him. He had the captured officer blindfolded with his hands tied behind his back. Henderson signaled for them to get down.

Hanson and the men of the Second Squad fell to the ground.

He turned his attention back to the front and yelled, "Fire!"

The First Squad fired on the five approaching enemy combatants.

"Look out—RPG!" Bear yelled.

The NVA soldier stood, firing the rocket-propelled grenade. The flash from the rear of the launcher lit up the area. *Bam!* The RPG grenade exploded between the two squads showering shrapnel in all directions.

The enemy soldier fell backward after Bear fired two rounds into his chest.

"The rest of the gooks are coming!" Laurel yelled.

AK-47 muzzles flashed, with rounds whizzing and zinging around the American soldiers.

The two squads opened fire, killing the five enemy soldiers in seconds.

"Bear and Cain, go check the bodies." Henderson stood to survey the area.

Both soldiers jumped to their feet, running toward the dead NVA while Laurel covered them. They returned in minutes, reporting that the squad killed the five enemy soldiers.

"Ray, call the choppers to come and get us." Henderson glanced skyward.

"Rescue One, this is Animal One. Come and get us. Over," Laurel transmitted using Henderson's call sign.

"Animal One, good to hear from you; on our way. Out," the pilot said.

The second squad stopped near Henderson.

"Good work, Henderson." Hanson smiled. "We got the goods."

He pushed the NVA officer toward Little JJ, and the Second Squad followed, carrying equipment.

"Grab your rucks. Let's move to the LZ!" Henderson yelled as he guided the squad.

After the men slid their rucksacks on, they made sure the landing zone remained secured. While the helicopters approached, the sound of their blades slapping the air grew louder.

The pilots used the moonlight to direct them to the landing zone. Both choppers settled on the ground. Hanson loaded the prisoner onto his chopper while they loaded the broadcasting equipment on the First Squad's Huey. Then the men of each squad boarded their helicopters.

Once the squads were on board, the Hueys lifted, heading to Chu Lai for the fifteen-minute flight. Henderson looked down into the darkness, wondering if the risk that they took was worth it. The men remained quiet during the trip and waited to come down from their adrenaline high.

In no time, the helicopters set down on the helipad at the division firebase. The pilots cut their engines. The only sound was the blades slowly spinning down.

Hanson slid off the Huey first. One of his men handed off the prisoner, and then the rest of the Second Squad jumped to the ground. The First Squad unloaded the equipment and placed it into the waiting three-quarter-ton truck.

Henderson stopped in front of Hanson. "Second Squad is invited to our hooch for a drink."

"Thanks. When we get rid of the NVA and equipment, we'll join you." Hanson gave a mock salute. "Good job tonight, Henderson."

A jeep pulled next to the helipad. "Is that the prisoner, Sergeant?" a military policeman asked.

"He's all yours." Hanson shoved the prisoner toward the MP.

The two squads met at the hooch for a short celebration before calling it a night. Henderson broke out a new bottle of Jim Beam, Bear got the Coke, and Little JJ fetched glasses for everyone. Once the twelve men each had a full glass, Henderson raised his and said, "May we stay safe."

The men responded, "May we stay safe," and downed the drink.

"Well, First Squad, we'll work with you guys anytime." Hanson put his glass on the table.

"Same here, Hanson." Johnston took a sip of his drink.

"Time for some shut-eye." Hanson slapped Johnston on the back.

The men of Second Squad left for their hooch to get some rest. The First Squad squared their gear away. One by one, they quickly fell asleep.

DUSTOFF DOWN

From a deep sleep, Henderson bolted upright in bed. "Mitch, I'm coming; hold on!" He flipped to his side, falling to the floor. "Where's my rifle? I can't find my rifle!"

"It's okay, Henderson. I got you." Johnston had a hand under Henderson's arm, pulling him to his feet. "Only a bad dream, man."

Henderson wobbled on his feet. "I got it. Thanks." He slipped from Johnston's grasp as he walked to the wall locker. "I'm getting a drink."

"Do you think you should? It's zero one hundred." Johnston picked up the pillow and tossed it on Henderson's bunk.

"Yep, I do. Do you want one?" Henderson started pouring the Jim Beam.

Johnston picked up a glass, handing it to him. "Might as well."

After he poured him a drink, Henderson lit a cigarette. "Let's go to the porch."

The two soldiers walked outside. Johnston removed a cigarette from the pack. "Why did you come back to 'Nam?" While waiting for an answer, he lit the Kool, inhaling deeply. He exhaled, blowing the smoke into the breeze.

Henderson watched the waves run along the beach. He felt the cold, wet breeze on his face. "Shit, I don't know anymore." He took a long drag from his cigarette. When he exhaled, a cloud of smoke dispersed into the air. "I thought my old unit needed me. I felt guilty leaving them in the bush."

"Yeah, that's how I felt, but I didn't plan on coming back." Johnston eyed Henderson to watch for his reaction.

After Henderson sat on the steps, he took another drag from the cigarette. "That's cool. I understand your predicament." He ran his fingers through his hair. "You had no choice. I did."

"Do you regret coming back?" Johnston shifted his weight from one foot to the other. "Hey, I have to ask."

Henderson glanced up at Johnston while taking a drink. "Yeah, I do. I miss Cheryl."

Laughter filled the early morning air. "Man, you got a beautiful girl there."

"I do, don't I?" A smile crossed his lips as he set the empty glass on the step. "She's smart too—going to be a math teacher."

"I bet you're proud of her."

Henderson looked toward the full moon with the light reflecting over the sea. "I am." He felt calmness take over his body. "She'll make a good teacher. She has a lot of patience."

"She would need a lot of perseverance to be married to you." Johnston laughed while punching Henderson lightly on the arm.

"We still got time to get some shut-eye." Johnston yawned as he stretched. "What you say?"

Henderson stared at the ocean and then back at the bright night sky. "Yeah, let's go." He flipped his cigarette to the ground. "Thanks." He turned his gaze toward Johnston. "Thanks for listening."

He reached down and pulled Henderson to his feet. "Anytime."

•

While the men of the First Squad ate breakfast, Brighton approached their table with a coffee cup in his hand. "Sergeant Henderson, the squad can take a half day off today. Go swimming or whatever." He took a slow sip of the hot coffee. Then he peered over the rim of the cup. "Make sure the squad stays together in case there's a mission. Let me know where you plan to be."

"Sounds good, LT." Henderson picked up his tray. "I think this morning would be a great time for a swim."

The men at the table laughed.

"Let's go." Bear took long strides toward the door, and the squad followed.

Little JJ turned to face Henderson. "I don't know if swimming is a good idea, Sarge."

Henderson's eyebrows rose. "Why not?"

"Have you ever seen Bear without a shirt?" Little JJ tried to repress the smile that tugged at his lips.

"My feelings are hurt." Bear had an offended look on his face.

The laughter of the squad followed them out the screen door.

After they changed to swimming trunks, the squad walked along the sandy road toward the beach, with each man carrying an olive, drab-colored towel. The pace was slow as they laughed and joked about the simplest things in life.

Henderson strolled alongside Little JJ while they followed Bear. "Hey, I know what you mean about Bear." Both men laughed. "I don't see any skin on him."

Little JJ chuckled. "I told you." He made fun of Bear until they reached the beach.

Once at the seashore, Bear gave Little JJ a menacing glare. "I'm going to drown your little ass."

Henderson saw the fear in Little JJ's eyes. He didn't know if he was faking or not, but Little JJ ran like hell when Bear chased him down the beach.

After swimming for twenty minutes, Henderson walked from the water to the hot white sand. It seemed the morning sun's heat beat down on him like any other time of the day. He stretched out on the towel, letting the rays dry his body. While he looked out to the ocean, he thought of Mitch and the time they swam in the South China Sea. Sergeant Stahl, Doc, and Ronnie Porter were alive that day too.

Henderson's mind left the South China Sea, crossing the ocean while he thought about being with Cheryl. The love he felt for her made his body tingle. Her image floated before his eyes. He saw the twinkle in her green eyes, the freckles that ran across the bridge of her nose from one cheek to another, and how her dimples appeared when she flashed that gorgeous smile with her full lips.

"Hey, man, it's time to go." Cain kicked sand at Henderson.

Startled, Henderson jumped to his feet. "What the hell." When he said those words, he remembered where he was. "Sorry."

"No problem. Time to go." Cain directed Henderson's attention to a tall, lanky soldier, running down the road.

"Sergeant Henderson, Sergeant Henderson," the soldier yelled.

"It's the clerk." Henderson pointed toward him.

Cain signaled to the rest of the squad to come back to the beach. After the squad gathered, they collected their belongings. They jogged toward the clerk.

With Henderson in the lead, he reached the clerk first. "What's up?"

The clerk strived to catch his breath. "The LT . . . wants the squad . . ." He stopped talking while he bent over. "… to get ready for a mission." He looked up at the men that gathered around him. "He'll meet you at your hooch."

"Okay, tell him we'll be there." Henderson turned, waving his men to follow.

•

Once the squad reached the hooch, they burst through the screen door, stripping off swimsuits. After they pulled on jungle fatigues and boots and got their weapons, they waited impatiently for instructions.

When Henderson walked into the center of the room, he felt the soft panic grow inside him, but it quickly faded. "Take the basic rescue load. Bring extra ammo."

The men looked up for a second, listening. Then they packed their rucksacks with the required items for a rescue mission.

"Laurel, make sure you have a fresh battery for the radio. Hell, bring an extra one." Henderson stuffed more magazines into his rucksack.

Brighton opened the screen door, entering the room with a sense of urgency. "Gather around. New mission."

The First Squad stopped what they were doing. They bunched around Brighton as he spread a map across the card table. "This is going to be a hairy rescue." He pointed at a valley. "A dustoff was shot down here." He traced the ridgeline above it. "VC are entrenched along here."

Henderson cleared his throat. "How many VC?"

"Probably company size." Brighton glanced at the squad members. "There could be more by the time you get there." He rubbed his hand through his hair. "The VC isn't the only problem. The weather is bad, with low visibility." He stopped talking while he eyeballed the men gathered around the table.

"The dustoff has a crew of four, with one wounded soldier. The pilot reported that everyone was alive. No one injured in the crash, but the enemy destroyed the chopper." He lowered his eyes and started to fold the map. "We only have one rescue chopper available. It's refueling now."

"How's that a problem, LT?" Johnston asked.

Henderson reached into the ice chest for a cold Coke. "How are we going to get the crew on the dustoff along with the squad without making a couple of trips?" He tossed a Coke to each man.

"That's the problem." Brighton stuffed the map into his pants cargo pocket and studied his men. "You guys will need to stay behind until the second trip. It could get rough."

"Gawddamn it," Laurel said. He punched two holes into the top of the can and then took a long drink from the Coke. "Gawddamn it."

Bear looked around at the squad while waiting to get their attention. "Looks like the odds are in our favor."

Little JJ choked on his Coke. "How's that, you hairy animal?"

Bear grabbed Little JJ, pulling him into a hard hug, lifting him off the floor. "It's only a company of VC against the First Squad."

The room erupted in laughter with nervous amusement that didn't chase the fear away.

"Let me go!" Little JJ yelled, struggling to get free. After Bear dropped him, Little JJ gave him a friendly shove.

Once the laughter died out, Brighton took a drink of Coke. "I'm trying to get an ARVN infantry company for backup. But it'll take them a couple of hours to get there."

"That sucks." Cain looked at a picture of his wife.

Brighton glanced at the men. "You'll fly to the ground to where the crew crashed. Get off the chopper as fast as you can."

Henderson adjusted his bush hat. "By the terrain, we should be able to protect the crew for a while."

Brighton finished his Coke. "Any questions?" He crushed the can with ease in his large hand and then shot it into the trash can.

"Any air support?" Henderson asked as he raised his Coke for a drink. He wished he could pour in a shot of Jim Beam.

"Yes, a Cobra gunship will be on station." He stood erect, looking at the squad. "The Cobra should arrive at the same time you do." Brighton rotated his wedding band around his finger. "With the weather as bad as it is—I don't know how long he can stay with you." He shifted his weight. "It may be hard to get you more air support."

"Lieutenant, get more help as soon as possible." Henderson reached down to pick up his M-16 along with the rucksack. "Okay, grab your gear. Move to the helipad."

Brighton extended his hand to Henderson. "Good luck, Sergeant."

"Thanks, LT." Henderson smiled. "You know the area we are going to is the same area of operation we patrolled with First Platoon?"

Brighton placed his hand on Henderson's shoulder. "I saw that too. Be careful."

Once they reached the Huey, each squad member boarded. Henderson moved to his assigned spot on the chopper. The copilot looked to his rear. Henderson gave him the thumbs-up signal that they were ready. The pilot slid the collective pitch control lever and throttle forward. After the Huey climbed with the blades rotating faster, he banked the helicopter, accelerating as he left the Combat Center behind.

When the helicopter took flight, Henderson thought of Cheryl, wishing he had written to her last night.

THEY HAD TO LEAVE THEM

While the pilot flew low to the ground, Henderson ran the rescue scenario through his head. He kneeled behind Laurel, watching the rice paddies, hedgerows, and jungle growth zoom by the helicopter. The countryside looked familiar to him. The thought of the First Platoon humping the hills brought a thin smile to his lips. He missed his brothers from the old unit. However, Henderson appreciated the opportunity that Brighton gave him with this unit.

His headset crackled with static. Henderson heard the pilot. "In five minutes, we're going to drop fast to the landing zone. Everyone get ready."

"Roger, sir." Henderson motioned for the squad to prepare for landing.

When the chopper started to descend, he pulled the charging handle to the rear of his M-16, releasing it to chamber a bullet. Next, he slammed the palm of his right hand against the forward assist to ensure the round seated fully. He sat with his hand wrapped around the pistol grip and his index finger on the trigger. His thumb rested on the selector switch.

Henderson could tell the men were becoming tense by the way their eyes narrowed, darting from one location to another, or their knuckles turned white because of the death grip on their weapon.

He knew there was no way to relieve the fear. It probably was a good thing; it got their adrenaline pumping, which caused their senses for survival to heighten.

Suddenly a burst of enemy fire raked across the helicopter as AK-47 rounds tore through the Huey. The ripping of metal echoed inside the chopper. Henderson leaned forward, looking toward the ridgeline where the VC were entrenched. He observed the cloud cover was low, with light rain falling. The flashing of rifle muzzles sparkled like a night sky full of stars. *Oh fuck!*

The chopper weaved left then right as it descended to the landing zone. More rounds hit the helicopter, with the window exploding on the left front. The copilot jerked, wincing in pain.

Henderson screamed to the copilot over the radio, "You okay? Where are you hit?"

"I'm hit in the leg. I'll be okay." The copilot applied pressure to the wound.

The pilot calmly lowered the helicopter. "Get ready. I'll hold her at two feet."

Henderson signaled his men time to go. The soldiers of the First Squad, with every muscle at the ready, tensed for the jump to the ground. While firing their weapons, the downed crew covered the rescue squad's approach. The enemy's automatic fire threw chunks of earth into the air along the chopper's path. Little JJ lit up the ridgeline with his M-60.

While Henderson surveyed the landing zone, the downed crew, and the enemy, fear took hold of him. Sweat ran from his face as his stomach turned over, making his breakfast meal rise to his throat. Within seconds, he shook off the fear.

With a hand signal from Henderson, the First Squad jumped, hitting the ground hard. They sprang to their feet, running for cover. The pilot maneuvered the helicopter quickly from the hot LZ while flying to a higher altitude. He circled above the battle, waiting for Henderson to give the go-ahead to pick up the crew. Little JJ continued to fire his M-60 to protect the soldiers on the ground.

While Henderson crawled toward the downed crew, the ridgeline exploded. When he looked up, he saw a Cobra with all its armament. It fired its miniguns, rockets, and 40-millimeter grenades at the VC positions. The enemy gunfire died off when the Cobra attacked.

Henderson rolled onto his back. "Call the rescue ship. Tell the pilot to come in fast," he yelled at Laurel.

Laurel waved. "Rescue One, this is Animal One. Ready for pick up; come fast. Over."

"Animal One, roger that. Here we come. Out."

Within a minute, the rescue helicopter was on the ground with its blades still spinning fast, straining to rise off the ground.

Without a word spoken, the First Squad moved the downed crew along with the wounded soldier to the waiting bird. Little JJ gave Henderson a pleading look. He signaled that he should stay with the squad. Henderson shook his head while pointing at the M-60. He reached up, touching Little JJ on the knee. "We'll be okay."

Once loaded, Henderson gave the pilot a signal to take off. The pilot waved, and then the Huey shot straight up. When the pilot put the nose down, the chopper accelerated across the hills toward Chu Lai.

"Animal One, this is Warlord Two. Over," the pilot of the Cobra transmitted.

Laurel heard the transmission. "Go ahead, Warlord Two. Over."

"Heading back to base to refuel and reload ammo. I'll be back. Over."

"Roger, Warlord Two. Don't be gone long. Out." Laurel looked at his handset. "Shit, bad timing."

When the Cobra disappeared over the horizon, Henderson heard *whoosh*! He screamed at his squad, "Incoming RPG." The men of the First Squad hit the ground and sought cover.

Bam! The explosion rocked the surrounding ground. Henderson sat up. He scanned the area to make sure his men were not injured. Seconds after the RPG exploded, the squad started receiving AK-47 fire from the direction of the ridgeline. He sensed they were moving closer to their position. Henderson focused on the enemy, not letting the nervous anticipation he felt taking hold of his body to distract him from holding off the VC. After he surveyed the area, Henderson directed the four squad members to defensive positions. They returned fire at the invisible enemy.

Bear extended a light anti-tank weapon he carried as he rose to a kneeling position. He aimed at the location where he thought the VC fired the RPG. Once he checked to his rear, he shouted, "All clear." Flames shot from the back of the LAW. The rocket screamed to the aiming point. It exploded seconds after it left the tube. "Got the little bastard!"

"Animal One, this is Animal. Over," Brighton transmitted.

Laurel gave the handset to Henderson. "Go ahead. This is Animal One. Over." Henderson crept lower behind the rocks as rounds thudded into the ground on all sides of him.

"The Animal Two Rescue chopper is on the way; hang in there. Over," Brighton said.

Henderson remained calm. "What's the ETA? Over."

"Animal One, it should be there in five mikes. Good luck. Out."

Henderson gave the handset back to Laurel. "Chopper coming in five mikes. Give covering fire."

The squad could hear the whirl of the blades slapping the air. Cain looked skyward. He pointed. "Here she comes!"

When the chopper lowered to the ground, the enemy opened fire with everything they had. Rounds ripped through the fuselage and cabin, tearing holes. The copilot's head exploded with blood dripping down the cockpit window. The gunner fired as fast as the M-60 would load each round. Henderson heard a loud thump. As he looked up, the gunner secured by a cable slumped over the gun.

When the squad attempted to maneuver toward the Huey, the enemy concentrated their firepower on them.

Their only way out ascended quickly to the sky. Henderson heard the radio crackle. "Animal One, landing zone too hot. I can't land. Heading back to base. Sorry."

Enemy rounds ricocheted off the rocks or buried into the ground around the five soldiers. They returned fire to keep the enemy from advancing.

"Conserve your ammo." Henderson scanned the area. "We have twenty minutes until our chopper gets here with support."

Cain rose to a sitting position to see over the berm he hid behind. "Shit, they're coming for us."

"I got the fuckers." Bear fired at the advancing Viet Cong.

"Oh shit." Cain groaned while falling to his side. Henderson saw Cain take a slug to the shoulder and crawled to the wounded soldier. Once he reached him, Cain was already bandaging the wound.

"You need help?" Henderson asked.

Cain held the bandage over the wound. "Tie it off and give me my weapon."

Henderson tied the dressing tight. "That should hold." He handed Cain his M-16.

"Thanks." He placed his M-16 on the berm with one hand and quickly returned fire.

"Pull back, pull back," Johnston yelled as he crawled to the rocks fifty feet behind their position. He turned to give covering fire for his squad members.

Without much effort, Bear scooped Cain into his arms. He helped him toward the rocks. Laurel, with Henderson, was a few steps behind, turning every other step to return fire. Enemy AK-47 rounds whizzed by the two soldiers and thudded into the ground at their heels. While covering his friends, Johnston knelt behind a boulder firing his M-16.

When Henderson looked toward Bear, he saw Cain jerk in his arms. Bear couldn't hang on to him. Cain fell forward onto the ground. He lay sprawled in an awkward position facedown in a pile of stones.

Bear bent down to get him. "Fuck! Cain is dead."

The firing from the VC increased.

The four grunts took up fighting positions behind the rocks. Henderson looked toward the sky, thinking it was a little longer until they arrive. Then there was silence.

Johnston peered over the boulder. "They must be regrouping."

Henderson signaled for Laurel to hand him the handset. "Animal, this is Animal One. Where is the cavalry? Over."

"Animal One, hang in there for fifteen mikes. Over," Brighton transmitted.

Henderson frowned at the response he received. "LT, I don't know if we have that long. Over."

"The ARVN infantry element should be closer to you. Over."

At that moment, Henderson heard the booming echo of weapons discharging. It sounded like a full-scale battle about two klicks from them. The sounds of the firefight rolled through the valley, with the reverberation of the gunfire increasing. He knew the ARVN Company was getting hit.

"Animal, I don't think they're coming. Out." He handed the handset back to Laurel.

Henderson stared out into the jungle, searching for a way out of the ambush. He didn't want to lose any more men, but their prospects weren't looking good. He knew there was nowhere to go. They had to wait for help.

After leaning his back against a boulder, Henderson removed the picture of Cheryl from his breast pocket. As the light rain soaked his uniform, he stared at the photograph, thinking of the love he felt for her. As the dread grew inside him, he slid the picture back into its rightful place.

Johnston crawled next to Henderson. "What the fuck are we going to do?" His hand was trembling as he wiped at the dirt and sweat running down his face.

While still staring into the jungle, Henderson said, "Wait. Fight. Then wait. That's all we can do." He surveyed the area one more time. "Shit, nowhere to run to."

Bear carried Cain with him as he hurried to where his squad members were. He fell in a heap next to Henderson. "What are we going to do, Sarge?"

"Wait for our ride out of here." Henderson reached over to Cain; with a finger, he closed Cain's eyes.

The sun moved slowly, westward toward the mountain peaks. "Shit. Time check?" Henderson asked.

Laurel looked at his Seiko watch. "It's sixteen hundred." He chuckled when he remembered that he bought the wristwatch on his first stand-down. "Hey, Sarge, you remember when we bought our watches? I still got mine."

"Yeah, I do. It was on stand-down." To Henderson, it seemed like a lifetime ago. "Hell, you didn't even know what a stand-down was." The four soldiers laughed at the thought of Laurel being an FNG.

Henderson saw movement at the edge of the jungle. "Here they come." Laurel moved in closer to Henderson. "Bear, move to our right to the last boulder. Take Cain's ammo with you." Henderson grabbed Johnston by the arm. "Move to our left to the end of the boulders. Don't do anything stupid. I need you to take charge in case they get to me."

"Got it. Don't worry, we'll get out of this shit," Johnston yelled over his shoulder as he crawled toward the boulder at the far end.

"Stay right next to me with that radio." Henderson shook Laurel's shoulder. "We got this."

"I don't know, Sarge." Laurel looked scared.

Whoosh! An RPG round zoomed over the soldiers, hitting behind the boulders. *Bam!* The explosion rocked the ground and threw shrapnel, dirt, and rocks into the air.

"Gawddamn it." Laurel brushed off the dirt that covered his uniform. "That was close. Here they come!"

Ten VC sprang from the ground no more than thirty feet from Henderson's position. They ran toward the American soldiers while firing their AK-47s. Henderson was fixated on the enemy soldier in the center running toward him without showing any fear. He could see his twisted face, hate radiating from his eyes.

"Kill the sons of bitches." Henderson fired at the soldier he was obsessed with and watched him fly backward when three rounds thudded into his chest. "Kill all the bastards."

The First Squad fired at the exposed VC. Three more of the enemy fell to the ground in a heap. A grenade flew in their direction.

"Grenade!" Laurel yelled while he hit the ground, covering his head with his arms.

The explosion blinded Henderson for a moment. Neither Laurel nor Henderson could hear a sound. The movement around them was a blur in slow motion. Henderson felt like he was in a dream, with the sounds of the battle getting louder. He wanted to lie down and not deal with it. The enemy advanced.

Two enemy soldiers maneuvered around the boulder on the right side of their position. Bear turned, pointing his M-16 squeezing the trigger. Nothing happened. "Fuck, out of ammo!" He ran forward, snatching the first enemy soldier into a death grip before the VC knew what happened. Bear had him in a stranglehold, and within seconds, the soldier slumped in his arms dead. He threw the dead soldier toward the advancing enemy.

The other Viet Cong soldier swung his AK-47 toward Bear. Without hesitation, Bear grabbed the barrel, moving it away from him. The rifle discharged, and the round traveled harmlessly into the jungle. He then ripped the weapon from the VC's hands. As the soldier glared at him, Bear swung the stock of the rifle, hitting him in the right side of the head, knocking him to the ground.

"Fuck you! Fuck you!" Bear screamed while standing over the VC, hitting him, again and again with the butt of the rifle.

At the other end of the line of boulders, Johnston fired at another group of Viet Cong rushing their position. Several fell when he flipped the selector switch to automatic, emptying the magazine. After reloading, Johnston continued to fire. Suddenly he felt a burning pain in his right leg. His weapon sagged in his hand.

When he looked at his leg, he saw blood seeping through his pant leg. An enemy soldier was almost on top of him. He picked up his rifle and fired at point-blank range. The VC fell forward, landing on top of Johnston. With ease, Johnston threw the dead Viet Cong off of him. While enemy AK-47 rounds cracked over his head, Johnston crawled toward Henderson. "I'm hit. I'm hit."

Once he came out of the daze caused by the explosion, Henderson crawled toward Johnston. "Let me help." Henderson took the M-16 and Johnston's rucksack. "Come on, you can make it."

Henderson spotted an enemy soldier running around a pile of rocks. He lowered his rifle, firing three shots in quick succession. The VC fell back against a boulder, sliding to the ground.

Bear screamed, "You little fucker!"

He instinctively placed his hand over his left shoulder, where the VC had stabbed him with an eight-inch blade. Blood gushed from the wound. After the initial shock, Bear grabbed the VC's arm when he brought the knife down a second time. He snapped the enemy soldier's wrist with ease and took the weapon away. Bear grabbed the VC with his free hand, holding him around the throat with a firm grasp. "This is for you!" He sank the blade into the VC's heart. He lifted him by the throat, staring the soldier in the eye. While the enemy's last breath escaped from his lips, his eyes rolled back, exposing only the white. Bear released his grip, letting him fall to the ground.

After he grabbed his M-16 along with the rucksack, Bear ran bent over toward Henderson. "More VC coming!"

"The chopper is coming." Laurel dropped the handset.

The ground around the four soldiers turned upside down, with dirt and rocks flying through the air. Henderson looked toward the sound of the Huey. He saw Little JJ firing his M-60 nonstop at the enemy forces.

When the helicopter hovered a foot from the ground, the four squad members dragged Cain toward the chopper that was twenty-five meters away. The enemy opened fire at the struggling American soldiers.

Little JJ ducked as AK-47 rounds tore through the cabin of the Huey. The pilot slumped in his seat with a bullet through his chest. The copilot took over the controls. "We need to go now!" he yelled through the headset.

"Give me one minute!" Little JJ yelled as he fired at the approaching enemy.

The copilot held the chopper in its hovering position. "You need to hurry. I can't hold her much longer."

They lifted, pushing Cain onto the floor of the Huey. Then Henderson and Laurel lifted Johnston onto the helicopter, and Little JJ pulled him onto the deck. "Fuck, they shot me again," Johnston screamed as an AK-47 round nicked his right arm.

While they ignored the incoming fire from the enemy, the two soldiers on the ground with all their strength lifted Bear. He grabbed a pole, and along with Little JJ pulling and Henderson and Laurel pushing, Bear fell onto the deck alongside Johnston. Bear passed out.

Whoosh! "Incoming! RPG!" Henderson screamed at Laurel, and he hit the ground. *Bam!* The boulders behind them exploded. The Huey rocked violently while the copilot attempted to hold their position. The air filled with incoming AK-47 rounds thudding into the ground near Henderson. He heard metal tearing as the Huey took many hits.

When he raised his body from the ground, Henderson looked up at the copilot. Their eyes locked. Henderson waved him off. "Go now! Go now!"

The pilot moved the collective and throttle forward, shooting skyward. Little JJ screamed into the headset. "What the fuck are you doing?" A slug hit Little JJ. He winced in pain but continued to fire the M-60.

While the copilot raced for Chu Lai, he adjusted the headset. "Animal, this is Rescue One. Coming home with wounded. Animal One and Animal One-three left at the crash site. Need assistance. Over."

"Goddamn it, don't leave them! Do you hear me, Rescue One?" Brighton yelled into the handset."

"Roger, Animal. I don't have a choice. Heavy enemy fire. Out," the copilot transmitted.

The VC ran toward the American soldiers left on the ground. The two soldiers fired, aiming with each shot, not wanting to run out of ammo. The enemy rounds zinged overhead. Henderson winced, falling over onto Laurel. Laurel flipped Henderson onto his back. He discovered that a slug creased Henderson's head, knocking him unconscious.

"*Đầu hàng!*" *Surrender.*

Laurel looked up. There stood five enemy soldiers, their AK-47s pointing at him.

An important-looking Viet Cong scrutinized the two soldiers. "Surrender." Then a rifle butt connected with Laurel's head.

The radio filled with static and then a voice transmitted, "Animal One, this is Animal. Over." Then again, "Animal One, this is Animal. Come in, Animal One. Over."

Seconds later, the radio blared again, "Henderson, this is Brighton. Hang in there. We're ten minutes out."

The radio exploded as a VC soldier emptied his AK-47.

WHERE THE WOUNDED GO

The 91st Evacuation Hospital stood on a rocky bluff overlooking the South China Sea. It was the most active hospital in Vietnam with the most patients. When wounded soldiers arrived on stretchers, the medics placed them on sawhorse-shaped supports in the triage area. The nurses had all the medical supplies stocked the same. That way they didn't have to search for what was needed.

The dustoff settled on the helipad near the hospital. Medics were moving the wounded before the copilot cut the engine. One by one, the injured soldiers were transported to the emergency area. A team of doctors and nurses stood at the ready.

Brighton watched as the doctors checked his three men. When a medic wheeled each soldier to a surgical room, he stood by his side.

"You'll be okay, Bear; the doc got you."

"Hang in there, Little JJ."

"You might go home, Johnston."

After the medic wheeled Johnston away, Brighton looked at the emergency room. Bloody bandages littered the floor. He saw footprints in the puddles of blood. Out of nowhere, two young Vietnamese women appeared. They began cleaning the room. The metallic smell of blood soon gave way to the smell of disinfectant. Within minutes, Brighton couldn't tell his wounded had been there.

In the corner, Brighton saw a body on a gurney. He slowly walked toward the lifeless soldier. He slid the blanket back to expose his face. "Cain, I'm sorry," he whispered to the dead soldier. "I'll write to your family and tell them what a warrior you were." Brighton brushed the dirt off Cain's face. Tears clouded his eyes.

A medic walked to Brighton's side. "We need to take him, sir."

As Brighton pulled the blanket to cover Cain's face, he stopped to take a long last look. It was as if he burned Cain's image into his memory, never to forget. Brighton went to the waiting area to be there when his men came out of surgery.

Once the three soldiers were out of danger, Brighton returned to his office. The first thing he did was write the After Action Report. He wanted to make sure his commander knew that two of his men were missing.

He picked up the telephone handset and dialed the number. After he waited for the clerk to answer, he said, "I need to talk to Major Anderson."

Anderson picked up the telephone. "Yes, Lieutenant Brighton."

Brighton slid his chair out. "Sir, I'm submitting my report, but I want to let you know I have two men missing."

"Damn. Who are they?" Anderson asked.

"It's Sergeant Henderson and Corporal Laurel, sir." Brighton lit a cigarette.

"I'll have their families notified ASAP," Anderson said.

"Thanks, sir." Brighton set the handset into the cradle, which disconnected the call.

After the phone call, Brighton fumbled inside a desk drawer for several minutes. He retrieved a pen, paper, and an envelope. He picked up the pen and started to write.

Dear Mr. and Mrs. Cain,

I'm Brian's commander, James Brighton. I know the Army has informed you of his death, but I wanted to let you know what kind of man and soldier he became.

On the day Brian died, he served our country. He died a hero, who served others and treated all with respect.

You should be proud of your son . . .

THE SEARCH CONTINUES

Two Cobra gunships flew overhead, protecting the rescue Huey as it hovered over the battle area. The Second Squad leader, Sergeant Hanson, hung out the door, scanning the ground where the First Squad fought the VC. While the Huey lowered, Hanson leaned farther out the open doorway without any fear. He needed to find Henderson and Laurel.

Before the chopper touched the ground, six soldiers jumped. After he landed solidly on his feet, Hanson ran for cover behind the same boulders that the First Squad had used for protection. He could see the battle damage and bloodstains on the rocks and ground. At one end of the boulders, he observed several dead VC.

A soldier ran over to Hanson, handing him the handset. "Animal Two, this is Rescue Two. Where do you want me? Over," the pilot transmitted.

"Rescue Two, stay high above; we'll check the area. Over." Hanson looked skyward toward the pilot.

The Huey pilot transmitted, "Roger. Be safe, Animal Two. Going up. Out." The helicopter shot skyward.

Hanson turned, giving his attention back to finding the two missing soldiers. "Second Squad, spread out and check the area out to one hundred meters." He gazed at his men. "Work in pairs."

While they searched for the two missing soldiers, the rescue squad moved in different directions.

•

Forty minutes later, Hanson asked for the handset. "Rescue Two, this is Animal Two. Come get us. Over."

The pilot looked toward the ground. "Roger, Animal Two; you find them? Over."

Hanson stood silent for a moment, giving the area another scan. "Rescue Two, no, we didn't. Out."

The chopper settled gently on the ground while the six soldiers climbed aboard. While the Huey lifted to the sky, Hanson gave the battle area the once-over one last time. The helicopter banked right, heading toward Chu Lai.

When he flew away, Hanson saw a Loach flying low over the countryside, looking for the two men. High above, two Cobras protected the smaller helicopter. "Where was all the air support an hour ago?" Hanson asked.

THE NOTIFICATION

When he rolled over, Professor looked at the alarm clock on the nightstand. There it was again, the damn pounding on the front door. The sound was louder this time. While rubbing his eyes, he slid from the bed, staggering into the living area. Professor was a spectacle, wearing only jeans, his long brown hair was over his ears. His beard needed trimming too. He stopped at the front door, and after turning the lock, he threw the door open. He struggled to adjust his eyes to the bright sunlight. Finally, Professor made out a figure of a man standing on the porch.

"Good morning, sir. Are you Calvin Cox?" an unknown voice asked.

At last, his eyes focused on the man without answering.

"Are you Calvin Cox?" He handed him an envelope.

Professor became fixated on the yellow cab parked on the street in front of his apartment. "Oh no . . . oh fuck no, it can't be." He saw the envelope was from Western Union. "What happened to Henderson?"

The taxi driver's gaze fell to the porch. "My condolences. I don't know, sir. My instructions were to deliver the telegram to you."

Professor stumbled backward. "I'm sorry. Come inside."

"I can't do that, sir." The cabbie stepped off the porch.

Professor closed the front door. He sluggishly walked to the kitchen. "I need to make coffee."

Once he sat in a kitchen chair, he opened the envelope from Western Union and steadied his shaking hand to read the telegram:

> *Mr. Calvin Cox*
>
> *The Secretary of the Army has asked me to express his deep regret that Sergeant Eddie Henderson has been missing in Vietnam since 14 June 1970. He was last seen as a leader of a rescue squad for a downed helicopter and its crew. They were attacked by a large hostile force. A search is in progress . . .*

Professor jumped to his feet. "How in the hell am I supposed to tell Cheryl that he's missing? And the Army doesn't have a clue where he is."

When he slumped into the chair, the shock from the news he'd received hit him with full force. The feeling was similar to a boxer beating him with body punches, one after another. He couldn't breathe, think, or focus on a single thought, and then Eddie's face flashed before him. Professor wept.

After twenty minutes went by, he stared at the telephone on a small table near his chair. He tried to think about how he would break the news to Cheryl. She didn't know that Professor was the emergency contact.

He removed the handset from the cradle, holding it to his ear. After he heard a dial tone, he inserted his finger into the rotary dial for the first number. He rotated the dial clockwise until his finger hit the metal stop, and then he removed his finger from the opening, watching the rotor roll back to its original position. As he repeated the motion, Professor slowly dialed the next number, then the next, until he dialed all the numbers.

Once his finger hit the stop for the last number, he released his finger and listened. There was a moment of silence. While his eyes darted around the room, he heard a ringing sound. After the fourth ring, Professor heard a distinct click. "Hello, the Henderson residence."

Professor, uncertain if he could talk, hesitated, but the words came. "Cheryl, it's Professor."

She laughed. "Oh, Professor, I'm glad you called. I thought we could do lunch soon. Will you be on campus tomorrow? We can meet where we normally have lunch."

There was an uncomfortable silence. Professor was struggling to maintain his composure to formulate his next sentence. He had a feeling in his gut that urged him to run, to be a coward, but he fought to have the courage to do what was right, especially for Eddie.

"Hello? Professor, are you there?"

Professor fell back into his chair with tears streaming down his cheeks. "Yes, I'm here. I need to see you today. Can I come by your apartment in an hour?" He wiped at his tears while he took a deep breath.

"You sound serious. Is there anything wrong?" Cheryl asked.

Professor scanned the room, searching for help. "I need to . . . see you . . . today."

"I'll be here. Come on over."

"I'm on my way." Professor placed the handset gently into the cradle. The call disconnected.

He sensed the panic in Cheryl's voice. Unlike this conversation, Professor knew that he didn't stumble over his words or hesitate to use them. He didn't think he fooled her.

•

After he freshened up, Professor stared into the mirror. "This beard needs to go." He wore khaki slacks with a light-blue oxford shirt and loafers. The anti-war protester hadn't dressed this formally since the wedding. Professor wanted to be respectful to Cheryl. He rubbed his smooth face.

When he passed the table, Professor picked up his car keys along with the telegram. With a loud sigh, he left the apartment to deliver the awful news. With measured steps, Professor slowly walked toward his car, carrying the burden of the news about Eddie. How do you tell a wife that their husband isn't dead, but he probably is?

While he stood at the door, Professor made sure his shirt stayed tucked in his pants. Then he ran his hands through his long, thick hair. The bearer of tragic news squared his shoulders, attempting not to look serious. He knocked on the door. After the first tap, the door swung open.

Cheryl stood in the doorway, her gorgeous smile beaming. "Hi, Professor. What happened to your face?" She giggled. "I don't remember the last time I saw you without a beard. You do look handsome."

He dropped his gaze. "Thanks." He stepped across the threshold.

Cheryl walked to the kitchen table. "I'm having a Jim Beam with Coke. You want one?"

"Sure, but make it a double." Professor closed the door, hesitated, and then he followed her to the kitchen.

She handed him the glass. "Have you heard from Eddie?"

Professor pulled out a chair. "Not for a week." He sat, placing his elbows on the table. "That's why—"

"I got a letter yesterday." Cheryl sat across from Professor as she took his hand into hers. "I'm sure you'll get a letter soon."

"I'm sure I will." He squeezed her hand. "That's why—"

"Eddie seems to like his new job. I feel much better that he's on such a big base. He doesn't have to live in the jungle. What a relief to know he's not in any danger." After Cheryl took a sip of her drink, she looked into Professor's eyes. "Now tell me, why do you need to see me all of a sudden?" She took another sip. "Is Eddie hurt?" Cheryl tipped the glass back, emptying it. "I'm sure the Army would've told me if he was hurt."

Professor shifted in his seat. "No, the Army wouldn't tell you."

"What do you mean?" Cheryl leaned forward with elbows on the table while she looked intently into his eyes.

He picked up his drink, tipping it until there was only ice left in the glass. "Eddie made me his emergency contact." He set the glass down. "Cheryl, that's why I'm here."

With her hand trembling, she poured Jim Beam, spilling more than she got into the glass. After his words sunk in, her body shook as tears streamed down her cheeks. "Oh . . . Oh no. Eddie is dead."

Professor took the bottle from her. "No, he isn't dead."

"What are you telling me, then?" Cheryl screamed. She stared out the window as she wiped at tears. "If he isn't dead, then why are you here?"

"I don't know how to tell you." Professor grabbed her hand, holding it tight. "Eddie is missing." There he said it. Now she knows.

Her glass fell to the floor, shattering across the kitchen tile. "No, no, no." She fought to catch her breath as tears streamed. Professor walked around the table, taking Cheryl into his arms. "Is he dead? Is he in the jungle hurt? Is he all alone? Is he a prisoner somewhere being mistreated?" she whispered, sobbing into Professor's shoulder.

Professor pulled Cheryl closer. "I don't know."

NO ONE KNOWS

Before the sun dropped behind the jungle growth, Henderson stirred. His wet uniform clung to his body while keeping in the cool air. He shivered violently. A ringing sound echoed in his ears while waves of nausea rocked his body. He put his hand over the head wound. Once he discovered the injury wasn't bleeding, he pulled himself into a sitting position.

With his head throbbing and blurred vision, he could distinguish only strange dark shapes. Henderson's senses alerted him when the smell of rotting vegetables, mold, exotic food, and animals reached his nostrils. Fear ran through his body.

While his eyes focused, he looked through the bamboo bars of the cage and saw them—a group of VC eating. *Oh fuck!*

He began to scan the surrounding area, hope rising in his heart. The group of VC and his cage sat in a small clearing surrounded by tall trees and thick jungle vegetation. When he looked toward the sky, it was invisible, only the canopy of the trees was noticeable. He searched for a way to escape.

The sturdy cage was built with thick bamboo, inches apart, held together by rope. The entryway to the cage had a gate that was tied shut with a small slot underneath. Not big enough for a man to crawl through the opening. He figured, even if he managed to get out of his cell, the VC would be on to him in no time. Henderson didn't have a sense of how many enemy soldiers there were at the campsite.

His head sagged to his chest when he realized that his world had become a cage. The pit of his stomach knotted and bile rose in his throat. He knew death would be better than being a prisoner of war. The promise that Laurel and he made hit him with the force of a typhoon—another promise broken. Freedom felt a million miles away.

He patted his pockets, noticing that they were empty, even the picture of Cheryl he kept in his breast pocket was gone. There was an indentation where his watch had wrapped around his wrist, and his ring was gone too. *Shit, they even took my boots.*

After the shock wore off, Henderson knew he had to come up with a plan. *I need to quit feeling sorry for myself.* He figured that the VC couldn't have traveled far with him unconscious. All that mattered was putting distance between him and the enemy. Once he studied the jungle, Henderson realized he had no idea which direction to head when he did break free. That didn't matter; he knew to take one thing at a time.

Henderson heard a low moan coming from behind him. Slowly, he turned to see the source of the sound. "Shit, Laurel, you okay?"

Henderson scooted toward his friend, who lay helpless. "Let me get a look at your head." He ran his fingers around Laurel's head, thinking the wound was severe. "Wow, man, you have a big knot. The wound appears deep, but it's stopped bleeding."

Laurel peered up at Henderson. "Where are we?"

Henderson looked back at the VC and then said, "I think we're prisoners."

"Gawddamn it!" Laurel whispered. "Gawddamn, I thought we promised each other."

"Shit, Ray, we didn't have time—you know that."

"I know, I know. I'm sorry." Laurel attempted to pull himself upright.

One of the soldiers noticed the two Americans were talking. "*Ngừng nói!*" *Stop talking!* He jumped to his feet.

Henderson observed the enemy soldier who approached him was short, dirty, and appeared no older than fourteen, maybe sixteen at the most. He wore the uniform of the VC—black shirt and trousers. His footgear was sandals. In his hand was a four-foot-long, thick bamboo stick that he twirled as he strolled toward the cage.

Within seconds, he was at the cage. "*Ngừng nói!*" He poked the stick at Henderson.

"Okay, stop poking me!" Henderson attempted to avoid the stick.

Laurel rose to a sitting position. He leaned against the bamboo bars of the cage. "What is he saying?"

"I don't know." Henderson made eye contact with the soldier. "Don't hit us."

The stick struck Henderson in the gut, knocking the wind out of him, forcing him back. He lay against Laurel, bent over, holding his stomach, gasping for air. When he scrutinized the enemy soldier, Henderson saw the face that he learned to despise, hate, and sometimes fear. He no longer felt the fear because he knew that he was going to die this day. After his breathing became more comfortable, Henderson looked at the enemy soldier with hate radiating from his eyes. "You little son of a bitch."

A soldier, much taller than most Vietnamese men, walked from the shadows. "*Dừng lại,*" *Stop,* the soldier said in a soft voice. He wore a large belt buckle with a red star on it. He had the same type of uniform—black shirt and trousers—but he wore boots. There was some type of rank on his shirt collar. To Henderson, the soldier appeared to be in his midthirties and had an air of authority. He figured him to be an officer. When he turned, Henderson observed the large scar that ran down his left cheek.

"*Dừng lại.*" The officer squared his shoulders, his eyes turning cold.

The teenage soldier gave a rushed bow while avoiding the gaze of the approaching officer. He scurried off into the darkness.

The officer stopped at the cage and looked at Henderson in the eyes. "I apologize for my soldier." After his heels came together, the officer slightly lowered his head, dropping his gaze for a moment.

Henderson stared at the officer, not believing the words he'd heard. Hell, he spoke in English too.

"My name is Lieutenant Dang." He smiled.

Deciding to play along, Henderson said, "Thank you." He turned to help Laurel into an upright position. "He needs medical attention."

Dang stepped closer to the cage. "We have none to offer." A thin smile twitched at the corners of his mouth. "Let me offer you some food."

With a quick stride, the lieutenant strode over to his soldiers. Henderson heard talking but had no idea what was said.

A soldier, much older than Dang, strolled toward the cage carrying two bowls. Without a word spoken, he slid them through the slot at the bottom of the gate, and he immediately left.

Without warning, his stomach growled from hunger. Henderson picked up a bowl. First, he noticed it looked like rice, and when he smelled the contents, his nose wrinkled. He handed the bowl to Laurel. They used their dirty fingers to scoop the rice and stuffed it into their mouths, making sure they got every grain. Within seconds the bowls were empty. Laurel began to lick his dish clean. Henderson searched for his cigarettes, and then he remembered his pockets were empty.

He grabbed Laurel's leg. "You got any smokes?" Henderson knew it was useless to ask.

Laurel patted all his pockets and frowned. "No, nothing. All my pockets are empty. Shit, they took my Seiko watch too."

Out of habit, Henderson glanced at his left wrist. "Yeah, they took mine too."

When Henderson looked back at the enemy camp, he saw Dang approaching the cage. The officer stopped in front of Henderson. He pulled out a pack of Marlboros and removed a cigarette. While it dangled from his thin lips, he lit the smoke with a Zippo lighter. Henderson's face contorted. The officer had Henderson's cigarettes and lighter.

After taking a drag, Dang offered the cigarette to Henderson. "Here, for you."

At first, Henderson was going to decline, but his addiction got the best of him. He accepted the cigarette. He took a long drag from the smoke, and then he offered Laurel a drag. The captured soldiers felt a sense of peace for a moment.

"Was the food good? How is the cigarette?" Dang asked. "What unit do you belong to? Why were you in my area?"

The feeling of suspicion raced through Henderson's mind. "Thank you for the food and cigarette."

Dang ran his finger along his scar. "What about my second question?"

Henderson managed to stand. "You know we won't answer that question. We *can't* answer those kinds of questions."

Dang chuckled. "We'll see." He disappeared into the darkness.

Henderson couldn't tell if the smile was genuine, or if it was a smile of an evil person. The two POWs huddled together for warmth, falling asleep.

•

The sun barely rose above the horizon, when Henderson heard a noise at the cage. He saw a boy soldier, no older than twelve, slide two bowls of rice with two cups of water into the cage. Without saying a word or making eye contact, the boy left. Henderson shivered from the cold, damp morning air.

"Breakfast is served." He nudged Laurel. It took Laurel several minutes to wake. "You okay?" He seemed disoriented.

"I don't feel good." Laurel leaned against the bamboo bars.

Both soldiers wolfed down the rice. Henderson savored the water while he watched Laurel. "The water hit the spot. How you feelin'?" He couldn't remember the last time he had a drink. Henderson ran a dirty finger across his chapped lips.

"I'm okay." Laurel wiped his eyes.

Henderson put his hand on Laurel's wound. "How's the head?"

"Better. I'm not as dizzy or feel as sick as yesterday." He stretched his arms to get the blood circulating. "See, my arms work."

He figured that Laurel had lied so not to worry him.

With cigarette smoke trailing behind him, Dang strolled to the cage. "Was the food good?" the officer asked. "What unit do you belong to? Why were you in my area?"

Henderson gave Dang a brazen smirk. "You know the answer to that." He stood up in the cage to glare at the officer. "How did you learn English?"

Dang removed a cigarette from the pack. "I'll answer your question." He lit it with the Zippo. "I went to university in France. I studied English literature." A smile tugged at his lips when he handed Henderson a cigarette. Henderson accepted it and took a long drag, letting the nicotine soak into his bloodstream, and then he looked at Dang. *This fucker is messing with me.*

"Now, I answered your question. You answer mine." While Dang traced the scar on his angular face with his finger, he glared at Henderson. "What unit do you belong to? Why were you in my area?"

"I'm not answering that question." He handed the smoke to Laurel.

After Dang searched through his pants pocket, he pulled out a photograph. "Is this beautiful woman your wife?" He flipped the picture around where Henderson could see it, and then he held it to his nose, taking a whiff of her perfume. "She smells good too."

"That's mine." He shoved his arm through the opening in the bamboo cage, reaching for the picture. "You son of a bitch."

Dang stepped back from his reach. "*Cảnh!*"

The teenage soldier with the stick ran to the officer's side. "*Vâng thưa ngài.*" *Yes sir.*

"*Đánh hắn.*" *Hit him.* Dang nodded toward Henderson.

The young soldier thrust the stick hard into Henderson's stomach, and he fell to his knees, gasping for breath.

"Stop!" Laurel held Henderson.

This time Dang pointed toward Laurel. "Hit him," he ordered, in English this time.

The teenage VC rammed the stick into Laurel's stomach with all his strength. Laurel fell onto Henderson, fighting for air. Without a word, Dang, along with the soldier, walked back to the camp. The officer gave a command. The five soldiers started packing gear.

Twenty minutes later, the boy soldier slid two pairs of boots through the gate slot. He didn't make eye contact with the prisoners. The teenage soldier gestured for Henderson to move toward the gate of the cage while the boy held an AK-47 pointed at them. He motioned for him to kneel.

Henderson kneeled as instructed. "Stay cool," he whispered to Laurel.

The gate swung opened. The teenager held his hands to the front of his body, signaling for Henderson to do the same. He complied. The soldier looped the rope around Henderson's wrists, tying his hands together. Then, he took an eight-foot length of cord, binding it to the rope around Henderson's hands. He pulled Henderson from the cage, forcing him into a kneeling position.

The soldier did the same with Laurel. He used the end of the extra rope to tie to Laurel's rope. Now the two soldiers were bound together by the eight-foot cord. The teenager tugged on the line for the two prisoners to follow him to where the other VC soldiers stood.

When they stopped, Dang flashed the two prisoners a cordial smile. "I'm letting you wear your boots while we walk. You will take them off at night. If you try to escape, you'll remain barefooted." His dark, black eyes turned cold. "You will be punished."

When he turned to leave, the soldier tugged the rope for the two Americans to move along the trail into the jungle. The boy soldier led the way, and the two older soldiers followed him, and then Henderson and Laurel, with the officer and teenager behind them.

Henderson observed, by the sun's location, that the soldiers were moving them south, not north as he expected. He followed the men to his front while Laurel struggled behind him. At times, Henderson pulled on the rope to help his friend to keep the pace.

The trail snaked through the dense jungle growth along ridgelines. After several hours of walking, Henderson heard the sound of a helicopter flying low over the canopy. The small group of men moved off the trail into the jungle. The teenage soldier forced Henderson and Laurel to the ground. With the thick canopy of trees, the helicopter crew didn't have a chance to spot them. Henderson wanted to jump to his feet and yell, but he realized no one would see or hear him.

Tears clouded his eyes as he caught a glimpse of the Huey as it flew overhead. It appeared to be one of the rescue helicopters. A glimmer of hope surfaced while he listened to the chopper disappear behind the hills. He knew the Animals were still searching for him and Laurel. Although not religious, he said a short prayer that they would find them.

The heat, along with the humidity, was unbearable. Without water, the two American prisoners were weakening fast. Keeping up with their captors became increasingly difficult.

The adrenaline that pumped through his body was the only thing that kept Henderson moving. The pace, the heat, the humidity, and the lack of food and water were his enemy now. There was only one thing he could do, and that was to hope no one killed him. He needed to keep going forward. Escape will be his reward.

They marched until dusk. Once stopped, the teenager made both soldiers remove their boots and then tied them to a tree. Each received a bowl of rice and a small cup of water. They attacked the food like two starving dogs. When finished, each licked their bowl clean and then washed the rice down with the cup of water.

Laurel looked at the VC. "I need more food and water." He started to cry.

"We'll get more in the morning. Hang in there, Ray." Henderson touched Laurel's arm. "You okay? You don't look good." He observed that Laurel's face seemed flush with fever and his eyes were dull.

"I think I'm okay. My head hurts like hell." Laurel rubbed his wound. "Gawddamn it."

"Stay strong. We'll get out of this." Henderson watched their captors. "I haven't seen anyone on the trail, have you?"

"Nope, I haven't. Probably a good thing," Laurel whispered.

Henderson saw the teenager stroll toward them. "Be quiet. Get some sleep." He closed his eyes. The enemy soldier stood over the two Americans and lightly prodded each one. They didn't move.

They lay on the hard jungle ground with mosquitoes charging them and emitting a loud buzzing sound. It was nerve-racking. The damp night was cold. Henderson began to wonder if he would ever escape from the VC. He checked on Laurel, who was curled up, and then he fell asleep, exhausted.

THEY'RE NOT WATCHING

Before the sun peeked over the hills, the teenage soldier prodded Henderson. He stirred but didn't acknowledge that the enemy poked him. The VC gave Henderson one final stare, directing his anger to wake him. When he didn't move, the teenager kicked him in the back.

"Stop. I'm awake!" Henderson rose to a sitting position.

The teenager snickered, prodding Laurel until he was awake. When he sat up, Laurel leaned against a tree.

"You okay, Laurel?" Henderson moved closer. "Damn, you still don't look good."

His head hung against his chest with drool dripping from his bloody cracked lips. "My head hurts. But I'll be okay."

The boy soldier approached the Americans. He dropped their boots at their feet and then turned to head back to the VC camp. The teenager removed the rope that tied them to a tree. He poked Henderson one more time before leaving for his fellow soldiers.

The VC sat around a firepit, talking and eating breakfast. Henderson watched the lieutenant as he scooped rice into his mouth, washing it down with water. He was hungry for even the smallest amount of food. Henderson focused only on the food; nothing else mattered.

Henderson slid on his boots. "Come on, Ray, get your boots on."

"Give me a minute." Laurel lifted his head while wiping at the bloody spit running down his chin. After a minute or two, Laurel slid the boots on his feet. "I'm hungry and thirsty."

Henderson licked his dry lips. "Yeah, me too. Maybe the boy will bring us food." He continued to watch the VC eating.

While his stomach growled, Henderson sat straighter. "Look, Ray, the boy is filling two bowls!" He stopped watching the VC eat. Henderson realized that he had reached the point where he would do anything for food. He felt disgusted for having that thought. *Fuck them!*

The boy stood over the two prisoners. Without making eye contact, he set a bowl of rice with a cup of water in front of each prisoner and then bent to tie Laurel's boots. He stood and walked back to his fellow soldiers.

Henderson picked up the bowl, staring at it. He was determined to eat slowly to prove he wasn't hungry. He wanted to show them that food wasn't necessary to him. With his grimy fingers, Henderson scooped up a small amount of rice, taking his first bite. He finished the bowl in seconds. Before realizing it, he licked the bowl clean.

After much laughter, Dang said, "I guess you were hungry."

Henderson looked up, startled that the VC officer stood over him.

Dang removed Henderson's cigarettes and lighter from his pocket. Slowly, he lit a cigarette while staring at Henderson. He then removed a picture from his breast pocket. "Yes, you have a beautiful wife." He looked down at the American soldier. "I love the smell of her."

Henderson sensed at that moment that Dang enjoyed it. He got a kick out of humiliating or torturing another person. "Yes, she is." He decided to be careful in the way he talked to Dang; there was no need to provoke him unnecessarily.

After taking a drag, Dang dropped the unfinished cigarette at Henderson's feet. "We'll be leaving soon."

Without hesitation, Henderson picked up the cigarette. Again, he let his addiction get the best of him. He took a long puff. Then he exhaled slowly. "Here you go, Ray." He passed the cigarette.

Laurel seemed to perk up after taking a hit from the cigarette. "That does taste good." They took turns smoking the cigarette until the filter burned.

Henderson turned his attention back to the group of VC. He observed Dang walking away from the campsite, down the trail with the teenager. The older men appeared preoccupied with cleaning the eating utensils, while the boy packed the gear. It was as if they forgot about the two prisoners.

Within seconds, Henderson knew the window of opportunity to escape opened. "Now is our chance."

However, the fear of being caught overwhelmed him. Everything hinged on them getting away—their sanity and their lives were at stake. This opportunity could be the difference between being free or left in the jungle to decay. Henderson's hand felt his unshaven face. He wondered if he would starve to death if he didn't fade into the wilderness when he had the chance. The dread Henderson felt gripped him, and his heart pounded against his chest. He thought of escape or death. He'd learned while in this war that the Vietnamese people believed in reincarnation after death. *Fuck, what if I come back as a Viet Cong?* The thought made him laugh under his breath.

He nudged Laurel while pointing with his bound hands in the direction of the jungle away from the VC. "That way, now; keep low."

They crawled on their elbows and knees, into the jungle growth away from their captors. The morning air was crisp and damp, but Henderson's uniform became soaked with sweat in minutes. He and Laurel crawled over rocks, thorns, and brush that cut their hands and knees. The two soldiers twisted and turned on their bellies through a stand of bamboo. With hands tied, it was more challenging to maneuver away from the campsite, but they kept going forward.

Once Henderson thought they were out of sight, he stood. He ran with Laurel at his heels. Tree branches slapped him in the face, and thick brush attempted to trip him. While running faster than his tired legs would carry him, Henderson tripped, falling into thick brush. He rolled onto his stomach and pushed himself to his feet. Henderson continued to run downhill with Laurel right behind him.

He stopped, panting hard, with Laurel at his side. He looked at the sun. “Let’s head east toward the coast,” Henderson whispered.

Laurel gasped for air. “Go. I’ll follow you.”

While the two followed a ridge toward the valley below, they headed east. Laurel stumbled, hitting the hard ground face-first. “Gawddamn it.” He let out a loud moan.

“Be quiet.” Henderson reached down, pulling Laurel to his feet. “You okay?”

“Yeah.” Laurel wiped the blood from his face.

Voices speaking in Vietnamese filtered through the jungle growth. “They’re coming. We need to move.”

Henderson searched for the best route away from the VC. With his face soaked in sweat, his fear traveled to every muscle in his body while he held on to Laurel. For a moment, he froze to the spot where he stood. He released a sigh and then pushed Laurel forward.

With the weight of their bodies pushing them downhill, they broke into a run. Henderson dodged jungle growth with Laurel behind him. However, stands of trees covered in bamboo thickets slowed their progress. Out of breath, Henderson stopped. He leaned against a tree, struggling to slow his breathing. Laurel fell to his knees, having a harder time as he panted; his breathing was shallow.

The Vietnamese voices inched closer as Henderson’s heart thrummed against his ribs. While he scanned the area for a place to hide, he helped Laurel to stand. “Let’s hide over there.” He spotted a thicket of thick brush about fifty feet away.

They quietly crawled into the brush, lying as low as possible. Henderson covered Laurel with rotting vegetation from the jungle floor, and then he hid under the foliage. Both men attempted to slow their breathing and waited.

Henderson cringed as he watched through the leaves with frightened eyes. He glanced at Laurel, noticing his eyes shut tight.

While he lay there, Henderson began searching for a way out, but deep down he knew there was no escape. Maybe they won't see them. He knew that was wishful thinking.

The voices grew louder. Twigs snapped, and tree branches swooshed through the air. He felt the enemy closing in, taking away their only chance to get away. An imaginary weight laid on his chest, keeping him from breathing or moving. Henderson knew that to be free, he had to remain perfectly still, or he would become the prey for the VC.

When he peered through the growth, Henderson saw a pair of boots no farther than ten feet away from him. It had to be Dang. He tried to burrow his body lower into the earth. Henderson thought the sound of his violently shaking body echoed in the jungle. He was sure the enemy could hear it.

"*Tìm họ*." *Find them*. Dang scanned the area.

Henderson felt the panic, and his stomach tightened into knots. His breathing became rapid. The tension grew throughout his body as the boots stood in front of him. He wanted to run but dared not move a muscle. He squeezed his eyes shut, attempting to calm himself by thinking of Cheryl.

"*Tìm họ*." Dang walked downhill.

The two American soldiers remained hidden as the sun fell behind the mountains. Darkness crept through the silent, still jungle, cooling the air. After he quietly removed the vegetation from his body, Henderson stood. "Let's move." He felt the rope cutting into his wrist.

"Are they gone?" Laurel rolled over, pushing himself to his feet.

"Yeah, but I don't know which direction they went." Henderson helped lift Laurel to his feet. He held Laurel steady and felt his body shaking.

"Damn, that was close." He didn't know if it was fear or the cool of the night that shook Laurel's body. "Let's get these ropes off."

The two soldiers struggled for several minutes, untying the ropes that bound their hands.

Henderson rubbed his wrists. "Let's get moving before they come back." He ran his fingers through his filthy wet hair, and then he grinned through his chapped lips. He knew the VC would find their trail soon, but for now, it was Laurel and him running for freedom. Distance from Dang was all that mattered. He wasn't stopping for anything until Laurel and he were free. For the first time since being captured, he sensed that they would escape.

While they moved downhill, Henderson peered into the darkness, following his intuition for the best route. After thirty minutes, the clouds floated northward, leaving the full moon exposed. The moon provided ample light to follow an old trail toward the east.

Henderson understood that the illumination from the moon could reveal their position to the VC. He also knew he should avoid using paths, but the jungle was thick vegetation. He ignored his instincts. They stopped along the trail when he sensed danger. "To our front," he whispered. Laurel's eyes went wide as he nodded that he understood.

When Henderson saw a stick coming toward his body, it was too late. The thick bamboo stick hit him across the chest, causing him to grunt and fall to the ground. He heard a loud *whack*. When he turned, he saw Laurel lying facedown, blood streaming from his head. The teenager stood over them.

A pair of boots stopped inches from his face. "I told you not to escape." The two older VC pulled Henderson to his feet. "Now, you will be punished." Dang stared into his eyes.

Again, Henderson sensed the evil radiating from his captor. Panic overwhelmed him, like when a raging forest fire changes direction with the wind, heading toward you. He could no longer breathe. *Stay calm, stay calm*, Henderson thought.

Next, they lifted Laurel to his feet. "What happened?" His chin hung to his chest.

Dang gave the boy instructions. He immediately used rope to tie Henderson's and Laurel's hands as he had before they escaped.

"Carry him." Dang pushed Henderson toward his hurt friend. "Start walking."

Henderson put his arm around Laurel holding him steady. "Come on, Ray, you can do this."

The teenager pushed his bamboo stick against Henderson's back. Surprised by the direction the teenager pushed him, Henderson and Laurel started down the hill toward the valley. While they trudged along the trail, Henderson followed the two older VC as the lieutenant and the teenager followed. The boy walked ahead of the group.

After hours of walking, the sun rose over the horizon, spilling light across the jungle. Henderson heard Vietnamese voices echoing across the rice field. When he stepped from the edge of the wilderness, he saw the village. He halted because it seemed familiar. The teenager pushed him forward, prodding him with the end of the bamboo stick. When Henderson stumbled, he fell, grabbing hold of an ancient well to catch himself. Once he regained his balance, he looked around. "This is the same well Mitch and I got water from one afternoon."

Laurel didn't acknowledge that Henderson said anything. He followed along.

Henderson looked around the village, taking it in, as the villagers went about their daily activity. While he looked in amazement, he couldn't see any changes to the village. They still didn't have electricity, telephones, or indoor plumbing. Children ran around half-dressed. The women wore black or white silk-like pajamas; most wore a sizable conical palm-leaf hat to protect them from the sun. The villagers constructed their hooches of straw, bamboo, or hardened mud. The pigs and chickens roamed free, with the animal pens located behind the family hooch.

The teenager hit his leg with the stick. Henderson winced in pain, staggering and stopping in the middle of the village. An old woman with black-stained lips stared at him as a young mother pulled their children into her arms to protect them from the Americans. The old men waved their arms wildly, shouting at the two Americans. Dogs ran around them, barking and nipping at their ankles.

When Henderson scanned the villagers, he observed that they appeared frightened and angry. He wondered why they would be afraid of him since he was tied up and a prisoner of the Viet Cong soldiers. Then it dawned on him—they were fearful of the VC.

Dang shouted orders to the soldiers. They stormed into huts and returned with food and clothing. Henderson saw them push elderly men and women to the ground and yell at them. The two older VC brought three young boys, roughly twelve years old, to the lieutenant. Dang shouted at the boys. The women began to wail.

Within seconds, two VC soldiers that Henderson hadn't seen before walked toward Dang. The lieutenant gave orders. The three boys picked up the stolen goods and followed the soldiers into the jungle.

One of the older women ran to Dang, dropped to her knees, and pulled on his leg. To Henderson, it appeared she was begging him. The lieutenant attempted to shake the woman off him; she clung to him and wailed. He pulled his pistol and, without any hesitation, shot the woman in the head. He shook his leg to free himself of her dead hands that still clutched on to him. Then Dang kicked her body out of the way and walked toward Henderson.

Henderson's face contorted to the ugliest sneer he could muster. He glared at Dang. "I saw what you did. I didn't miss anything, you bastard." The sight of the cruel lieutenant made him sick; he knew evil when he saw it. Hate never came easily, but now it filled his heart.

Once Dang stopped in front of Henderson and Laurel, he said, "That can be your fate if you don't obey me." He flashed his wicked smile. "Now, get moving."

When he stumbled past the last hut, Henderson saw a boy who was missing a leg and a hand. "GI number ten." The boy glared at the two Americans.

Henderson lowered his head, thinking that this was the same kid during his earlier tour that thanked him for the candy and said "GI number one" to him. This time the boy's mother didn't pull her son into her bosom. She looked into Henderson's eyes with a smirk. It appeared to Henderson she got her revenge for her son.

Since the forced march began, Henderson's face showed signs of wear with no way to cope. His feet moved faster until he stumbled. The teenager prodded him with the bamboo stick.

While staying in the tall grass that ran along the trail, the group made their way across the two-lane road known as Highway 1. To his front stood a hill, overgrown with bamboo thickets, elephant grass, brush, a dense growth of thin trees, with slopes running to the hilltop. All of which looked impossible to climb.

Henderson struggled to keep up with the three VC to their front. When they fell behind, with encouragement from Dang, the teenager poked them with his stick.

Henderson felt the rope tightened. "Come on, Laurel, you can make it. Stay with me."

After an hour, they crested the top of the hill. Dang moved the group through the clearing to the edge of the jungle growth facing west. Henderson noticed old C-ration cans strewed around the area. His heart sank as he recognized the spot where Mitch received the Dear John letter. *Fucking Sandra!*

In the distance, Henderson heard the sound of helicopter blades hitting the air. The teenager grabbed the rope that held the Americans. He pulled the two soldiers under the jungle canopy, forcing them to the ground. The rest of the VC group ran for cover too.

Henderson's brain came alive with the thoughts of being rescued. A smirk crept into the corners of his mouth as the sound grew louder. Any minute, he could jump to his feet to signal his savior. His dull eyes lit up; they could be free today!

Dang put his boot against Henderson's head. "Go ahead, run for it. Yell out." He laughed.

•

"Animal, this is Animal Two. Over," Hanson transmitted as he hung out the chopper side with his feet on the skid.

"Go ahead, Animal Two. Over," Brighton transmitted.

The rescue Huey for the Second Squad slowed its flight as they reached the hill.

"Animal, we've searched the grid pattern; still nothing. The hill is the last checkpoint. Over." Hanson scanned the hill for any indication that Henderson or Laurel were there.

"Animal Two, come on back. Over," Brighton said.

•

One of the older soldiers sat on Henderson, pushing him into the ground. Henderson fought to get to his feet. The teenager hit him on the back of the legs with the stick.

"We're here. We're here. Over here." Henderson sobbed.

The teenager hit Henderson again across the legs.

"Fuck you!" Henderson muttered.

With his foot, Dang pushed Henderson's face into the hard ground. "I told you."

The helicopter lifted, flying north.

"Gawddamn it." Laurel looked skyward, watching the silhouette of the helicopter fly away. He cried.

"When are you going to learn that you two belong to me?" Dang gazed at the Americans, and a hateful smile lifted at the corners of his mouth. "You belong to me."

THE LIEUTENANT LEAVES

While the sun beat down on Henderson, he woke to the sound of the VC talking. He found the singsong tone of their language unnerving. When he surveyed the area for food, his stomach growled and rumbled, demanding nourishment. Henderson salivated at the thought of a bowl of rice; he looked again but didn't see the soldiers cooking.

Next, he shook Laurel. "Time to get up."

Laurel rolled over, dried blood caked to his face. "I'm hurt." His eyes rolled back. After several seconds, they came back in focus.

"Hang in there. We'll get out of this." However, Henderson didn't believe it. He squeezed Laurel's shoulder. Henderson had lost his strength days ago, but he wasn't going to give up trying. His hatred kept him alive; his only thought was of revenge. He eyed Dang, and the hate he felt toward him fueled his body. Henderson wanted Dang dead; he wanted all of them dead. He had to stay alive.

Dang approached the two prisoners. "Get up. We are moving." He lit a Marlboro, blowing the smoke toward Henderson. "I warned you, but you wouldn't listen."

Henderson swallowed his pride. "We need food and water." He looked up at the VC officer. "Please."

Dang smiled. "You will get nothing to eat or drink today."

"What about medical help for Ray?" Henderson's eyes pleaded for help.

"Maybe if you do what I tell you, I can help him." He flashed a menacing smirk. "We'll wait and see."

Henderson hadn't felt this much rage in his lifetime. He knew if he released his anger that Dang would have the teenager beat him into compliance. The only solution was to act as an obedient prisoner. That's what the VC lieutenant wanted. Henderson kept his anger inside for his ticket to freedom. He decided to use his rage to kill Dang.

Fuck you! Henderson yelled in his mind. "Thank you." He looked up at Dang with a shit-eating smile.

The teenager walked past his lieutenant. He used the eight-foot rope, tying Henderson to Laurel. "*Di chuyển.*" *Move.* The teenager tugged hard on the line.

Before Dang walked away, he said, "Move now."

•

They walked at a quick pace, and the day got hotter. Sweat poured off Henderson as he strived to keep up while pulling Laurel. After hours of continuous walking, Henderson stumbled, falling hard to the ground. He found it difficult to get to his feet. He had no energy because his captors hadn't given them food or water since late evening yesterday. His adrenaline had quit pumping through his veins.

Dang towered over Henderson. "Get up."

He clenched his fist so hard that the knuckles turned white while gritting his teeth to not yell at Dang. They needed rest and food. Surely, he knew that. Henderson's face slowly turned red while he struggled to control his anger. He lifted himself to his feet. He glared at Dang. When he tugged the rope for Laurel to follow, it went taut. Laurel lay on the ground, moaning.

Dang moved to stand over Laurel. "Get up." He kicked Laurel in the side. "*Thức dậy.*" *Wake up.* Laurel didn't flinch or make a sound from the kick.

"Stop kicking him, you son of a bitch!" Henderson yelled.

"You mean like this?" Dang kicked Laurel again in the back.

Henderson took a step forward, but the teenager yanked on the rope, pulling him backward. Dang grinned at Henderson. The lieutenant motioned for one of the older soldiers to come to him. They talked a moment. The soldier bent over Laurel to check his condition. Then he stood, shaking his head, saying something to Dang.

The soldier untied the eight-foot rope that bound the two Americans together. He threw the end of the rope to the teenager. The older soldier continued to talk to Dang.

Henderson stared, trying to figure out what they were discussing about Laurel. He moved toward his friend. The teenager yanked the rope hard, making Henderson walk backward toward the enemy soldier. When he regained his footing, Henderson saw Dang remove a pistol from his holster. In horror, he saw him point it at Laurel.

Ray turned his head as his eyes fluttered open. He stared at Henderson with wide, horrified eyes. "Promise you'll kill the bastard, promise," Laurel muttered. His body shuttered, and then he attempted to slither away from Dang.

Frightened by Ray's expression, Henderson took a deep breath. He stumbled backward, his shoulders shaking in fear. In that split second, every nerve in his body felt on fire. There was nothing he could do.

"I'll kill the fucker, Ray. I promise!" Henderson screamed.

Ray Laurel looked into the barrel of the pistol. "Gawddamn it."

Dang smirked and squeezed the trigger.

Bang!

"No!" Henderson screamed.

Gripped in panic, Henderson stood frozen, wanting nothing more than to get to Dang. Sweat covered his body, and his heart thumped against his chest, like it was going to explode. *Revenge is coming.*

The teenager hit him with the stick. Henderson fell to his knees. He saw Laurel staring at the sky with lifeless eyes and blood oozing from his forehead. Dang stood over him with a pistol in his hand, smiling.

"You didn't have to shoot him, you son of a bitch." Henderson fought to get to the officer. "I'm going to kill you!" He crawled toward Dang.

The thought of the hundred different ways he could kill Dang flashed before his eyes. *Maybe I'm not human anymore*, thought Henderson. "Who cares if I lose my soul? I'm going to kill the son of a bitch," Henderson muttered.

The stick hit Henderson in the back of the head. He fell unconscious three feet from Ray Laurel.

•

Sunlight peeked in and out behind the leaves of the trees, while a light breeze blew through the jungle. A soft drizzle trickled through the canopy. Henderson's eyes opened. He watched the sunlight dance around the leaves and felt the refreshing rain splash on his face. Then he remembered. *Laurel!*

When his vision cleared, he saw Dang standing over him. Henderson struggled to stand but found his hands were tied to a tree, holding him on the ground. His head hurt. "You son of a bitch. You didn't need to kill Ray."

"He was going to die anyway." Dang flashed a grin that Henderson had seen too often from this enemy soldier. "You should try harder—that way you can stay alive."

Henderson watched as Dang's pupils appeared to glow red while the whites of his eyes grew smaller. It seemed his glare could kill him quicker than the pistol he used on Laurel. Henderson gave a final glance at those eyes and knew Dang was going to kill him too.

The smile disappeared while Dang ran his finger down the length of his scar. "You will stay here for two days. I'm leaving you with three comrades. I will return soon." He walked away.

The lieutenant stopped to talk to a group of soldiers. After much laughter, Dang, the two older soldiers, and the teenager disappeared into the jungle. Only the boy soldier, a different older soldier, along with a child soldier, remained. He hadn't seen the two soldiers before now.

The three VC huddled around the fire with a pot heating in the center of the pit. Henderson studied the group. The older soldier was ancient, probably in his sixties, while the boy soldier was no more than twelve. Henderson guessed the child soldier's age at eight or nine years. He had an unhealthy slender build and was barefoot and dirty. *Maybe this will be my chance to get the hell out of here.* Henderson's mind raced with an escape plan.

The child soldier filled a bowl from the contents of a large pot. The old soldier handed him a wooden cup. As the child strolled toward Henderson, he balanced the bowl and cup, making sure not to spill the contents. He held his head down with his conical hat hiding his face.

When he reached Henderson, he kneeled to place the breakfast meal on the ground next to him. The child looked into Henderson's eyes. He seemed familiar.

"Vinh," Henderson whispered.

Henderson could see the recognition in his eyes. They knew each other. Vinh was the boy from the small village where the typhoon hit during his first tour. His mother, Mai, died from the hands of the Viet Cong.

The boy nodded. "Eddie boo-coo dinky dau." Vinh smiled. He placed his finger on his cracked lips for Henderson to be quiet. His eyes showed the kind of soothing apprehension his mother used to have. Vinh laid his hand softly on Henderson's leg. Instead of recoiling, as he had with his captors, the boy's touch calmed him. He remained sitting next to Henderson while he ate.

"Vinh!" the ancient soldier yelled.

Vinh stood without looking at Henderson and walked toward the two soldiers.

It was a long day; the silence was unnerving. Henderson remained tied to the tree without the VC checking on him. The sound of a soldier's voice or the rattling of the cooking pot made his heart beat faster. The thought of food made his mouth water. He felt his strength draining without nourishment from enough food to eat or water to drink. While he stared at the stars, he thought of Cheryl. A smile crossed his lips until he fell into a deep sleep.

Henderson felt tugging at his hands. When he opened his eyes, he saw a shadow of a person kneeling over him. He tensed his muscles to protect his body, thinking that Dang or the teenager had returned to beat him.

"Shhh," the shadow said. Vinh untied the rope that bound the prisoner. Henderson sat up, rubbing his hands, and then he embraced the boy. The child placed a pair of boots next to Henderson. "You go." He pointed toward the east. "Mama-san."

When Henderson digested the instructions, it finally struck him what Vinh meant. Henderson made a face, hunching over like an old person.

"Yes." Vinh shook his head up and down. "Mama-san." He grinned at Henderson.

Henderson grabbed the boy's arm to take him back to the village and Mama-san. Vinh jerked away.

"No." He walked toward the sleeping soldiers.

He could feel the fear in his chest, wanting to take charge of his mind. Maybe the fear wants only to protect him because of the danger that waited for him. To move, he needed to defeat the fear. To be free was what he wanted. With his heart pounding, Henderson slid into the jungle, crawling as fast as he could to put distance between him and his captors.

MAMA-SAN HUMS A LULLABY

While he crawled east, Henderson didn't look back. Once the camp was behind him, he stood, wobbled, and began walking. With only the moonlight to guide him, Henderson attempted to stay off trails. His only thought was of freedom while he made his way through the jungle.

The destination was the small village where the old woman lived. It was the same woman that cared for Vinh after the VC killed his mother. Henderson thought of the time she washed his and Mitch's dung-covered uniforms; they had stood naked, waiting, with a palm leaf covering their manhood. The corner of his lips tugged upward into a smile.

While following an eastward direction, Henderson slid down the hillside, barely missing trees. When he came to a stop, he found a small stream running around the base of the hill. The beauty of the three-foot-wide bubbling brook of fast-moving, clear water energized him. He collapsed face-first into the water, gulping mouthfuls. In the back of his mind, he heard Sergeant Stahl order, "Drop in your iodine tabs." Henderson didn't care. Satisfying his thirst was his only thought.

A low growl resonated through the brush roughly twenty meters from Henderson on the other side of the stream. He recognized the sound. *Fucking tiger.* His eyes flew wide. The only thing in his mind was to protect his place at the creek. After all, it was his water. In seconds, he decided that he would fight the tiger for the water. "I was here first. It's mine," Henderson said loud enough for the tiger to hear. It appeared that Henderson's threatening voice frightened it, and the tiger ran away. He lapped at the water until he quenched his thirst. With his belly full, Henderson rolled onto his back.

The absolute horror of getting caught by the Viet Cong paralyzed him. The more he thought about his escape, or only moving a bit, the more terrified he became. Henderson didn't remember being this scared in his life, but he knew he had to keep moving. He wasn't going to let them catch him this time. To Henderson, dying seemed a better option than going back to Dang.

At least I won't have Laurel slowing me down this time. Henderson realized what he thought. *I'm sorry, Ray.* Tears rolled down his cheek. *What am I becoming?* Still lying on his back, staring at the stars through the trees, Henderson heard the call of the tokay gecko lizard echoing to his front. "Fuck you. Fuck you." He couldn't contain an inward laugh.

After a brief rest, Henderson walked in the creek for about three hundred meters. He then stepped on the ground, staggering toward the ville. Near nightfall, he heard Vietnamese voices. Once he found concealment in a thicket of brush, Henderson watched. He listened for any sound. The talking slowly faded. As the night quieted, he fell asleep.

Crack, a twig broke. *Swoosh*, a tree branch swung in the air.

Henderson woke, staring into the darkness. Then he saw them. A Viet Cong patrol walked no more than twenty feet from the thicket of brush that concealed him. He felt the sweat soak his skin as his heart thumped against his chest. Henderson's fingers curled around a thick tree branch. His muscles tightened, ready to attack the VC. The fear seemed to give him strength.

They passed, heading in the opposite direction he was going. A flood of relief washed over his body.

Within twenty minutes, Henderson heard all hell break loose. He recognized M-16 and AK-47 rifles, firing roughly two hundred meters away. He smiled. "They're coming for me." The firing of guns and explosions lasted for ten minutes. Then nothing but silence fell over the jungle.

He waited for what seemed an eternity—then crawled from the brush. To shout out to the American soldiers was his first instinct, but he knew better without knowing who the victor was. Henderson slowly made his way toward the area where the battle occurred. The smell of death and gun smoke hung in the humid air.

When he neared the site, he dropped to the ground, crawling toward bodies sprawled around the area. After he crept up to the first man, his gut tightened. He realized there were five dead American soldiers, stripped of personal items, equipment, and weapons. The only thing left on them were two dog tags hanging around their necks attached to a chain. A sense of hardness overcame Henderson as he moved body to body, removing the dog tags. He placed them in his pants pocket.

When he yanked the chain off the fourth body, Henderson heard a soft moan. He looked at the soldier as his eyes opened and he gasped for air—then his head fell to the side. Henderson placed his ear against his mouth but couldn't detect him breathing. He moved to the last body. After he removed the dog tags, he stayed on the ground among the dead, waiting until he thought it was safe to leave.

Thirty minutes later, Henderson decided it was time to continue his trek toward the village. As he walked, thoughts of Cheryl flashed through his mind. He knew she must be going crazy not knowing what's become of him. His heart ached for her. He wanted to hold her and to comfort her. With guilt, Henderson realized what he needed was for her to console him.

After hours of walking, the sun peeked over the horizon. Henderson made his way to the edge of the jungle growth. When he peered through the thick vegetation, he saw farmers. They worked in the cornfields several hundred meters away. What got his attention wasn't the farmers, but the ears of corn that hung from the stalk.

The rows of corn stalk seemed to run forever, while each one held an abundance of corn. Once Henderson crawled into the field, he snapped off several ears. When he rolled onto his back, he removed the husk around the corn. He began gnawing the kernels off the cob. This was his first food in what seemed like days. He crawled back into the jungle growth. He continued to bite the kernels off like an animal. After he consumed five ears of corn, his eyes closed.

Two hours later, the voices of the farmers leaving the field woke him. Henderson crawled into the field. He snatched the fresh corn and stuffed it into his shirt pockets. He managed to cram in four ears. After sliding back into the jungle, he buried the remains of the eaten cobs into a shallow hole. He knew he needed to find water, and soon.

Henderson reached up, grabbing a low tree branch, pulling himself to his feet. Even though his belly was full, it wasn't enough to regain his strength. Once he recovered his balance, he faced eastward, staggering along the edge of the jungle.

Before sunset, Henderson saw the hill where the platoon stayed for several days when the typhoon hit. With newfound energy, he picked up the pace as the ville was between him and the Song Lai Giang River. He remained on the hillside in the dense brush as he weaved along the hidden trail. It was a slow process. By dusk, he could see the outline of the village. He stopped at a stream for a drink.

When Henderson splashed water on his face, he heard a rustle along with a twig that snapped. While striving to act as if all was normal, every muscle tensed in his body. With his adrenaline pumping, Henderson found renewed strength. He slowly picked up a large rock from the creek, clasping it hard in his right hand.

Another branch snapped right behind him. Henderson wondered if the enemy sneaking toward him could hear his heart pounding. He felt the oxygen pumping inside his lungs but was afraid to exhale. With his fingers curled around the rock cutting into his hand, fear overwhelmed his body. He wanted to run from the source of the sound.

Henderson sprang to his feet. When he turned, he threw his body weight behind the hand that held the rock. The rock smashed into the VC's face with brutal force. The sound of bursting flesh and breaking bones echoed in the jungle. After Henderson followed through with the punch, they fell to the ground, with him on top of the enemy. The VC struggled to push the American off of him. Henderson swung the rock, hitting him on the side of the head. Again and again, he slammed the soldier's head with the stone. The VC didn't move, and blood poured from the wounds with a gray substance dripping to the ground.

Henderson rolled to his right, falling to the ground, gasping for air. While his erratic, deep breathing prevented him from moving, he lay there. Henderson knew he had to keep going. To stop meant he would die in this godforsaken jungle.

He didn't know how long he lay next to the dead VC, but he knew it was time to move. After he splashed water on his face to clean the blood away, he washed his hands. Next, Henderson searched the soldier but didn't find anything of use. *Hell, the VC didn't even have a weapon.*

Henderson grabbed the soldier's ankles. As he used the last of his energy, he dragged the dead VC into the thick bushes to conceal the body. In a daze, he stumbled toward the ville. He realized that making it to the ville was his only chance for survival.

After walking another klick, Henderson reached the outskirts of the village. Once he determined it was clear, he maneuvered to the backside of the hut where the old woman lived. He waited.

Thirty minutes later, the lamps and candles went out, and the sounds of the ville went quiet. While Henderson crawled under the hooch toward the steps, he hoped that she still lived here. As silent as possible, he pulled himself up the steps into the large room to discover a candle burned as it cast a dim light. Henderson couldn't stand.

"Mama-san," he whispered.

The floor creaked as the occupant tiptoed toward the door with a broom in their hand. The villager looked at the body lying on the floor. Puzzled, the figure moved closer to stare into Henderson's eyes while he lay helpless.

"Eddie." She squatted next to him.

A smile crept across his face, ear to ear. "VC, Vinh."

She hadn't changed. Henderson saw the same old woman who cared for Vinh and mourned for Mai. She stood less than five feet, with a small frame, and her long, gray hair was tied, hanging down her back.

She took his arm and pointed to a corner in the small room. He held on to her while they made their way toward the back of the hooch. Once Henderson reached the far side of the room, he crumpled to the floor. The woman covered him with a blanket.

"Thank you." He curled under the blanket.

She placed a finger over her mouth. "Shhh."

The woman left the room but returned within a minute, carrying a large cup of water. Henderson reached for it, gulping its contents before the bowl reached his mouth. Once he drank the water, he lay his head on the floor.

She reached down, stroking his hand. Then the old woman pulled the blanket over his head. While humming a lullaby, she sat next to Henderson, holding his hand. Her tender touch and soothing voice calmed him. His heartbeat slowed, and the fear slowly left his body, and he fell asleep to the unknown words of the song.

•

Whop! Whop! Whop! The familiar sound jolted Henderson awake. "It must be a dream," he muttered.

The noise of the blades slapping the air drifted closer. Henderson detected the pitch changing while the rotors slowed; it was a Huey landing, landing close. He crawled from under the blanket, moving toward the doorway. With hesitation and fear, he lay at the opening, while the sunlight blinded him. Then there was a commotion.

"Where is he?" an American voice said.

At first, Henderson didn't respond or move. His ears seemed sharper, but his mind paranoid. Fear gripped his body. *What if it was a trap? What if it was that fucking Dang?* He whispered, "It can't be him." He pushed his body to the porch. Henderson called out in a low, hoarse voice, "Over here, over here." He cried, "I'm here!"

Heavy boots thudded up the steps. Henderson couldn't lift his head. While he lay in the doorway, he watched the boots approach him. A large black hand touched his cheek. "Sergeant Henderson, it's time to go home."

"That you, LT?" Tears poured down his cheeks. "I knew you would come for us." When Brighton removed his hand, Henderson felt more optimistic than ever.

He lay there, giddy like a little boy. Happiness touched every nerve in his worn, beaten body. Henderson wasn't ashamed one bit for having these feelings. All his worries of being a captive, the evil lieutenant, and even Ray dying disappeared when he felt the touch of Brighton's hand on his face. He knew that he would live to see Cheryl.

"Bring the stretcher!" Brighton rolled Henderson onto his back. "You hurt anywhere?"

"I think everywhere." Henderson attempted a laugh.

Brighton stepped inside the hooch, looking for any sign of Laurel. When he came back to the porch, he asked, "Where's Laurel?" He peeked back inside. "I don't see him anywhere."

When he turned his head to the side, the memory of how Ray died flashed through his mind. The hatred was all he had for Dang; he wanted to kill him with his own hands. Henderson swore at that moment that he would.

"The fucking Lieutenant Dang executed Laurel, LT."

"What!" Brighton stood stunned with his mouth open. "We'll talk about it later."

Two soldiers carried a stretcher up the steps. With Brighton's help, they rolled Henderson onto the litter. They picked him up, ready to take the steps to the ground.

The old woman walked to Henderson, placing her hand on his. "Eddie."

Henderson looked into her eyes. "*Cảm ơn bạn*, Mama-san." He grinned. "Thank you, Mama-san."

The men with the litter stepped down the steps. They walked toward the helicopter, carrying a free man. Brighton towered over Mama-san and put his hand on her shoulder. "Thank you." He turned and followed the men who carried Henderson.

Within minutes, the Huey shot into the air. The pilot rotated the chopper one hundred eighty degrees. He took a flight path to Chu Lai.

While Henderson lay on the deck of the helicopter, he heard the familiar sound of the blades slapping in the air. He couldn't believe that he had survived his ordeal and was going back to his squad. The memory of Ray lying on the ground yelling, "Gawddamn it" echoed inside the chopper. He shivered as Laurel stared at him with lifeless eyes with a bullet hole in his forehead. Henderson stared at the heavens through the open doorway and said, "Ray, I'm going to kill the bastard."

THE RECOVERY

When the Huey settled on the hospital helipad, two soldiers rushed forward. Each grabbed an end of the stretcher, lifting Henderson from the chopper. They walked with a quick pace to the emergency area. Two doctors with several nurses stood ready. The medics lifted him onto a gurney. After he hit the clean sheets, the medical staff examined him.

Henderson fell asleep.

One of the nurses started cutting Henderson's pants off. The other nurse pulled them from under him. Once she cut his shirt off, the nurse covered him with a sheet. The first nurse's nose wrinkled as she took a deep breath. "Those clothes stink. Never smelled anything like that before."

A medic picked up the clothing to dispose of them. "Wait a minute. There's something in his pants pocket." He reached inside the pocket, pulling out the dog tags. "What the hell."

"Give them to his lieutenant," the second nurse said as she started to wash Henderson.

The doctor swabbed Henderson's head wounds. "Not bad, not bad at all." He cleaned the areas. When he turned toward the second nurse, the doctor said, "Let's get bandages on those." Once the doctor finished the examination, he turned to face the first nurse, who held a chart. “He has several wounds to the head that should heal in a couple of weeks. The other injuries are cuts and bruises. He had several severe blows to the abdomen. Need to watch for internal bleeding.” The doctor stopped, waiting for the nurse to write. “He’s malnourished. Other than that, he should be healthy in five to ten days.”

When the nurse finished writing the doctor’s observations, she hung his chart at the foot of the bed.

“First, let’s get X-rays of his chest. Take one of his back too.” The doctor looked up at the medics. “Then, get him to a room for fluids and observation.”

The two medics wheeled Henderson to radiology.

“That poor boy.” The first nurse looked worried.

•

When Brighton reached the hospital room, he paused to gather his composure. “We found Henderson.” Three soldiers beamed with relief. Bear, Little JJ, and Johnston lay in their hospital beds. They shared a small room that Brighton had arranged for them.

Johnston maneuvered into a sitting position. “How’s he doing? Is he hurt badly?”

“He isn’t bad, considering what he went through. I don’t have all the details yet.” Brighton sat in a chair.

“What about Laurel?” Johnston rubbed the wound on his leg.

Brighton stared at the floor, deep in thought. “He didn’t make it.” He felt responsible that the VC captured Laurel because he didn’t get there fast enough. “We haven’t recovered his body yet.”

Bear rolled to his side to ease the discomfort of his wound. “That sucks. Ray was a good kid.”

“It don’t mean nothin’.” Little JJ looked at Bear for confirmation.

Johnston winced from the pain. “Gawddamn it,” he said in his best Laurel imitation.

The room echoed with laughter.

“Ray was a good man.” Little JJ had droplets of tears blurring his vision while waves of sadness flowed over him.

Brighton stood. "Well, the good news is that Henderson will recover." He shifted his weight. "Hell, you three will be reporting back to duty soon. You better go see him."

"We'll do that." Johnston rearranged his pillow.

"Thanks." He eyed his soldiers, the men of the First Squad, with respect etched on his face. "You men are true warriors." Without another word, he left the room.

•

"How are you feeling?" A nurse stood over Henderson, inserting a needle into his arm. "This is to give you nourishment."

He glanced up, struggling to smile. "Thank you. I am better."

The nurse adjusted the bed. "This afternoon, an operator from the Military Auxiliary Radio System will allow you to call the States from your room. I understand you have a wife. I bet she would like that." She pulled the blanket up to cover his body.

"I would like that too." Henderson's face cracked a boyish grin that hadn't shown in a long time.

Within an hour, the medics rolled the three wounded soldiers to Henderson's room. They placed the three wheelchairs to the left side of the bed.

A loud, rough voice said, "Wake up, soldier."

Henderson almost jumped from the bed. "What the hell." He looked around the room and saw his squad members. "I knew it had to be you, Bear."

His smile grew larger as he saw Little JJ along with Johnston sitting in their wheelchairs next to Bear. "You guys look pitiful."

After the laughter subsided, Johnston asked, "You doing okay, Henderson? You need anything from us?"

"Not right now." Henderson fidgeted with the tube running into his arm. "I'll be okay."

"We're going to be discharged soon. Let us know if you need anything." Little JJ rolled his chair closer.

Henderson was asleep.

Bear signaled the medic they were ready to return to their room.

•

When he walked out of the hospital, Brighton quickened his pace to the MARS station, where they relayed a call over amateur radio stations. He had a call to make.

The soldier in charge of the station said, “Use the term ‘over;’ that way, the receiver understands it’s their turn to talk. They need to do the same.” He looked at Brighton to make sure he understood. “Two people can’t speak at the same time.”

“Got it.” Brighton’s brows lifted. “Not my first time to use a radio.”

Once it was his turn, Brighton sat next to the telephone. He dialed Professor’s number. After several rings, a voice answered, “Hello.”

With a smile, Brighton said, “Professor, this is Brighton. Over.”

“Damn, LT. How are you doing?” He hesitated. “Over.”

“We found Henderson. He’s alive and doing okay. He needs some rest and good food.” Brighton rubbed his hand through his short hair. “Can you tell his wife? Over.”

Professor slowly exhaled a breath. “Thank God! Yes, I can. Over.”

“Great!” Brighton breathed deeply. “One last thing, I don’t know if he’s coming home or not. His wounds aren’t that bad. Over.”

The soldier responsible for monitoring the calls stood over Brighton.

“You should receive a telegram today or tomorrow. My turn is up. I have to go.” The call ended.

NOW SHE KNOWS

Professor dropped the handset into the cradle. He stood in amazement; he'd learned that they found Henderson alive. Tears of joy rolled down his cheeks. There was a certain sense of warmth, a fullness that Professor hadn't experienced in a week. He was thankful that Henderson survived his ordeal.

On a whim, Professor decided to go to Cheryl's apartment instead of calling. After he grabbed his keys, he ran down the steps to his car. Within twenty minutes, he pulled into a parking spot. Professor ran up the stairs, taking them two at a time.

This time he wore jeans with a T-shirt. He had even begun growing his beard back. The news about Henderson was more important than how the man looked who delivered it. Once at the door, Professor stood silently for a moment before he knocked lightly on the door.

He felt her staring at him from the peephole. "It's me, Cheryl." Professor grinned.

The door swung open. Cheryl stood in the doorway, with her puffy eyes red, hair unkempt, and wearing pajamas. With a dull stare, Cheryl said, "What, Professor?"

Professor peered around her into the living area. "Can I come in?" Before she could respond, he blurted, "They found Eddie!"

He caught Cheryl before she hit the floor. He scooped her up into his arms, kicking the door closed. Gently, he carried her to the sofa. While Professor kneeled next to her, he asked, "Cheryl, you okay? Cheryl?"

She moaned. Then her eyes fluttered open. "Is it true, Professor? Is it?"

He took her hand into his. "Yes, it's true. He's in the hospital. Lieutenant Brighton told me he wasn't hurt too bad." His eyes darted around the room. "But . . . he doesn't think Eddie will come home right away."

"That's bullshit!" Cheryl screamed. "Fucking bullshit!"

He tightened his grip on her hand. "Let's give it some time. At least he's alive, and we know where he is."

"I know, but I want Eddie home. He deserves to be home."

The phone started ringing. Cheryl stared at it.

Professor walked to the table and picked up the handset. "Hello, Henderson residence."

"How are you doing, Professor? Over," a distant voice said.

With a laugh, Professor handed the telephone to Cheryl. "You want to take this call."

She snatched the phone from his hand. "Hello."

"I love you. Over," Eddie said.

It took her seconds to recover from the voice. "Oh, Eddie, I love you. I miss you. Are you okay?"

Professor whispered, "You need to say *over* when you finish speaking."

"Over." Cheryl stared at Professor.

"I'm doing good. I'll be back to the unit in a week. Over."

Cheryl's lips turned downward as she gazed out the window. "Why aren't you coming home?" She hesitated. "Damn. Over."

"I need to finish my tour. There are a couple of things I need to take care of before I come home. Over."

"Oh, Eddie. How come Vietnam is that important to you? Over." She stomped her foot and glared at Professor.

"Need to end the conversation, Sergeant Henderson," the soldier said.

"Cheryl, I have to go. I love you. I'll write soon. Over."

"I love you too. Come home!" There was a click.

The silence was unbearable while she held the handset to her ear.

Professor took the phone from her, placing it into the cradle. He wrapped his arms around Cheryl as she sobbed. He didn't know if she cried from happiness or pure anger.

•

When Professor pulled into his parking place, he noticed a yellow cab sitting across the street. As he approached his home, a man stood on the porch.

"Can I help you?" Professor asked.

He turned to face Professor. "I hope you can." He smiled. "You Calvin Cox?"

"I am." Professor climbed the steps.

"You have a telegram. I hope it contains good news." The cabbie handed him the envelope. He turned to head toward his car.

After he read the telegram, Professor grinned. "It's official."

THEY FOUND HIM

While Brighton headed back to his office, he recalled the conversation with the doctor. He was astounded to learn the wounds that Little JJ, Bear, and Johnston received wouldn't send them back to the States. He needed to find replacements for Cain and Johnston. He wanted Johnston to take over the Third Squad.

Once he was seated in his chair, he began going through orders of soldiers reporting to Vietnam. After several moments, he stopped and pulled out the dog tags. He read the name inscribed on each one. Tears welled in his eyes.

The clerk knocked on the door. "LT, the major is on the phone."

"Thanks." Brighton held out the five sets of dog tags. "Take these and give them to the commander."

"You got it, LT." The clerk took the tags.

He picked up the handset. "Lieutenant Brighton, sir."

"Brighton, I received word that an infantry platoon found Laurel. Well, they think it's him," the major said.

"When will he be taken to the hospital?" Brighton stood with his hands shaking.

"Should be there in about ten minutes," the major said.

Brighton was already heading for the door when he slammed the handset into the cradle.

While Brighton ran along the road toward the hospital, his conscience gripped him as he fought the feeling of how he felt—he had failed to be the leader his men needed. It was his fault that Laurel was dead.

Once he arrived at the hospital, a dustoff settled on the helipad. Two medics ran to the chopper. They removed the litter; one was at the head, another one was at the foot. They walked briskly toward the emergency room area. Brighton followed without speaking a word. They placed the poncho-covered body on a gurney. A nurse pulled the poncho off as a doctor examined him.

Brighton rushed to the gurney, staring down at the lifeless body. Tears slowly rolled down his cheeks.

"Do you know this soldier?" the nurse asked.

Brighton wiped at his tears. "That's Corporal Ray Laurel. He's from Montgomery, Alabama. Eighteen years old. His dad served at Bastogne, with the One Hundred and First Airborne Division. Laurel was a hell of a soldier." He touched Laurel's arm as a father would.

Brighton turned to walk down the hallway. "Now, I have to tell Henderson." Once he got to Henderson's room, he observed a nurse adjusting his bed. "Can I talk to him?" Brighton asked.

She stepped away from the bed. "Only for a minute."

Brighton pulled a chair next to the bed. "They found Ray." His lips trembled. "He's back with us."

Henderson squeezed Brighton's arm. He fell asleep.

After Brighton returned to his office, he sat alone, contemplating Laurel's death. How hard it had to be to die that way.

He picked up the pen and wrote.

Dear Mr. and Mrs. Laurel,

I'm Ray's commander, James Brighton. I know the Army has informed you of his death, but I wanted to let you know what kind of man and soldier he became.

On the day Ray died, he wasn't alone. He died a hero, who served others and treated all with respect.

You should be proud of your son . . .

THE TEAM IS BACK

While the doctor examined Henderson, he said, "You look like you're putting on more weight. I'll have the nurse weigh you." He placed the stethoscope on his stomach, listening. "Sounds good. I don't believe you have any internal injuries." The doctor wrapped the stethoscope around his neck. "You've been here for ten days. I'm going to release you tomorrow if your weight has improved."

Henderson sat on the edge of the bed. "It's about time."

"Okay, let's get you on the scale," the nurse said.

After he jumped to the floor, Henderson headed for the scales. "I'm ready." He walked without assistance from the nurse. Once Henderson stepped on the scale, the nurse moved the lower bar weight to the right.

"One hundred thirty-five pounds." She read from the upper bar on the scale as she slid it to a stop. "Congratulations."

"I hope he didn't break the scales," a voice boomed from behind them.

Startled, Henderson turned toward the voice. "Damn, LT, you can scare a man to death." Henderson stepped off the scales.

"Sorry, I didn't mean to." Brighton strolled forward, placing his hand on Henderson's shoulder. "You doing okay?"

"The doctor said I'm checking out tomorrow." Henderson rubbed his jaw. "I'm ready to go back to work."

"Great to hear." Brighton dropped his hand from Henderson's shoulder while he glanced around the room. "Bear and Little JJ were released yesterday. Johnston should be released next week."

"Yeah, they stopped by to tell me they'd see me at the hooch."

Brighton stood a little taller. "You guys will take it easy at first. I figure the squad will be ready for a mission in a couple of weeks."

Henderson's dull eyes had deadness to them. "I want to find the fucking gook that killed Ray."

Brighton knew that anything he said wouldn't help. "I'm going to check on Johnston. I'll be back later." Brighton walked out of the room. Once he got to Johnston's room, he observed him working the wounded leg. "Don't overdo it."

"Hello, LT." Johnston looked up, wiping at the sweat that ran down his face. "I'm almost ready to come back."

Brighton sat on the edge of the bed. "That's what I want to talk to you about."

"What's that, sir?" Johnston lifted his injured leg.

"Third Squad has a squad leader position open." Brighton sat back, feeling relaxed. "I want you to take it."

Johnston, his face stoic, remained silent, staring out the window.

"Well?" Brighton's brows furrowed. "I thought you would be excited, Sergeant."

Johnston started to walk around the room, stretching his leg. "I want to stay with the First Squad. I'm a good fit there." He stopped in front of Brighton. "Henderson will need my help. He's a good leader."

"If that's what you want, you got it." Brighton stood. "I'll see you soon." Brighton slapped Johnston on the shoulder before walking out of the room.

•

The next morning Henderson strolled into the hooch, allowing the screen door to slam shut with a loud bang. Bear and Little JJ jumped from their bunks.

"Who is making all that noise?" Little JJ rubbed the crust from his eyes.

Bear was already making a beeline for Henderson. "Oh no, you don't. I'm still fragile." Henderson dodged Bear's grasp.

"You're all healed up now?" Bear stood with his arms crossed while wearing an ear-to-ear smile.

Henderson punched Bear in the arm. "Yeah, I am." He stopped to give both soldiers an appreciative once-over. "You guys look healthy too."

When he walked to his bunk, Henderson saw the M-16 on the blanket. Next, he opened his wall locker. His jaw went slack when he saw it was stocked with the needed combat gear and ammunition for any mission. Clean uniforms were hanging from the rack. A bush hat sat on the shelf. Best of all, an unopened bottle of Jim Beam sat next to the hat. Henderson wanted to enjoy the moment, knowing that Bear, Little JJ, and probably the lieutenant took the time to re-outfit him with the equipment he needed. He turned to face his squad members.

"I don't know what to say. Thank you."

Little JJ threw a pillow at Henderson.

When Henderson ducked the pillow, Bear grabbed him, holding on hard. "You're still too little for me." They tussled for a moment.

Bear let out a howl.

"See, I know your weak spot." Henderson smiled.

Bear was holding his manhood. "Come on, man, that ain't fair."

"I'm free, aren't I?" Henderson put his arm around Bear's shoulder.

"Let's go eat. I'm hungry." Little JJ rubbed his stomach while making a troubled face.

The three soldiers grabbed their M-16s, and then they strolled to the mess hall. They talked and laughed as if nothing had happened in the last month.

•

The next morning Johnston walked through the hooch door. He pulled it closed, not wanting it to slam with a loud noise. He strolled quietly to his wall locker, hoping not to wake his sleeping squad members.

"That you, Johnston?" Henderson asked as he sat up in bed.

Johnston peered over his shoulder. "Yeah. I got them to release me at zero dark thirty. I couldn't stay in the hospital another minute."

"I don't blame you. You'd think being laid up at the hospital was a good thing. But I started to feel useless after a couple of days." Henderson lit a cigarette. "Glad you stayed with us."

Johnston faced Henderson with rage in his eyes. "I thought you might need some help killing that son of a bitch lieutenant that murdered Ray."

"I do. We need to kill him." Henderson stared out the window for a moment, watching the sun climbing over the South China Sea, painting the sky in different colors. "I have to kill him."

From the darkness, a booming voice said, "I'll kill him with my hands."

"I'll use my M-sixty on his ass," another voice said.

"Okay, guys, thanks. Get up. Say welcome home to Johnston." Henderson turned on the lights.

Bear and Little JJ were already tussling with Johnston. He broke free from the two squad members.

"You guys win. Let's get breakfast."

"We need to get back in shape. First, let's eat better. Then do some training." Henderson walked out the door of the hooch to the mess hall with the First Squad following.

While eating, Brighton approached the table, with a corporal following him. "Can we join you?" Brighton pulled out a chair without waiting for a response. He nodded to the corporal to sit too.

Henderson stuffed a forkful of eggs into his mouth. "Sure, go ahead, LT." He gave an open-mouth smile with eggs showing.

Brighton looked away. "Damn, Henderson, that's disgusting."

Henderson grinned. "I know."

Brighton surveyed the men seated at the table. "This is Corporal Marvin Williams. He's an M-sixty machine gunner, and . . ."

"... Wait a minute, LT, I'm the gunner," Little JJ blurted, not giving him a chance to finish.

Brighton nodded at Little JJ. "You still are, but for now, you'll carry the radio." He mopped at the sweat running down his face. "The plan is to have a five-man squad until I find another replacement. No one stays on the chopper." Brighton leaned back in his chair, taking a drink of coffee. "Williams will take Little JJ's place but carry the M-sixty. Everyone is on the ground. I'll coordinate with the aviation unit to have a gunner on the chopper." He leaned the chair back on two legs, setting his cup on the table.

"What do you think?" Brighton studied Henderson.

"I like it." Henderson glanced at the new soldier. "Welcome to the squad, Williams."

Brighton stood and then pushed his chair under the table. "Great. I'll let you men get to know each other." He headed to his office.

•

After the tenth day of training, the men of the First Squad wore sweat-soaked jungle fatigues, while taking short, boot-dragging steps toward their hooch. Their shoulders slumped, heads hanging while they walked.

Little JJ lifted his head and rubbed the sweat from his face. "When are we going on a real mission?"

"I believe we're ready." Henderson put his arm around Little JJ. "I know the training has been hard, but we needed to get back in shape."

Johnston pushed Bear from the back. "Well, I think we are."

Little JJ shot a look at Williams. "You're a pretty good shot with that M-sixty."

"Thanks." Williams slapped Little JJ on the back. "You're not bad yourself."

Henderson walked backward, facing the squad. "I'll tell the LT tonight that we're ready."

He saw only smiles coming from his men.

Once the soldiers ate, they sat around the card table, enjoying a Jim Beam and Coke. Johnston poured the new guy another drink.

"Keep it light." Williams smiled. "I'm not a big drinker."

"Well, Williams, this is a good a time as any to tell us a little about yourself. You've been pretty quiet the last couple of weeks." Johnston set the bottle of booze down.

Williams took a slow sip from the glass. "In short, I'm from Bearsville, New York."

"No shit." Bear busted into laughter. "I'm sorry, but your accent is a dead giveaway."

"No offense taken." Williams set his glass down. "I lived there all my life. I got my draft notice right after I graduated from high school. I'm not married, but I do have a girlfriend, Cindy." He removed a picture from his breast pocket, sliding it toward Johnston.

"Wow, she's a looker." Johnston passed it to Henderson.

Henderson looked at the picture. "Yes, she is." He handed it to Bear. While Bear looked at the picture, Henderson studied Williams as if it was the first time seeing him. He observed a twenty-year-old with thick arms and a bull neck, but no taller than him. He wore his caramel-color hair short. His thick mustache covered his upper lip. Henderson thought him an excellent addition to the squad.

"Where in the hell is Bearsville? You mean you're not from New York City?" Little JJ stood, taking a drink. "I thought everyone was from the city."

Williams laughed. "Bearsville is near Woodstock." He surveyed his squad members. "Everyone knows Woodstock."

"Damn, you a hippie, Williams?" Bear asked.

The men broke into laughter at his remark.

Williams's mind wandered back to the good old days of August 1969. "Well, Cindy and I did attend. Shit, it was in our front yard. We had to go. Jimmy Hendrix was awesome."

"Damn. I heard over four hundred thousand people attended. That's too crowded for me." Johnston poured another shot of bourbon.

Henderson decided to change the subject. "How did the lieutenant find you?"

Williams downed his drink. "I've been in-country about seven months with the One Hundred and Ninety-Eighth Infantry Brigade. I heard about the opening in your unit. Shit, I volunteered. The lieutenant interviewed me, and within a couple of days, I'm here."

After he stood, Henderson put his empty glass on the table. He liked Williams and thought him an excellent addition to the squad. For the first time since leaving the hospital, Henderson believed the First Squad was ready to get back to work.

"Listen up, everyone." Henderson moved to the center of the room. The men stopped talking and eyed their leader. He rubbed his hand through his thick hair. "Training is over. We've healed from our wounds and trained hard."

"That's what I'm talking about!" Bear yelled.

Henderson smiled. "I'll tell LT that we are ready for a mission."

BACK TO THE VILLE

While the men of the First Squad sat around the hooch cleaning their weapons, the screen door swung open. "You have a mission." Brighton stepped into the room, letting the door slam shut with a loud bang.

The men stopped what they were doing to listen.

Henderson walked to the table. "What's the mission, LT?"

"A dustoff crashed." Brighton spread the map on the tabletop. "There's an infantry platoon protecting it right now." He pointed to the location on the map.

"Hell, sir, that's the ville where the old woman and Vinh live." Henderson placed his finger on the map.

"Yes, it is." Brighton scanned the men to make sure they were attentive. "It was reported that villagers were killed by the VC too." Brighton eyeballed Henderson. "I don't know how many."

Johnston bent over the map. "What's the mission, LT?" He knew Henderson was concerned about the villagers but wanted to get the mission details.

Brighton stood, squaring his shoulders. "The dustoff crew is safe. They're back at Chu Lai. Our mission is to rig the Huey for transport back here."

"Piece of cake." Henderson walked to his wall locker. "Grab your gear, and let's go." He felt a strong urge to get to the village now. Henderson hoped the old woman wasn't one of the dead. *Fucking VC!*

Within ten minutes, the squad jogged to the helipad. The Rescue Huey sat with the engine running, and the blades cut through the air. The men rushed to take their assigned seats, except this time, Little JJ sat where Laurel usually sat. Williams sat next to Henderson, which was Cain's position. Henderson surveyed his squad. They seemed anxious. He adjusted his headset. "Ready to go."

The copilot turned in his seat to look at the passengers. "Welcome back, Henderson. Taking off."

Henderson raised his right hand to signal the squad ready to lift off. While the helicopter rose into the air, Henderson pictured the face of Dang. For a fleeting moment, he hoped that the VC lieutenant would be there.

As the Huey flew across the landscape, Henderson watched the jungle, rice paddies, and hills disappear behind him. It appeared all too familiar. He felt the weight of his tormentor sitting on his shoulders. Henderson's hands began to shake, and sweat soaked his uniform. He knew there was no use avoiding the fear, and he needed to accept it. He would do what had to be done.

After twenty minutes in the air, the chopper settled on the hard-packed paddy field. Henderson observed the platoon guarding the perimeter around the landing zone. Within seconds, he was thankful he wasn't in the bush anymore. The men of the infantry platoon were thin, dirty, and wearing filthy uniforms. They appeared exhausted. He felt a twinge of guilt for being clean and wearing fresh clothes.

With a signal from Henderson, the men of the First Squad grabbed their gear, including the sling load equipment to attach to the downed dustoff. They hit the ground running. The rescue chopper lifted, flying high above the field, waiting.

The infantry platoon leader strolled toward the squad while they set up around the dustoff. "Who's in charge?"

Henderson stood erect. "I am. Sergeant Henderson, sir."

"How long will this take?" The young-looking lieutenant stopped in front of Henderson.

Henderson grinned and stuck his hand out to shake hands. "About thirty minutes to fix the sling, then wait on the Skycrane."

The lieutenant briefly shook Henderson's hand. "We have a mess to clean up at the ville. Then we're moving."

"What do you mean *mess*?" Henderson asked.

The lieutenant's eyes darted toward the ville. "The VC killed a bunch of villagers."

"You guys finish up. I'm going to check the ville out," Henderson said as he walked away.

The lieutenant fell in step with Henderson. "I'll go with you."

Henderson picked up the pace as they neared the village, knowing what he was about to witness would haunt him forever. When he approached the entrance to the village that sat along the riverbank, Henderson noticed that it looked the same as the last time he was there. The huts were on stilts, nearly three feet above the ground. He always thought this appeared to be one of the smallest villes he had been to, with a little over fifteen hooches and a small community building. There were roughly forty-five villagers.

"What's special about this ville?" the lieutenant asked.

"They're good people." Henderson stopped as he observed dead bodies lying in bizarre positions throughout the village. "These villagers saved my life more than once."

"Sorry that this happened." The lieutenant took his helmet off and ran his hand through his damp hair.

While he strode through the ville, Henderson had to avoid the dead bodies. "They must've killed half the village." His eyes darted from one dead body to another.

The smell of death was overwhelming. He tied a handkerchief over his nose and mouth, with only his eyes exposed. Tears flowed into the cloth below his eyes. Henderson couldn't imagine how one human could do this to another. However, he knew Dang and how he had complete disregard for life. He used fear and death to get what he wanted. What Henderson witnessed was murder, pure and simple. His hatred for Dang grew stronger.

He increased his gait toward the old woman's hooch. Had she survived the mass murder of the village? What about Vinh? Did he escape from Dang too? His mind raced, remembering his captivity, the cruelty of Dang, and how he almost didn't survive. Mama-san had to be alive. She had risked everything to save him.

Once he reached her hooch, Henderson saw a body lying at the bottom of the steps. His heart thumped against his chest while he gasped for air. Tears burned his eyes. He ripped the handkerchief from his face.

Henderson reached down, gently rolling her over.

"Eddie," a soft voice from the porch called out.

When he looked up at the porch, Henderson saw the old woman. "Mama-san." Henderson laughed. He ran up the steps. "Thank God you are safe." He embraced her as he would his grandmother.

She raised her head and flashed Henderson a toothless smile. "Eddie."

The lieutenant stood at the bottom of the porch. He wanted to give Henderson the time he needed, but the mission came first. "We need to get back, Sergeant."

"Wait a minute." He looked into the woman's eyes. "Vinh?"

She wiped at a tear. "VC."

"Come on, Sergeant, let's go." The lieutenant paced around the dead body.

After he released the woman from his embrace, Henderson bounded down the steps. Once he hit the ground, he froze. The hair on his neck stood on end with every nerve in his body screaming danger. He surveyed the hedgerow behind the hooch inch by inch. His warning system told him that an enemy was watching him. Henderson imagined that Dang lurked in the thick brush or behind the trees. He saw a shadow move.

Henderson ran back to the downed chopper, with the lieutenant striving to keep up with him. The squad finished attaching the last cable to the dustoff when Henderson arrived, gasping for air. "Bear, I need you to come with me."

"Sure, Sarge." Bear handed his end of the cable to Williams.

The lieutenant reached where Henderson stood. Breathing hard, he adjusted his rucksack. "We aren't staying much longer, Sergeant."

Henderson faced the lieutenant. "You can leave anytime, sir."

The lieutenant walked away, shaking his head.

Henderson turned to the squad. "Bear, let's go." The two soldiers ran back to the ville.

Once they reached the old woman's hooch, Henderson stopped. She sat on the porch, staring down at the two Americans. Slowly, Mama-san turned her head toward the hedgerow behind her home. "VC." She gave a sideways glance.

Henderson nodded at her. "Let's go check it out, Bear."

While he led the way, Henderson took quick steps to the rear of the hooch. To his right was the same animal pen that Mitch and he had jumped into with Vinh and Mama-san a year earlier. Behind the pen was the hedgerow, where he killed a VC while protecting the two villagers. They continued toward the hedgerow.

Henderson saw a shadow move in the trees. "Move this way. To my right." The two soldiers slowly approached the overgrowth, walking side-by-side.

"What do you see?" Bear asked as he scanned the brush.

Henderson stopped. "He's here." A shadow moved away from them. "Over there!" Henderson pointed toward the north.

When he saw movement again, Henderson ran toward the VC that evaded them. He raised his rifle. As he moved the barrel of his M-16 to different aiming spots in the hedgerow, he stopped with his sight on a VC. Sweat ran down his face, stinging his eyes. When he moved forward, his blood pulsed fiercely through his body. Then he saw the face with a scar.

"It's him!" Henderson screamed. "It's fucking Dang!" He fired round after round at the shadow, until his rifle no longer recoiled when he squeezed the trigger.

Bear ran to Henderson's side. "I don't see anything." He stared into the hedgerow. "Man, are you sure?"

Ignoring Bear, Henderson ran to where the VC had stood. "He's gone! He's gone!"

Henderson knew he'd been under a lot of stress. The shadow made him afraid. Was his brain reacting to fear? "Damn it, I know it was Dang!" The fear caused him to want to hide, to be silent, waiting to kill.

"What in the hell is going on?" Johnston asked as he panted.

Bear stood by Henderson and put his arm around his shoulder. "He saw the VC lieutenant."

Johnston's jaw went slack. "You kill the son of a bitch?"

"He got away." Henderson walked toward the dustoff.

Whop! Whop! Whop! The three soldiers looked skyward as the Skycrane started to descend over the downed Huey.

"Let's go help." Henderson broke into a run, with Bear and Johnston behind him, arriving in time to help Little JJ and Williams attach the sling. The Skycrane lifted with the dustoff swaying under its belly while heading toward Chu Lai.

Henderson couldn't stop thinking of Mama-san. How will she survive this war from the VC? He couldn't abandon her, leaving her fate to Dang. He had to find a way to help keep her from certain death. He wished that Vinh was here; he could save him too.

"Bear, come with me." Henderson ran back to the village with Bear at his side.

Once they got to the hooch, Henderson ran up the steps with Bear following. "Mama-san, Mama-san."

She appeared at the doorway, frowning, her head tilting to the side. "Eddie?"

After several minutes of using broken English, he had her gather a few belongings that she stuffed into a burlap rice bag.

"Ready to head back." Henderson ran down the steps. "Bear, carry her."

"I got her." Bear lifted her with ease into his arms.

The two soldiers ran past the infantry troops as they picked up bodies to carry to the community building.

Once at the crash site, Henderson said, "Little JJ, call our chopper." He scanned the hedgerow one more time. "It's time to go home."

Little JJ picked up the handset. "Rescue One, this is Animal One. Ready for pickup. Over."

"This is Rescue One; we are coming in now. Out," the pilot transmitted.

Within minutes the chopper settled on the ground, kicking dirt at the waiting squad. They ran toward the Huey with heads down, holding on to their hats.

Bear placed the woman on the deck, climbing in after her. The rest of the squad scrambled aboard. The men shifted to give the old woman room.

Henderson slid Mama-san next to him and wrapped an arm around her, pulling her close. He adjusted his headset. "Ready to go, sir."

The pilot turned in his seat, looking at Henderson. "Do you know what you're doing, Henderson?"

Henderson nodded. "Let's go. I'm not leaving her."

The chopper rose high into the air. The pilot put the nose down, accelerating toward Chu Lai.

The old woman squeezed her eyes shut, moaned, and trembled. She burrowed closer against Henderson. He held her with a firm but loving grip. Mama-san began humming the same lullaby that she sang to Henderson when he escaped. He smiled and stroked her hand.

What seemed like minutes later, the copilot transmitted, "Arriving home, landing in three minutes."

Henderson signaled the squad that they were landing.

Once the skids touched softly on the helipad, the men jumped to the ground. Henderson passed Mama-san to Bear, grabbing her bag as he slid off the deck. They jogged back to the hooch. The woman wasn't even visible in Bear's arms.

Seconds after the screen door slammed shut, the squad started rearranging the hooch to accommodate her. Within fifteen minutes, there was a bunk in the corner with poncho liners hanging like curtains.

Johnston put his hand on Henderson's shoulder. "You think we'll get away with this?"

"I don't know." Henderson surveyed the room. "Hey, guys." The squad stopped what they were doing to look at their leader. "We'll take turns bringing her meals until I get this figured out."

"What about when she needs to go to the bathroom or shower?" Little JJ asked.

Henderson rubbed his hand through his hair. "Let's take one step at a time."

The screen door slammed shut. "Welcome back." Brighton stood at the doorway with his feet spread apart with hands on his hips.

"I was going to explain, LT." Henderson knew that Brighton was aware that the old woman was here.

Brighton relaxed his stance. "Yes, I know, Henderson." He strolled to the poncho liners pulling them back. "I'll get an ID made for her. She'll officially be the squad's hooch maid." He grinned at the woman. "However, she'll stay at the girls' hooch by the office."

Henderson's smile broke across his face. "Thanks, LT."

Brighton pulled out a chair sitting at the table. "Intel informed me of what happened at the ville."

"It was a massacre." Henderson shot the LT a glance. "Fucking VC."

The rest of the squad gathered around the table to listen intently to the conversation.

Brighton placed his elbows on the table, leaning forward. "The report stated that the VC took out retribution for them helping American forces in the area." He made eye contact with Henderson. "It's not from them helping you. They assisted other units too. Don't go thinking it was your fault." He reached for a Coke from the ice chest.

After punching two holes into the top of the can, Brighton took a long drink. "Like you, I remember these villagers from our first tour. They're good people."

"I understand, but that doesn't change the fact that Dang was taking his anger out on the villagers because of me." Henderson shifted in his chair. "He's pure evil."

"All units in the area have been given a description of the lieutenant. He will pay for the way he killed Corporal Ray Laurel." Brighton stood. "The gook will pay." He finished the Coke, crushed the can in his hand, and then shot it into the trash can. "You guys get some rest. I'm sure tomorrow will bring another mission."

Henderson frowned. "Yes, LT, will do."

Brighton stopped at the door. "Oh, Sergeant Henderson, don't bring any more civilians back with you." The screen door slammed shut with a loud bang.

A LITTLE VACATION TIME

Henderson whimpered in his sleep. "Ray, follow me!" He flipped onto his stomach, crawling toward the foot of the bed. "Let's go, Ray." When Henderson slid to the floor, he yelled, "Run, it's the fucking lieutenant." His legs moved as if he was running. His body trembled and sweat soaked his clothes. He watched Laurel stare into the barrel of the pistol and say, "Gawddamn it."

Henderson's heart beat hard against his chest. "I'm going to kill you!" he screamed at Dang.

"Eddie, it's okay," Johnston said in a soothing tone. "It's a dream."

"No, don't hurt Ray," Henderson whispered.

While he talked, Johnston placed a hand under Henderson's arm. "Let me help you back in bed." He guided Henderson to the bunk. After he sprawled across the bed, Johnston covered him with a blanket.

He looked down on Henderson and sadly shook his head. "Poor son of a bitch."

•

The next morning, when the sunlight spilled through the screened window, Henderson woke his squad. "Let's get breakfast."

After some grumbling, they rolled out of their bunks. They dressed and then slid on their boots.

"Let's go." Johnston patted Henderson on the back.

When he finished chow, Henderson strolled to the hooch. Mama-san was already cleaning the squad area. He gave her a quick hug before he collapsed on his bunk.

Henderson felt as if a demon raged inside him because of the damage caused by his past. He knew the fear came from another place, and at times he couldn't control it. Henderson tried to find a moment of calm in the storm. He knew he had to repress the guilt to fight the anger.

After he rolled out of his bunk, he straightened his uniform. Henderson took quick, long strides to Brighton's office. He opened the screen door, letting it slam shut.

The clerk jumped in his chair. "What the hell." He spotted Henderson in the doorway. "You don't have to scare a man to death. The lieutenant is in his office. Go on in."

For a second, it felt right to Henderson to see another person face fear. He laughed while walking into the office. "Good morning, LT."

"How are you doing, Henderson?" Brighton stood, lighting a cigarette.

"I'm doing okay, sir." When Henderson removed a cigarette from the pack, he looked at Brighton.

"Sure, go ahead; light up."

"Well, we've had this conversation before." Henderson lit his cigarette and took a drag. "When Mitch died."

"Yeah, I remember." Brighton seemed sad for a moment. "You want to go on R and R?" He took a hit from the smoke, and then he blew a dense cloud of smoke toward the ceiling.

Henderson looked down at the floor. "Yes, sir, I do. I think seeing Cheryl will help." He eyed Brighton while taking a drag from his cigarette. "Besides, going in July works better because Cheryl starts teaching in August."

"I get it. You've gone through hell these last couple of months. More than most." Brighton stood gazing out the window. "A little downtime will probably do you some good. I'll get the approval."

"Thanks, LT. It means a lot."

Henderson left the office, letting the screen door slam.

"What the hell!" the clerk yelled.

Henderson chuckled as he walked along the path to his building.

Once he got back to the hooch, Henderson found Johnston sitting at the table. "I'm going on R and R. You'll take over the squad." Henderson lifted his brows. "Take care of Mama-san too."

"Take all the time you need." Johnston stood. "Maybe we'll find Dang while you're gone. I'll kill the little son of a bitch for you."

"You better save him for me." Henderson clenched his jaw.

Johnston laughed. "You got it, Henderson."

Henderson packed and changed to his khaki uniform for his trip to Hawaii. A horn blew, and he saw the jeep waiting in front of his hooch. Without a lot of celebration, Henderson walked to the door. "See you guys in a week. Stay out of trouble."

The men of the First Squad stood by the doorway, slapping Henderson on the back and told him to have a good time while he was on R and R.

Once he climbed into the passenger seat of the jeep, the driver put it in gear and drove to the division airfield for his flight to Da Nang. After he landed in Da Nang, he waited several hours before he boarded the flight to Hawaii. When he was comfortable in his seat, Henderson closed his eyes, ready for the seventeen-hour trip. Before he knew it, the aircraft taxied down the runway and then lifted to the skies.

The hum of the aircraft as it flew through the clouds reminded him of the lullaby that Mama-san hummed to him. He slept like a baby.

•

The captain of the aircraft announced over the intercom, "We will arrive in beautiful Honolulu in thirty minutes. Please fasten your seat belts and prepare for landing."

The pilot's announcement woke the soldiers from their restless sleep. They cheered, knowing that they would be landing. Henderson felt his excitement building. Unlike the last time he landed on the island, he would meet a loved one after he stepped from the plane onto American soil.

Once the wheels squealed on the runway, the servicemen cheered as one. Thundering laughter boomed throughout the aircraft. After the pilot pulled into the terminal area, the passengers stood to retrieve their bags. When the doors opened, Henderson rushed forward to get off of the aircraft.

He couldn't focus because the anticipation he felt made him giddy, like a school kid with his first crush. When Henderson walked down the steps, he imagined holding Cheryl. A tingling sensation spread across his body.

While Henderson followed the group of servicemen along the airport corridor, he recalled the last time he took this journey. He had formulated his plan to carry out the promise for Mitch. But Henderson couldn't get off the island, which was fortunate because he met Cheryl. A smile tugged at his lips.

They were rushed through immigrations and then received a fifteen-minute briefing. After the orientation, the soldiers were herded to waiting buses to take them to Fort DeRussy Rest and Rehabilitation Center. Once the buses arrived, Henderson walked along a long corridor lined on both sides with wives and girlfriends. It was pandemonium with the women calling out to their man. He searched both sides for a beautiful woman with red hair.

"Eddie! Eddie!" Cheryl called out.

For a moment, he forgot his name was Eddie. Their eyes met across the walkway. As she ran toward him, he grinned, waving to her.

She jumped into his arms, almost knocking him down, but he held her tight. He twirled her round and round. He nuzzled her neck, taking in her aroma like he did before he left for 'Nam. The softness of her cheek felt warm and welcoming against his.

He gently let her slide to the floor, while gazing into the depth of her green eyes. "I missed you. I thought of you every day."

Cheryl met his gaze. "I missed you." She stood on her tiptoes, planting a lengthy kiss.

They walked arm in arm to the parking area to catch a cab to the Reef Hotel. Within minutes they slid onto the back seat of the cab.

While the car rolled along the roadway, Cheryl said, "I'm happy we are together. And wow, we're staying at the same hotel where we met. How exciting."

"I was surprised they had a room available." Eddie stared out the window. Cars, buildings, and people flashed by as the cab drove to the hotel. He had thoughts of Laurel and the way he died.

"It will be nice to be in a familiar place." Cheryl giggled, squeezing his hand. "I've missed you."

He turned his attention back to Cheryl. "This will be the best six days of the year. I missed you too."

•

Several hours after they checked in, Eddie asked, "You ready for dinner?"

"I'm starving. I've been too excited to eat since leaving the mainland." She ran the brush through her hair one more time.

Eddie opened the room door. "I'm ready for anything other than roast beef with mashed potatoes."

"I thought that was your favorite meal," Cheryl said.

"It is if the Army isn't cooking it."

Their laughter followed them as they strolled along the hallway, heading to Duke's for dinner. After dinner, it was a show.

"I'm looking forward to the Don Ho show." Cheryl giggled.

Eddie put his arm around her waist, pulling her in close. "I've heard it's a great show."

"I hope he sings the song that made him famous."

"Okay, you know I don't know anything about music or performers. What's the song?"

Cheryl smiled. "Oh, I know you've heard the song 'Tiny Bubbles.'"

"Sure. You want me to sing it for you?"

"Oh for heaven's sake, no! You can't sing."

The two newlyweds quickened their pace.

•

When they returned to the hotel, they shared a nightcap of Jim Beam and Coke.

Eddie took her hand. "Did you bring the photograph?"

"Yes, I did." She searched through her purse and eventually found it. "Here it is. I can't believe you lost my wedding picture."

Eddie's gaze fell to the floor. "I know. It must've fallen out of my pocket during a mission."

"I put the perfume that you liked on the back, just like the last picture." Cheryl handed the photograph to him.

"Thanks." He put the picture into his shirt pocket. "Let's get ready for bed."

Once in bed, Cheryl kissed Eddie on the cheek. "I love you. Good night." She rolled onto her side, turning the lamp off. Eddie was already asleep. Not more than an hour after she fell asleep, he tossed and rolled as if he was running through the jungle.

He whimpered in his sleep. "Ray, follow me!" Eddie flipped onto his stomach, crawling toward the foot of the bed. "Let's go, Ray." When Eddie slid to the floor, he yelled, "Run! It's the fucking lieutenant." His legs moved as if he was running as fast as he could. While sweat soaked his underclothes, his body shook violently. He watched Laurel stare into the barrel of the pistol and say, "Gawddamn it."

Eddie's heart beat hard against his chest. "I'm going to kill you!" he screamed at Dang.

"Eddie, it's okay," Cheryl said in a soothing tone. "It's a dream. I have you. You're safe."

She helped him back into bed, all the while talking softly to him. She curled up next to him. "What have they done to you?"

•

During the next five days, the young newlyweds made sure they got out to see the sights that the island of Oahu had to offer. The last time they were in Hawaii, they hung around the hotel the entire week.

They spent the mornings frolicking on the two-mile stretch of the Waikiki Beach. Eddie chased Cheryl along the hot white sand and into the clear blue-green water. They played like teenagers at the beach for the first time.

One evening, they had a full-course dinner at Prince Kuhio's in the Ala Moana Center. Another evening, they watched a show at the Queen Surf while eating a buffet meal. Eddie couldn't get enough to eat. Although he ate most meals in the mess hall, it wasn't anything like the food he found on the island.

In the afternoons, they visited tourist sites like the Polynesian Cultural Center at Laie. The couple found the village and culture exhibits of the Polynesian people's the most entertaining but informative. They attended Kodak's free hula show at the Waikiki Natatorium. Of course, the Pearl Harbor tour was a must.

One night, like most nights, they walked along the beach barefoot, sipping a Jim Beam and Coke. As the waves rolled toward the shore, they held hands while strolling at a leisurely pace, talking about their future.

"Do you want to have children?" Cheryl blurted.

Eddie was quiet, not expecting that question.

She released his hand. "Well, do you?"

Eddie laughed a loud belly laugh.

Cheryl stopped. "What's funny?" She stomped her foot.

"Recently, I pictured how great it would be to have a little Mitch running around the house."

She picked at his shirt. "So, if it's a boy, you already named him—Mitch?"

"Yep." Eddie leaned down to kiss her.

While they spent every moment together, Eddie couldn't talk to Cheryl about Vietnam like he had when they first met. It wasn't he didn't want to share with her. Eddie desperately tried to tell her about Laurel, Cain, and the evil Lieutenant Dang. He didn't know how he could explain it in a way that she could accept what happened to him—how he was held captive, Dang murdering Laurel, and him beating another man to death with a rock.

On the last morning, the two ate breakfast in silence. Eddie had packed his civilian clothes. He donned his khaki uniform. Eddie felt refreshed, more relaxed than he'd been in months. He attributed that to Cheryl because she had a calming effect on him.

After taking a sip of coffee, Eddie said, "We need to finish. I catch the bus in twenty minutes."

"That soon?" Cheryl wiped at tears.

"The week went by fast for me too." Eddie reached for her hand. "I'll be home before you know it."

Cheryl took his hand. "I wish you would've talked to me."

"I will when I come home." Eddie wiped a tear from her cheek. "I promise."

"You better!"

Eddie stood. "It's time to go."

He walked around the table to embrace Cheryl. He placed his cheek against hers, taking in her smell. "I love you."

When he stepped onto the bus, he looked back one more time. He saw Cheryl, standing with the other women, wearing a brave smile. Henderson knew that in the world of war, where cruelty and death is the outcome, his love for Cheryl was the reason he could survive another seven months.

When the plane took to the air, the beautiful, caring woman with flowing red hair and the cutest freckles flashed before his eyes as his last memory of Hawaii. He fell asleep smiling.

A PROMISE MADE

Henderson sat on his towel, watching the tide push and pull the water along the shoreline. The hot sun beat down with little mercy on him. The aroma of the sea air in his nose and the sand between his toes reminded him of being with Cheryl in Hawaii days earlier. "Damn, I miss her," he said out loud.

When he scanned the beach, he observed Bear chasing Little JJ into the water. Then without warning, Bear picked him up high in the air. He threw him toward the sky, like a two-handed basketball shot. As Little JJ descended, he extended his body. He completed a perfect dive into the water. *Now that's teamwork*, Henderson thought.

Johnston pulled himself into a sitting position. "Did you see that? What a dive."

"Yeah, I can't believe Bear threw him that far." Henderson leaned forward. "Damn, how strong is that guy?"

"Well, I'm no weakling, but Bear has to be the strongest guy I know." Johnston stood while watching the two soldiers. "I wouldn't want to tangle with him."

"Hell, he would kill me in two seconds." Henderson jumped to his feet. "It's too damn hot. I'm going back to the hooch." He picked up his towel.

"I'm ready too." Johnston grabbed a small bag.

The two soldiers walked along the road back to the hooch. At one point, Henderson looked over his shoulder. He saw the rest of the squad following about fifty meters behind them.

He laughed. "The rest of the squad is behind us."

"I know." Johnston smiled.

When he entered the hooch, Henderson saw Mama-san sweeping under his bunk. He strolled over to her. She stopped cleaning and lay her head against his chest while he gave her a gentle hug. She looked up into his eyes. "Eddie." After he released her, she touched his hand and then continued to sweep.

The squad went about the routine of cleaning weapons and checking gear. Once Little JJ installed a fresh battery, he went through several radio checks. The PRC-25 was ready for a mission.

The room was quiet except for the sound of the bristles of the broom gliding across the floor. When Mama-san swept one of the squad member's areas, she would gaze into his eyes, smiling. It was her way of saying thank you.

Henderson collapsed on his bunk, staring at the ceiling. He removed the photograph of Cheryl. While he looked at the image, anger started to boil his blood. He wanted the picture that Dang stole from him. It was on their wedding day when the photographer took the picture. She was beautiful, wearing a white wedding gown. She had her hair pulled into a bun, and her smile lit up the room. Henderson didn't want to share the picture, especially with Dang. "I'm going to kill the son of a bitch."

Williams put the writing material away. "I'm getting hungry."

Johnston stood, stretching. "Me too." He glanced at Williams. "You writing Cindy?"

"Yeah, I try to write two or three times a week." Williams walked toward the door.

"What a good boyfriend you are," Little JJ chimed.

Henderson rolled out of his bunk. "Let's go, First Squad."

The men moved as one, jogging toward the mess hall.

•

Once they were in line to load their trays with food, Little JJ said, "Damn, it seems every meal is roast beef and mashed potatoes."

"It does get old." Bear playfully pushed his friend. "At least the milk isn't powdered milk."

While they ate, Brighton stopped at their table. "There will be a mission briefing at eighteen hundred. Make sure everyone in the First Squad is there."

Henderson stopped his fork midway toward his mouth. "No problem, LT." He took a bite. "What's the mission?"

"You'll get the details at the briefing. Wait until then." Brighton strode off toward a table where the officers sat.

Once the squad got back to the hooch, they arranged the table first and then began getting their gear organized.

"I wonder what the mission is?" Little JJ asked.

Bear put his hand on his friend's shoulder. "Probably a downed chopper in the jungle."

"Sure hope it's not a night mission." Williams raised his eyebrows.

Henderson surveyed his squad. "No use speculating. The LT will be here in twenty minutes. Let's wait. We'll see what he has to say." He sensed they were getting nervous.

Johnston reached into the cooler. He threw a cold Coke to each squad member. Henderson caught the Coke. "You might as well open one for the lieutenant. He's always taking one when he's here."

At that moment, the screen door creaked. Brighton entered the room. "Okay, gather around." He placed a map on the table.

"That Coke is yours, LT." Henderson pointed at the can on the table.

Brighton chuckled. "Thanks. How did you know?" He smoothed out the map. The squad gathered around the table, ready for Brighton to start the briefing.

"Well, Henderson, we're going back into our old area." He pointed at the ville where Dang murdered the villagers. "There has been a large number of NVA and VC spotted in the hills around the village. Intel has it that they are bringing supplies down the river too. The Navy has been patrolling but hasn't found anything yet."

Henderson studied the map. "How do we fit in, sir?" He eyeballed Brighton. "You haven't said anything about a downed chopper or crews that need rescuing."

"That's not the mission." Brighton smiled.

"Hell, sir, what are we doing, then?" Bear slammed his hand on the table. Brighton's Coke almost fell over.

Startled, Williams took a step backward. "What the fuck?"

"Take it easy, Bear." Henderson put his hand on his shoulder. "LT will tell us in due time."

Bear's action didn't faze Brighton. "Now this is the interesting part." The men leaned forward to hear the rest. "You're going on a snatch-and-grab mission." Brighton grinned.

Henderson's eyebrows cocked upward. "I thought the other squads did those missions." He rubbed his jaw. "Why us? Why now?"

Brighton couldn't contain himself any longer. "We found Dang." He scanned his men's reaction. "Yep, it's Lieutenant Dang. He'll be at this location at zero eight hundred tomorrow morning." He pointed to the hilltop right outside the ville.

"That's the same hill where we hid out from the typhoon, LT." Henderson laughed out loud. "I'm going to kill the son of a bitch."

Brighton's brows furrowed. "No, you're not." He took Henderson's arm. "You have to promise me you won't kill him, or you're not going. Command wants him alive for interrogation."

Henderson stood straighter, staring at Brighton, challenging him.

"Promise, Sergeant Henderson." Brighton stared back, accepting the challenge.

"Okay, sir. It's a deal. I promise." Henderson's lips tugged into a venomous sneer. "I can't guarantee that he might not be hurt when we bring him back."

"I can live with that." Brighton relaxed his stance.

Brighton finished his Coke. "Look at the map. I'll go over the details of the mission." He shot the can into the trash basket.

•

After thirty minutes of explaining the mission, he answered questions. When the briefing was over, Brighton gathered his map and several markers. "Okay, check your gear. Then get some rest." He wiped the sweat from his face. "Don't forget, be on the helipad by zero seven thirty hours."

Henderson surveyed the squad. "Bring plenty of extra ammunition and grenades."

"You promise?" Brighton stuck his hand out to Henderson.

Henderson shook Brighton's hand. "Yes, LT, I promise."

Before he left the room, Brighton faced the squad. "Good luck tomorrow. Get the son of a bitch."

The room remained quiet as he turned to leave. The men of the First Squad knew they didn't need to respond to Brighton verbally. They recognized he understood what they were thinking. The screen door slammed closed when Brighton left the hooch.

Henderson sat on the edge of his bunk. He felt the revenge gnawing relentlessly at his gut. The only way to stop the festering was to strike out at his tormentor. He knew that when faced with Dang, he would be unforgiving, probably brutal toward the Viet Cong officer. The thought appealed to his savage sense of retribution. However, he did promise not to kill him.

GRAB AND SNATCH

With their stomachs full from the morning meal, the First Squad grabbed their weapons and rucks. One by one, they filed out the screen door of their hooch, heading for the helipad. Once on the path, they broke into a jog, moving with a sense of urgency.

The first to arrive at the helipad was Henderson. He observed a Loach, two Cobras, and the Rescue Huey waiting, their blades slowly turning. The noise from the engines was deafening. Henderson and the squad moved toward the Huey.

While he stood waiting to board, Henderson ran his hand lovingly over his M-16. He knew it was better that he survived and the VC received what was due them. With the firepower of the helicopters flying over the enemy, the VC will be looking up with a sense of insecurity and anticipation as the choppers unloaded their ammunition on them. Hopefully, they won't notice the Animals jumping to the ground. *Everyone needs to die—except Lieutenant Dang.*

The door gunner waved for the squad to board. Each man rushed forward, sliding onto the deck to their assigned position. Henderson surveyed the men as they adjusted equipment or checked their weapon. Each one had a way to calm his nerves before a mission.

Henderson put on the headset. "Ready to go, sir."

The copilot turned in his seat to scan the infantry soldiers. "Welcome aboard. Good luck," the copilot said into the headset.

"Thanks, sir." Henderson signaled the squad they were taking off to their objective.

The Loach rose from the helipad first, staying low to the ground. Then the Cobras lifted, and, as the pilots accelerated, they climbed higher into the sky. The Huey shot straight up, and then the pilot pushed the nose down, flying south. When they crossed the perimeter wire, the Huey flew higher, and soon Henderson could look down on the three helicopters. The Loach flew beneath the Cobras.

While in flight, it appeared that the grunts were taking a nap. Their heads bobbed with each bit of turbulence the Huey flew through. Henderson knew that they were mentally preparing for battle.

For Henderson, this was the day he wanted but dreaded. Everything hinged on surprise and what the squad did once they arrived at the hill. Whatever happened cannot be undone. He knew that he promised not to kill Dang, but what if he had to, then what? He chuckled at the thought. All he could do was watch the jungle, rice paddies, and hills zoom by him. He'll know when the squad hits the ground.

Henderson heard a crackling in his headset. "Get ready. At the landing zone in five mikes."

The wind rushed through the open deck of the Huey as it descended.

After he nudged Williams, Henderson gave the signal to prepare for landing. Each man tapped the soldier next to him to make sure he was alert. The door gunner checked the belt of ammunition that fed into the M-60. He began to swivel the barrel, pointing at different objects on the ground.

"This is Skeeter One, dropping yellow smoke. Over," the Loach pilot transmitted.

"Dropping smoke." The observer released a smoke grenade.

Within seconds, yellow smoke drifted from the jungle canopy as the Loach climbed higher. Henderson could hear the chatter of the pilots as they communicated their intentions.

From high in the sky, the two Cobras tilted the nose of their aircraft toward the ground. As one, they accelerated toward the enemy. Once the target was in view, the pilots opened fire with miniguns and grenade launchers firing in rapid succession.

Henderson peered out the open doorway. He witnessed the two helicopters firepower tearing the earth apart where the yellow smoke drifted skyward. He could observe them making one run after another while leaving a trail of destruction.

The Loach pilot transmitted, "This is Skeeter One. Moving back in for a closer look. Hold your fire. Over."

"Roger, Skeeter One. We'll move higher up. Out," the Cobra lead pilot said.

Once the two Cobras flew to a higher altitude, the Loach descended, flying low over the jungle canopy. The observer had a purple smoke grenade ready to drop to pinpoint the enemy.

Enemy AK-47s, along with a .51-caliber machine gun, opened fire on the Loach ripping holes through the fuselage. The gunner on the Loach fired toward the ground, where the enemy green tracer rounds originated. Then his gun went silent as an enemy round tore through his chest. The wind whistled through the hole in the canopy.

"Thompson is hit. Damn, he's dead!" the observer yelled through his headset.

"Warlord One, Warlord Two, this is Skeeter; shit, there must be over a company-size element in the jungle on the other side of those boulders. That's a lot more than what Intel reported."

"Roger, Skeeter One, we see them. Over." The Cobra pilots maneuvered for a better position.

"I'm getting lower." The Loach lost altitude. "Drop smoke."

The observer leaned out the window. He dropped a purple smoke grenade on the enemy on the ground. The crews of the helicopters, along with the squad of grunts on the Huey, watched the purple smoke as it drifted through the canopy.

Without hesitation, the two Cobras strafed the enemy forces firing with all of their armament, to include the 2.75 rockets. The Loach pilot, while flying low out of the battle zone, watched the VC fall one after another. He spotted a small group of enemy soldiers moving to the boulders for cover. The observer saw that one of the VC seemed taller than the rest. It appeared he was giving orders.

"Rescue One, this is Skeeter One. I believe your target is hiding in the boulders to the south of the hill. Over," the observer transmitted.

Henderson surveyed the area, deciding to keep the original landing zone on the south side. He calculated that they could sweep to the north, coming in behind the enemy hiding in the boulders.

"This is Animal One. Thanks, Skeeter One. Good eye." Henderson scanned the area where the enemy hid.

Next, Henderson spoke to the pilot. "Rescue One, drop us at the planned LZ. We'll move from there."

"Roger, Animal One. Going to landing zone now." The Huey flew toward the designated location.

The other pilots heard the conversation between Henderson and the Huey pilot. They immediately flew higher over the hilltop to get out of the Huey's approach. The pilots remained vigilant, watching for the enemy to move on the squad of grunts.

"Warlord One, Warlord Two, this is Animal One; keep any enemy forces from moving south to assist the small unit held up there. Over," Henderson transmitted.

"This is Warlord One. Wilco, Animal One. Good luck. Over."

"Here we go, Animal One. Get ready." The Huey pilot pushed the nose down, accelerating to the landing zone. When he got closer, he changed the pitch while reducing the throttle. The helicopter slowed to a stop one foot off the ground. He held the Huey in a hover, waiting for the grunts to dismount.

The squad jumped from the helicopter, landing hard on their feet. They rushed forward to a stand of trees near the large rocks for cover. Henderson motioned for the squad to form in a line. The squad members knew their positions, moving without hesitation.

Enemy forces moved toward the boulders that hid the small group of VC that was the target for the Animals. The Cobras swooped from the skies, blowing holes into the ground at the advancing enemy. Bodies went flying in all directions. The VC quickly retreated, leaving twelve comrades lying in the open.

After the VC retreated, Henderson peered through the trees toward the boulders where the target hid. He didn't see any movement. With a signal to move forward from Henderson, the squad crouched, working their way through the trees and rocks. When they were within twenty-five meters of the boulders, Henderson whispered, "Hold up here. It doesn't feel right."

The smell of the enemy reached his nostrils as his nose wrinkled in disgust. Henderson drew his head backward while the color drained from his face. "The VC are close; be on the lookout."

After he spoke those words of warning, the enemy opened fire on the grunts from two sides. Henderson gauged the situation. "Johnston, take Little JJ and Williams. Move to our left. They're trying to flank us."

Johnston opened fire on the left flank. "Let's go—move." The three soldiers ran crouched low to the ground while firing at the enemy.

Henderson's eyes widened as he looked around. "Bear, you're with me. We're moving to the front."

The two grunts moved toward the incoming AK-47 bullets as the Viet Cong fired at them. Rounds zinged overhead, tearing off small tree branches, and thudded into the ground while they crawled forward. Henderson rolled onto his back to reload his M-16. He looked skyward at the two Cobras flying toward the ground, providing covering fire. They weren't allowing the enemy soldiers behind the boulders to receive any reinforcements or escape from their hiding place.

There was a lull in the enemy firing at the advancing soldiers. Henderson seized the opportunity.

"Bear, let's run like hell to the boulders to our front." Henderson crouched.

Bear looked at the boulders and acknowledged the order. "Got it, Sarge."

"Move now." Henderson ran forward, staying low to the ground.

Bear sprang to his feet, running behind his squad leader. They ran, zigzagging from the tree line to the boulders. Once the enemy spotted them, they opened fire. It was too late; they found concealment and cover behind the rocks.

While panting, Henderson checked to his front. "One more time. We'll be in their position. You ready?"

Before Bear could reply, the left flank filled the air with gunfire. "You son of bitches better run!" Johnston yelled.

Little JJ leveled the M-60, burning through several belts of ammunition as he fired at the Viet Cong.

The Loach followed the retreating VC, killing one after another.

"Let's go, Sarge." Bear stood with his face contorted with hatred.

They crawled from behind the boulders toward the waiting VC. After crawling for twenty feet, Henderson pulled himself up by a large tree. He eyed Bear and then glanced toward the rocks they needed to get past.

"Ready anytime you are," Bear whispered.

Henderson pushed the magazine release button, allowing the magazine to fall to the ground. He removed a fully loaded magazine from the bandolier and inserted it. Henderson pulled back the charging handle, releasing it to load a round in the chamber. Next, he hit the forward assist with the palm of his right hand. Bear emulated his squad leader.

Over the noise of the battle, Henderson yelled, "Now!"

After scrambling over the rocks, they fell into the waiting enemy. Two VC soldiers immediately jumped Bear. One was on his back, while the other held on to his left shoulder. He seemed not to notice the two enemy soldiers that clung to him.

"You can't run, you little bastard." He swung his rifle to his left, shooting one VC that was trying to run away. Bear shook his massive body, striving to dislodge the two Viet Cong that hung on to him. The one hanging on to his shoulder bit him hard on the neck. "You little shit!" Bear plucked the VC off him. He broke his neck in one smooth move. Next, Bear slammed his body back into the rocks, smashing the enemy that held on to him. When Bear felt him release his grip, he turned, putting his survival knife into his heart. The blade sunk to the handle.

An AK-47 fired with the sound echoing along the rocks. Bear's head exploded as he fell to the ground. He lay with open eyes blankly staring at the sky, half his skull missing.

At last, Henderson saw Dang. He froze as his hatred for the VC officer pulsed through his veins. He understood that the hate that existed between him and Dang would have one kill the other. At that moment, Henderson knew what he had to do to live.

He ran toward Dang, hitting him full force with his body weight, knocking him to the ground and the lieutenant's rifle flying in the air. Henderson sat on his chest, struggling to pin his arms. The two men were in a death grip, fighting to be the survivor. The Viet Cong lieutenant threw wild punches at the American soldier's head. Henderson took as many blows as he avoided.

While placing his hands around Dang's throat, Henderson screamed, "I'm going to kill you."

"Go ahead if you can." Dang sneered at him.

While Henderson grasped his throat with one hand, he removed the knife that hung from his belt with the other hand. He pushed hard on Dang's head, forcing the left side of his face into the ground. Henderson placed the blade against his right cheek "This is for Laurel, you little bastard." He moved the blade downward, cutting deep from the right eye to the chin. "Now, you'll have matching scars, mother fucker."

Dang screamed in pain. He reached for his pistol. It took him several seconds to work it free of the holster—then he forced the barrel into Henderson's stomach. "Now, I'll see you die." He pulled the trigger; the sound was muffled by Henderson's body.

Henderson winced in pain. He fell on his back to the right of Dang, holding his stomach. "Goddamn it," he grunted. As he stared at the sun, Henderson couldn't believe Dang would win. "I'm sorry, Ray," he whispered.

Dang rolled to his side with blood streaming down his face. He pointed the pistol at Henderson's head. A smile grew on the lieutenant's face.

At that moment, Henderson knew he was going to die. His body relaxed, accepting death. An image of Cheryl floated above him while her aroma filled the air. He could see her talking but couldn't understand the words.

A foot stomped down on Dang's hand, forcing the gun from his grasp, falling to the ground. A hot M-16 muzzle touched his temple. Dang's smile disappeared while he groaned in pain.

"Go ahead, I want you to, mother fucker." Johnston smirked at the Viet Cong officer. "I didn't promise *not* to kill your sorry ass."

Williams ran to Henderson. "You'll be okay, Henderson. You'll be okay." He started treating the wound.

"Is he dead?" Henderson was conscious but in pain.

Johnston chuckled. "No, you left him alive, as promised."

"Thanks, Johnston." Henderson struggled to stay awake. "Dang killed Bear."

Little JJ kneeled next to Bear. "No, it can't be!" he screamed.

He reached down, closing Bear's eyes. "I'll miss you—you big hairy animal." Tears ran down his cheeks. After he stood, Little JJ walked to where Dang lay on the ground and kicked him with all the force his hatred could muster. Dang screamed in pain.

"Need to call for extraction before the VC return." Johnston scanned the area.

With a shaky voice, Little JJ transmitted, "Rescue One, ready for extraction near boulders. Over."

"Wilco, Animal One, coming in now. Be ready to load." The pilot searched for the squad on the ground.

Little JJ looked skyward. "Roger, Rescue One. We have one KIA, one WIA."

"Roger that, Animal One, almost there," the Huey pilot transmitted.

"Hey, all you birds up there, we have the prisoner," Little JJ announced.

Laughter, along with congratulatory remarks, was heard over the handset as Little JJ held it out for all to hear.

Brighton had been listening to the conversations since the First Squad boarded the chopper for the mission. "Animal One, this is Animal. Great job. Come on home."

"Roger, Animal, chopper coming in now. Animal One is WIA. Out." Little JJ looked over at Henderson, his face reflecting sadness.

The chopper descended until the skids settled on the hard ground next to the boulders.

"Okay, blindfold him, then tie the fucker up," Johnston ordered.

Williams removed the blindfold and the rope from his rucksack. He slammed the VC lieutenant onto his stomach. Williams tied his hands behind his back. Next, he yanked him up by his hair, sliding the blindfold over his eyes.

"He's ready." Williams pushed Dang forward.

"Little JJ, get the weapons. Put them on the chopper." Johnston pointed at Dang. "Then come back to guard this piece of shit."

With his eyes darting around the ground, Little JJ collected the weapons. With arms full, he headed to the waiting Huey.

Johnston grabbed Williams by the arm. "When he gets back, I want you to help me carry Henderson. Then we'll get Bear."

Williams nodded that he understood.

As soon as Little JJ finished, the two soldiers picked Henderson up, with Williams at the legs and Johnston holding him under the arms. Williams stumbled to the chopper. "Damn, he's heavy."

They slid him onto a litter on the deck. The door gunner moved Henderson against the pilot seats and started to treat his wound. The copilot watched from his position. "He doesn't look good."

Next, the two soldiers returned for Bear. They strained with all their strength, barely getting him off the ground. They struggled to carry Bear to the helicopter. The door gunner jumped from the Huey to the ground. With the three of them, they lifted him. Finally, they got Bear on the chopper.

Johnston turned, signaling Little JJ they were ready for the prisoner.

"Get up." Little JJ yanked on the rope, making the lieutenant stand. He walked behind him, prodding him toward the helicopter. Johnston grabbed Dang. He tossed him into the chopper head first.

He faced the remaining squad members. "Load up. Let's get the hell out of here."

Johnston heard the cracking of AK-47s firing, and rounds hit all around the squad while they dove into the chopper. The door gunner returned fire with his M-60 as Little JJ boarded last. Johnston signaled the pilot to take off.

A .51-caliber machine gun joined in firing at the departing Huey. Rounds tore into the helicopter as it rose into the air. The squad hung on to the deck, knowing a bullet could strike them at any moment.

Out of nowhere, two Cobras flew low, firing their miniguns and rockets into the jungle growth where the VC hid. The jungle exploded into the air as the rockets hit their targets. The enemy guns went silent.

The four helicopters raced, flying back to Chu Lai.

The Huey pilot transmitted, "Animal, this is Rescue One; need medics on standby to carry WIA. Have hospital ready. Over."

"Roger, Rescue One. They're ready to receive WIA. Over," Brighton transmitted.

"Need litter for the KIA too. Out." The pilot moved the throttle forward.

•

Brighton threw the handset down. While he walked out of the screen door, he stopped. He lit a cigarette and then took long strides toward the landing pad. While Brighton stood next to the helipad, the four helicopters approached the base. The Huey came in first with the First Squad. Once they were on the ground, the medics removed Henderson. They strode to the emergency area.

A team of orderlies slid Bear off of the chopper. The soldiers holding the litter were having a hard time managing Bear's weight.

Little JJ slid off the chopper. "Let's give them a hand with Bear."

"Roger." Williams jumped to the ground.

They each took a handle of the litter, and the four men walked away with Bear.

Johnston grabbed Dang roughly by the arm. "Get on your feet, asshole." He yanked him to his feet. With a shove, the enemy soldier fell off the chopper, hitting the ground face-first. "Shit, I'm sorry, Dang." Johnston slid off the helicopter.

"We got the prisoner." A fresh-faced lieutenant wearing a military police band around his upper right arm approached Johnston. "Let go of him, Sergeant." He gave Johnston a disapproving look.

"Take care of him, sir." Johnston raised his right hand like he was going to salute. His right elbow smacked Dang on the left side of his face. "Sorry, sir." He gave the lieutenant a challenging look. Johnston walked away, leaving the prisoner under the watchful eye of the MP.

The soldiers carried Henderson and Bear into the hospital. Within minutes, the Loach and the two Cobras landed softly on the helipad. The pilots cut their engines. The area became eerily quiet as the blades rotated slowly to a stop.

Brighton followed the litters into the hospital. He sat alone, watching the scene unfold. With his eyes darting around the room, he lit another cigarette before he finished the last one. He turned his focus to the hallway. Brighton mentally walked through the mission from start to finish. He felt the tension and anxiety build up inside him. The thoughts of what he could've done differently bounced around his mind. His foot tapped faster, with his eyes never leaving the hallway to the surgical rooms.

"LT, he'll be okay." Johnston glanced down at Brighton.

"Yeah, I know. But Henderson has had a rough tour." Brighton lowered his eyes, staring at the floor.

Johnston pulled out a chair, sitting next to Brighton. Little JJ and Williams both nodded at the two leaders. They, too, pulled out chairs. The soldiers waited in silence.

After two hours, the doctor came into the waiting area. "Are you men waiting on Henderson?"

The chairs slid across the floor as the four soldiers stood at the same time.

"I'm his platoon leader." Brighton pointed at the three soldiers. "These are his buddies."

"Well, first off, he's going to be fine. We removed the bullet. There was no damage to any of his organs. Blood loss was the biggest problem." The doctor surveyed the faces of the soldiers.

"I guess he'll be going home?" Johnston stared down the hall.

The doctor squared his shoulders. "That's my recommendation. I'd say he'll be in Japan in two days. They have better equipment to treat his wound. The biggest concern at this point is an infection."

"At least he'll go home this time." Brighton's shoulders slumped.

"He deserves it." Little JJ put his hand on LT's shoulder.

"Okay, you guys go get cleaned up. Then get some sleep." Brighton hesitated. "Sergeant Johnston, don't tell Mama-san what happened. I'll have another girl translate when I tell her."

"Yes, sir." Johnston turned to walk away.

The other two members of First Squad followed Johnston.

The medic wheeled Henderson into a room with four other soldiers. He was still unconscious. A nurse hooked up an IV to his arm and then pulled a blanket over him. She looked down on him and patted his shoulder. "They're all too young."

DO IT ALL OVER AGAIN

When he walked out of the hospital, Brighton quickened his pace to the MARS station. He dreaded making the call to Professor a second time, but he did promise Henderson. "Shit, Henderson did keep his promise not to kill Dang."

The soldier in charge glanced up from his desk at Brighton. "You back again, sir?"

"I'm ready to make a call." Brighton ignored the soldier's remark. He dialed Professor's number. After several rings, a familiar voice answered the phone, "Hello."

"Professor, this is Brighton. Over." Brighton ran his hand over his sweaty brow.

"Damn, LT, how are you doing?" He hesitated. "What happened to Eddie? Over."

"Henderson was wounded this morning. He's alive. He's doing okay. I believe he will be going to Japan in a couple of days." Brighton's eyes darted around the room. "Can you tell his wife? Over."

Brighton heard Professor take a deep breath and slowly exhale.

"I don't want to, but yes, I can. Over," Professor said.

"Thank you." Brighton gulped in air. "One last thing, I don't know how long he will be in Japan. Over."

The soldier responsible for monitoring the calls stood over Brighton. "You should receive a telegram today or tomorrow. My turn is up. I have to go." The call ended.

While Brighton headed back to his office, he thought of Bear. What a good soldier he was. Once he was seated in the chair, he placed a sheet of paper on the desk and picked up the pen.

Dear Mr. and Mrs. Russel,

I'm David's commander, James Brighton. I know the Army has informed you of his death, but I wanted to let you know what kind of man and soldier he became.

On the day David died, he served our country. He died a hero, who served others and treated all with respect.

You should be proud of your son . . .

•

Professor placed the handset into the cradle. Numb from the news, he sat in the chair. "At least he's alive. He's coming home."

After ten minutes had passed, Professor picked up the phone.

On the second ring, Cheryl answered. "Hello, Henderson residence."

"Good evening, Cheryl. This is Professor." He shifted his weight in the chair.

"Is this about Eddie?"

"Eddie is alive." Professor stood, looking out the window. "Can I come over?"

"Please, tell me what happened to Eddie," she cried.

It wasn't the news he wanted to deliver over the phone. Knowing how Cheryl would react was eating at him worse than learning that Eddie was wounded. Professor decided it best to tell her. "Eddie was wounded this morning. He's fine and at the hospital in Chu Lai."

"Oh my God, he's going to die, isn't he?" Cheryl wailed.

"Listen to me, Cheryl. Eddie is doing fine. The hospital will transfer him to Japan in a couple of days. Then he will be moved to the States."

"Are you sure, Professor?"

"I was on the phone with Lieutenant Brighton. This is what he told me." Professor collapsed back into the chair. "I'm sure Eddie will call you when he can. You'll see he's okay."

The line was quiet except for Cheryl's heavy breathing. Professor gazed around the room. Their wedding picture on the telephone table caught his attention. He sat slowly into the chair, staring at the happy, smiling faces of Eddie and Cheryl.

"Oh, please let him come home," she whispered.

"Let me come over. We can get dinner and talk about Eddie." Professor stood picking up the car keys.

Cheryl opened the refrigerator to see if she had enough food for a meal. "Okay, come on over. I'll make dinner here. Pick up Jim Beam on your way, please."

"I'm on my way." Professor dropped the handset into the cradle, and he grabbed a pack of cigarettes before going out the door.

•

The next morning Professor sat in his chair, watching out the front window. He didn't know what time the cabbie would show, but he knew the driver would. After he drained the coffee cup, Professor walked into the kitchen for a refill. While he poured the fresh coffee, there was a knock on the door.

Professor set the cup on the counter when he walked to the door. He took a deep breath and swung it open. First, he observed the yellow cab on the street, then the cab driver standing on the porch.

"Are you Mr. Calvin Cox?" he asked and extended his hand, offering an envelope.

"Yes, I am." Professor took the telegram.

The driver looked down. "I'm sorry." He turned, walking to his cab.

While he opened the telegram, Professor knew what it said. He hoped the information he received from Lieutenant Brighton hadn't changed overnight.

He read the telegram:

> *Mr. Calvin Cox*
>
> *The Secretary of the Army has asked me to express his deep regret that Sergeant Eddie Henderson was wounded in Vietnam on 28 July 1970. He was a squad leader of a rescue squad responsible for the capture of a high-value enemy soldier. They were attacked by a large hostile force . . .*

TIME TO RECOVER

Brighton had another hooch girl tell Mama-san what happened to Henderson. After the girl translated, Mama-san's shrill cry echoed in the room. She fell to her knees, the weight of sorrow pressing onto her. He knew she had felt the sadness many times during the war. All Brighton could do was join in her pain. He reached for Mama-san, pulling her up, holding her for a moment.

While he took slow, calculated steps toward the hospital, Brighton held on to the old woman. She seemed so fragile in his hands that he was afraid to hold her too tight, but he didn't want her to stumble or fall on the uneven pathway. Mama-san gazed at him as if she was saying thank you for the help.

Once they entered his room, she saw him. Mama-san flashed a toothless smile and shuffled to Henderson's bedside. Brighton remained at the door. She took Henderson's hand into hers. "Eddie." She lay her head on his shoulder.

"Hello, Mama-san." Henderson stroked her long gray hair. "Thank you."

She squeezed his hand. "*Cảm ơn bạn.*" Tears rolled down her cheek, dripping onto the blanket. She began to hum the lullaby.

Henderson touched her face, wiping the tears away. "*Cảm ơn bạn.*"

The doctor entered the room. "Sergeant Henderson, you'll be going to Japan the day after tomorrow. Your wound is serious, but I expect a full recovery without any complications."

Henderson forced a smile. "Thanks, Doc."

Brighton reached for Mama-san. "Well, I guess we should get going. I bet you need some rest." They turned to walk toward the door. "I'll see you tomorrow before you leave."

•

The next morning Brighton, Johnston, Little JJ, and Williams entered his room.

"We came to see you off, Henderson." Johnston handed him a carton of Marlboros and a bottle of Jim Beam. "We brought you a farewell gift."

"Man, thanks. I've been out of smokes since last night." Henderson opened a pack. He removed a cigarette and lit it, inhaling deeply. "Take one." He offered the open pack to his friends.

They passed the pack around, removing a cigarette. Within seconds, the room filled with smoke. The four soldiers were uncommonly quiet.

Henderson surveyed his friends, noticing it didn't feel right. The corner of Brighton's right eye twitched, and Johnston stood with his arms folded across his broad chest. Little JJ drummed his fingers on the nightstand. Williams gazed out the screened window.

"Okay, what's going on, guys?" Henderson's eyes darted from one friend to the next.

The squad members turned their gaze toward Brighton.

"Okay, I'll tell him." He wiped at the sweat on his forehead.

"Shit, tell me what, LT?" Henderson tried to sit up in his bed. "What's going on?" He grimaced in pain while his mind ran through different scenarios. "What happened to Cheryl?"

"No, Cheryl is fine." Brighton approached the bed. "This isn't easy." He placed a hand on Henderson's shoulder. "No other way to tell you . . . Dang escaped last night."

"Come on, LT. You're fucking with me. No way could he escape!" Henderson yelled.

"No, I'm not messing with you. Dang had a confidant on the inside. We believe it was a Vietnamese interpreter. He was gone for hours before the alarm sounded."

"Goddamn it. It was all for nothing!" Henderson threw the carton of cigarettes at the wall. "I'll kill the son of a bitch." He cocked his arm to throw the Jim Beam, but Johnston grabbed his arm, stopping him. Henderson fought to get out of bed.

"Stay in bed." Brighton held him down.

"Damn it. Stop, Henderson. You're bleeding." Little JJ applied gauze against the wound.

Williams stepped into the hallway. "We need a nurse in here ASAP."

Henderson's anger grew in his gut. He'd never forget Laurel's eyes, or how Dang executed him because he couldn't keep up with his men. The inferno inside him was more than his mind could manage. His face turned red with the bottled-up rage he struggled to hold back. All he wanted was to kill Dang.

Within seconds a nurse came into the room. "Lie still, Sergeant. You tore open some stitches. You're bleeding. Please stop fighting me." She stepped next to Brighton. "Watch him while I get the doctor."

After a minute or two, she marched into the room with the doctor. "Everyone needs to leave." The nurse crossed her arms, staring at the soldiers. "The doctor will take care of your friend."

Johnston set the cigarettes and the Jim Beam on the nightstand. "Take care of yourself, Henderson."

"Here are our home addresses and phone numbers." Williams placed an envelope between the cigarettes and the bottle of bourbon. "Stay in touch, Henderson."

The men filed out of the room, following Brighton back to the hooch. Johnston plopped on his bunk. "That didn't go well."

"Nope, it didn't." Brighton reached into the ice chest for a Coke.

THE HOSPITAL STAYS

That afternoon, the medics placed Henderson on a C-141 medical aircraft for the trip to Tachikawa Air Force Base in Japan. His eyes darted around the plane. He saw stretchers attached to the metal framework, stacked four high on both sides. Litters were everywhere. A wounded serviceman lay on each one. *My God, how many wounded are there?*

While the aircraft flew to Japan, nurses, medics, and doctors tended to the wounded. Henderson heard groans, moans, and crying coming from the injured. He tried to close his eyes, but sleep never came. The sounds of pain echoed throughout the aircraft.

The soldier next to him stared at the litter above him. "What unit you with?" He rolled to his side.

"I'm with Bravo Company, One Hundred and Twenty-Third Aviation." Henderson didn't look at the soldier.

"Oh, you're a chopper guy." The soldier sounded disappointed.

Henderson turned his head to look at the soldier. "Hell no. We're grunts assigned to the unit." He observed the soldier was young. *Damn, he is thinner than I was.*

"What about you? What unit are you in?"

"I'm in Alpha Company, Third of the First, Eleventh Brigade."

"No shit. That was my unit during my first tour." Henderson smiled at the thought of his platoon brothers. "They're good men."

"They still are." The soldier closed his eyes. He fell asleep.

Henderson checked the sleeping soldier, discovering that he was missing his left arm. *Poor kid.*

•

After the C-141 landed, the medical personnel unloaded the patients. An administrator assigned every patient to a bed in a hospital ward. As the nurses walked by, they stopped and picked up the chart hanging at the foot of each bed. They read the medical information about each service member.

Before lights out, a nurse stopped at Henderson's bed. "Time to change your bandage." She reached to pull the sheet down. Henderson observed the way she cared for him. He felt the warmth of her soft hands as she tenderly removed the bandage.

He chuckled. "Thank you for being gentle with me."

"Sergeant, it's the least I can do after what you've been through." She reached to the tray to get clean gauze. "Your wound is healing nicely. I don't see any infection. That's a good thing."

"The pain isn't as bad." Henderson tried to sit up higher.

She adjusted her hat. Then she stuffed stray strands of blond hair underneath it. "This will sting a little. I'm going to clean around the stitches."

Henderson winced as he pulled back. "That's more than a little bit."

The nurse laughed. "Don't be such a baby." She taped on a new bandage. Then she pulled the sheet over him. "Now, get some sleep." Before she left to attend to the next soldier, she said, "We are reducing your pain medication. Let me know if the pain increases."

"I will. Thank you." Henderson watched her walk to the next soldier.

•

After two days, the orderlies placed Henderson on a bus full of stretchers. The doctor transferred him to the 106th Hospital in Kishine in Yokohama. He strained to see the city as they drove along the road, but the pain medication kicked in and he fell asleep.

When they arrived, it was the same process, and the administrator assigned him to a bed in a ward. His healing accelerated because he didn't have any infections. The nurses and orderlies tended to his wound. Each day the doctor checked on him.

The soldier next to him was the same man with the missing left arm who was on the flight from Vietnam. Henderson turned to see how he was doing and found him staring at the ceiling.

"Good morning. I remember you from the flight." The soldier didn't move. "We were in the same unit. I'm Henderson."

He rolled onto his side to face Henderson. "My name is Lawton." Tears dripped down his cheeks.

Henderson noticed the tears. "Well, Lawton, today is your lucky day. The nurse said I could start using a wheelchair." He smiled. "Now I can get out of this goddamn bed, but I need someone to push me. They don't want me ripping my stitches out, rolling it myself."

"Man, I don't know if I can do it with one arm."

"Hell, you fought the Viet Cong. You can do it." Henderson let out a loud laugh. "Come on, man—give me a hand."

Lawton smiled and slid from his bed. "Okay, let's do it."

From that day forward, the two were inseparable. They went to physical therapy, the mess hall, and the movie theater together. Henderson helped Lawton recover mentally from his wound, and Lawton did the same for him.

Henderson found himself getting stronger each day.

•

Two weeks later, the doctor stopped at his bed. "Sergeant Henderson, you will leave this afternoon for the States."

Once he digested the news, Henderson sat up. "Thanks, Doc. You have any idea where I'm going?"

"Your records indicated that you are from Berkeley, California; therefore, you are going to the Letterman Army Medical Center."

Henderson thought for a moment. "That's great, sir. Letterman is about twenty miles from my wife."

The doctor placed his hand on Henderson's shoulder. "Good luck, Sergeant."

Now that he was going home, he decided to call Cheryl. He desperately wanted to hear her voice. The only way to talk with her was to call collect, which was expensive. Henderson sat next to the telephone with anticipation and then dialed the operator.

A woman with a thick Japanese accent answered, "This is the operator. How can I direct your call?"

"I want to make a collect call, please." Henderson gazed down the hall.

"Who is making the call, and what number are you calling?"

Henderson gave the operator his information and heard her dial the number. His body began to tingle, knowing he would talk to Cheryl. Then he listened to the phone ring.

A voice on the other end said, "This is the Henderson residence."

Henderson's face lit up when he heard her voice.

"You have a collect call from Eddie. Will you accept the charges?"

"Oh yes, oh yes, of course," Cheryl said.

"Go ahead, Eddie." The operator no longer listened to the call.

"I hope it's not too early to call," Eddie said.

"No, of course not. Eddie, how are you? Professor told me you were wounded. I'm so worried."

"Don't worry. I'm healing fast and in good hands." Eddie smiled, hearing the concern in her voice. "I have good news. I'm being moved to Letterman and should be there tomorrow."

"Oh, Eddie, I can't wait. I love you. I'll be waiting at the hospital."

"I love you too. We better hang up. This call will cost a fortune." Henderson's smile disappeared.

"I'll see you tomorrow. I love you. Good-bye," Cheryl said.

Henderson heard the click of the call ending when Cheryl placed the handset into the cradle. The line went dead. He sat for a moment holding the handset while he savored the sound of her voice. *I'm going home!*

THE WAR IS OVER

The trip from Japan to Oakland, California, was tediously long. Again, the aircraft held many wounded men who were going to various hospitals in the United States. During the flight, the medical staff worked tirelessly to make the wounded as comfortable as possible. Henderson attempted to sleep, but the cries of pain or men screaming from within their nightmares kept him awake.

Once the plane landed, the orderlies loaded the wounded onto redesigned buses that held stretchers. As the bus traveled along the highway, he saw buildings, concrete, asphalt, and glass. Henderson smiled—he didn't miss the jungle, rice paddies, or mountains of Vietnam, not even the comforts of the firebase at Chu Lai.

After arriving at Letterman Army Medical Center on the Presidio of San Francisco, an administrator assigned Henderson to a ward and bed. He found this hospital to be larger and cleaner than the others where he was a patient. Within two hours, the nurse tucked him into the hospital bed. While he lay on his back, the smell of vomit, piss, shit, and disinfectant attacked his nostrils. Once Henderson shut out the smells, he began to get excited about Cheryl's visit.

A nurse approached his bed. "Sergeant Henderson, you have a visitor."

He glanced down the ward and saw Cheryl running toward his bed, her red hair trailing behind her. Henderson let the happiness cover him like a blanket. For a brief instant, he savored the moment, allowing his mind to relax while watching Cheryl approach him. He was home; he'd made it—he survived the war.

She stopped at his bedside. Cheryl leaned over to kiss him. "Eddie, are you okay?" She kissed him again. "I missed you."

He held on to her, not wanting to let go. "I'm doing fine." It felt good to be called Eddie. It made him feel normal. "I should be out of here soon."

With his face smothered into Cheryl's neck, he heard a voice, "Oh my, Eddie, are you hurt bad?"

When he glanced up, Eddie saw Martha and John standing behind Cheryl with concerned but loving expressions etched on their faces. All he could think about was the people he loved and cared for the most stood in front of him.

"You didn't have to come." Eddie wiped at his tears. "I'm fine."

"We couldn't leave you and Cheryl alone at a time like this." Martha bent over and kissed Eddie on the forehead.

John put a hand on Eddie's shoulder. "Damn, son, I told you not to go back." With a smile, he gave a gentle, caring squeeze.

Eddie grabbed John's arm. "How long are you staying?"

"We're here for two more days. Then we need to go back home." John glanced at Martha.

"We need to get back to feed the cats." Martha leaned over and kissed Eddie on the cheek.

•

During the next two weeks, Cheryl visited almost every day until the doctor discharged him.

On the day he was discharged, the doctor stood at the foot of his bed. "Eddie, I'm releasing you today. I'm also recommending a medical discharge. No doubt, it will be approved."

Eddie had a confused look. "You mean I'll be out of the Army?"

"That is correct. Once you leave here, you are a free man." The doctor laughed at his joke.

FACE THE TRUTH

Once home, Eddie became anxious. He'd failed to find a job or enroll in the university. The television was continuously blaring, and he got up from his chair to change the channels after five or ten minutes. Nothing could hold his attention but the memories of Vietnam.

No longer did he feel the calmness, only the restlessness and fear. His mind wandered back to Vietnam, recalling the night Mitch died, along with the promise he didn't keep the day Ray died. And he thought of the day Dang almost killed him by shooting him in the gut. These events played over and over, forbidding him to rest.

Eddie downed his fourth Jim Beam and Coke.

Cheryl pressed the off button as she passed the television. "It's time for bed. You need your rest."

"I'm not sleepy yet. I think I'll stay up a while." Eddie walked toward the television.

"You need your rest." Cheryl moved in front of the television, blocking him.

"Okay, you win." A small grin tugged at his lips.

It didn't take Eddie long to fall asleep.

Cheryl knew he hadn't been sleeping well. She thought that might be why he was feeling down. She'd talked to Professor in an attempt to learn how to help Eddie cope. The only advice he'd given was to be patient and eventually Eddie would snap out of it. She thought there had to be more to it than that. With these thoughts looping through her mind, she fell asleep.

Not more than an hour after she fell asleep, Eddie tossed and rolled as if he was running through the jungle. When she woke, Cheryl knew what was coming next, another nightmare, but she didn't know if it would be about Mitch or Ray.

He whimpered in his sleep. "Ray, follow me!" Eddie flipped onto his stomach and crawled toward the foot of the bed. "Let's go, Ray." When Eddie slid to the floor, he yelled, "Run, it's fucking Dang." His legs moved as if he was running. While sweat soaked his clothes, his body shook violently. He watched Laurel stare into the barrel of the pistol and say, "Gawddamn it."

Eddie's heart beat hard against his chest. "I'm going to kill you!" he screamed at Dang.

"Eddie, it's okay," Cheryl said in a soothing tone. "It's a dream. I have you. You're safe." She helped Eddie back into bed, all the while talking softly to him.

Curling up next to him, she whispered, "What have they done to you? What have they done?"

•

The next morning Eddie was up early, as usual. He sat at the kitchen table, looking at the strange landscape of buildings. When he picked up his glass, Cheryl walked into the kitchen.

"Good morning, beautiful." He downed the Jim Beam and Coke.

"Eddie, I'm worried about you. You're not talking to me. You're drinking too much." Her eyes narrowed and deep lines creased her forehead. Tears ran down her cheeks. "You haven't been out of the house for days. Let's go for a walk, then get breakfast."

"I don't feel like getting out." Eddie placed his hand on the healed wound.

Cheryl stood by his chair. "It's not a request." She folded her arms across her chest. Her eyes revealed the same concern that

Mama-san had shown him. She placed her hand on his shoulder. He felt soothed by her touch—it calmed him. Guilt overcame him for his actions and behavior since coming home.

"Okay, let's go." Eddie reluctantly stood, heading for the door.

While they walked along the park path holding hands, Eddie unloaded the memories that haunted him. He decided to tell Cheryl everything about his capture, and Cain, Ray, and Bear dying. He cried when he talked about the cruel VC Lieutenant Dang. The words spilled out as if a dam had opened. He no longer had control; he wanted to share his darkest days with Cheryl.

They shed tears, stopped, and hugged while they walked along the path. Strangers gave weird or sympathetic glances at the young couple as they passed them. The couple didn't care; they felt isolated from the rest of the world.

Eddie stopped. "Let's eat. I'm starving."

He felt a sense of freedom. Now he didn't have to hide behind a persona, concealing how he wasn't coping with his time in Vietnam. Their talk was a release valve they both needed. He knew that his friends' sacrifices gave him opportunities they would never have.

EPILOGUE

May 1st, 1975

From a deep sleep, Eddie Henderson bolted upright in bed. "Mitch, I'm coming; hold on!" He flipped to his side, falling to the floor. "Where's my rifle? I can't find my rifle!"

Cheryl slid out of bed. She sat on the floor in front of him, as she had done many times over the years. "Eddie, it's okay. You'll be okay."

He jerked away. "Help Mitch!"

She took his hands into hers. "Eddie, you're home. You're safe. It's me, Cheryl."

He sat upright, looking around the room, with sweat dripping down his face. His pounding heart pushed blood through his veins until he thought it would explode.

She cradled him in her arms. "It's okay. It's okay." She rocked him softly.

Then, he realized. "Shit. I'm sorry, Cheryl."

"It's okay. We need to get ready for work, anyway." Cheryl stood.

Looking embarrassed, Eddie walked toward the kitchen. "I'll get the coffee started."

After Eddie graduated from college, he became a history teacher; his life had seemed normal. But he still had fits of anger. He would become angry at car drivers, or when his food wasn't prepared quite right at a restaurant. Eddie even got mad at store clerks when they didn't seem helpful enough. He did his best to keep the anger hidden. Most days, he did.

While waiting for the coffee, Eddie stared at the newspaper. He stood transfixed with the paper in his hand.

"What's wrong?" Cheryl poured a cup of coffee. "Is it bad news?" She handed him the cup.

"Look at the headlines, 'Saigon Falls.' You believe it?" Eddie took a sip of coffee. "Here it is May first, nineteen seventy-five. It sure didn't take the Communists long to take over the country."

She took a drink and looked over the rim of the cup. "I'm glad it's over for us, and we aren't sending our boys to war."

"Yeah, I am, too, but it means we fought in that madness for nothing. All those men died for no reason, no reason at all." Eddie dropped the paper on the table. "I'm going to call Professor. I want to invite him to dinner on Saturday. Is that okay?" He blew on the coffee to cool it. "I'm sure he will be excited too. I wonder what he'll protest now."

•

It was a usual workweek for the young couple. Once they got home, Eddie watched the news while Cheryl fixed dinner. After dinner, he would do the dishes while Cheryl graded papers.

When they sat on the sofa, she took his hand. "You remember when we were in Hawaii and talked about having children?"

"Are you pregnant?" He asked with a surprised look creeping across his face.

She giggled. "Well, do you want to?"

"I've thought of a little Mitch running around the house. But this time, I get to be the boss." Eddie laughed while he brushed the hair from her eyes. "Yes, I would like to have kids with you."

"You still think you can pick a name without consulting me?"

"Well, I think Mitch would be a great name. Besides, his grandparents would love that too, don't you think?"

"Yes, I do." Cheryl squeezed his hand. She leaned forward to kiss him. "I'm pregnant!"

"Gawddamn it!" He said with his best Ray Laurel imitation. "I'm going to be a father."

Since returning home from Vietnam, Eddie hid his emotions, but the news that Cheryl was pregnant was different. The smile that spread across his face hadn't appeared since he gazed into Cheryl's eyes on their wedding day. He felt almost giddy, like a little boy at Christmas. Yes, the news excited him.

As they got ready for bed, Cheryl said, "Don't forget tomorrow is Friday. We meet at our restaurant."

"How can I forget a date with the mother of my child?" Eddie yelled from the bathroom.

•

The next evening Cheryl and Eddie met at their favorite place for dinner—a weekly ritual for them. Eddie arrived first, sitting at a table located at the large storefront window. He enjoyed watching the pedestrians as they strolled along the sidewalk.

When Cheryl approached the table, he watched her, realizing how beautiful and graceful she was. Eddie thought how sad it would've been if he didn't answer her when she stood at his table while on R and R in Hawaii. What if she didn't even see him? He would've never become the person he is today if she hadn't.

He stood, pulling a chair out for her. "I already ordered myself a Jim Beam and Coke. Just a Coke for you, little momma."

She kissed him. "Thank you." Then she sat in the chair he offered. "How was your day?"

"It was pretty much the same. You know how wild those seventh graders are. Sometimes I wonder why I chose to teach at the junior high school level." Eddie lit a cigarette. "Heck, some days I wondered why I choose to teach." He laughed.

Cheryl's forehead wrinkled. "I wish you would quit smoking."

"Maybe someday. I can go outside if you want." Eddie held the cigarette away from her to let the smoke to drift in a different direction.

"No, stay here with me." She picked up the menu.

Eddie stared out the window at the street as he took a hit from the cigarette. He gazed at people as they walked past the window. Watching people bustle about had always been a favorite pastime for him. He would try to guess a secret about their lives. All of a sudden, his face paled, and the cigarette fell from his fingers to the floor. Eddie started to shake uncontrollably.

Cheryl looked over the top of the menu. She gasped. "What's wrong, Eddie? What's wrong?"

While he struggled to breathe, Eddie pointed at the window. "Look . . . see . . . the man?"

"Yes, I do. Why is he staring at us?" Cheryl asked, her voice starting to crack.

An Asian man with a scar running down each side of his face stared at the couple. The scar on the right side was more profound and longer than the scar on the left side of his face.

As Eddie looked through the glass, his panic grew. His body trembled uncontrollably and tears ran down his cheeks. Then he saw Laurel looking at him with eyes wide, asking for help. Eddie attempted to stand, but his legs wouldn't obey the command. Fear, anger, and the urge to kill seized him. His hate, along with the rage, defeated the fear. Eddie jumped to his feet, spilling his drink. "It's the fucking Viet Cong Lieutenant Dang that killed Ray!" He pointed at the window. "Kill the mother fucker!"

The restaurant became disconcertingly quiet.

The man on the other side of the window flashed an evil smile. Dang reached into his jacket pocket, removing an object. He placed it against the window. While he stared at Cheryl, the man held it to his nose as if smelling the photograph. His lips tugged into a wicked smile.

Cheryl struggled to breathe. "Oh my God, it's my wedding picture! The one I gave to you. You told me you lost it." She looked at Eddie.

Dang removed a Zippo lighter. He flashed it as he lit a Marlboro cigarette. He showed Eddie the lighter before he slid it into his pocket along with the photograph.

"I'm going to kill you!" Eddie's voice echoed in the restaurant. "I'm going to fucking kill you!"

Dang turned, fading away into the crowd on the busy sidewalk.

The fear had turned into rage, then revenge. Eddie knocked his chair over as he ran outside to the sidewalk. He stood, looking in both directions, with sweat running down his face. Dang was nowhere in sight. "I will find you, you little son of a bitch . . . if it's the last thing I do."

ABOUT THE AUTHOR

Glyn Haynie enlisted in the United States Army at the age of eighteen. His military career spanned twenty years, during which he served his country until his retirement in March of 1989. Glyn Haynie turned nineteen soon after arriving in Vietnam, where he found himself fighting with the Americal (23rd) Infantry Division. Before retiring, Haynie served as a drill instructor, a first sergeant and, finally, as an instructor for the US Army Sergeants Major Academy (USASMA).

After retiring from the army, Haynie earned an AAS degree in Management, a BS degree in Computer Information Systems, and an MA degree in Computer Resources and Information Systems. He worked as a software engineer/project manager for eight years before teaching at Park University as a full-time instructor. Haynie continued as an adjunct instructor for thirteen more years.

Glyn Haynie and his wife of thirty-three years, Sherrie, currently reside in Texas. They have five children, fourteen grandchildren, and four great-grandchildren. Three of their sons have served combat tours in either Iraq or Afghanistan. This is a family in which service to their country is a tradition.

To learn more about Glyn Haynie and his work, please visit his website:

http://www.glynhaynie.net
Email: glyn@glynhaynie.com

I hope you enjoyed this book. If so, would you do me a favor?

Like all authors, I rely on online reviews, and your opinion is invaluable. Would you take a few moments now to share your assessment of my book on any book review website you prefer? Your opinion will help the book marketplace to become more transparent and useful to all.

Thank you very much!
Glyn

Made in the USA
Middletown, DE
08 September 2020

19117133R00144